The Barque of Bulleyn

The Hoye Barcke Image by permission of the Pepys Library, Magdalene College Cambridge

K. C. Isted

The Barque of Bulleyn
Published by The Conrad Press in the United Kingdom 2016

Tel: +44(0)1227 472 874
www.theconradpress.com
info@theconradpress.com

ISBN 978-1-78301-919-9

Book jacket design and typesetting by:
Charlotte Mouncey, www.bookstyle.co.uk

The Conrad Press logo was designed by Maria Priestley.

Printed by Management Books 2000 Limited
36 Western Road
Oxford
OX1 4LG

Author's Note

The *Barque of Bulleyn* is about the adventures of a real-life Elizabethan privateer - Captain Robert Isted of Hastings - and is based on events that occurred between April and July 1574.

The primary sources for this are:

- Correspondence between Sir Henry Killigrew - an English ambassador who had been sent to Scotland, in 1574, to deal with 'the Great Matter'- and Sir Francis Walsingham, Queen Elizabeth's principal secretary and spymaster. These records are contained in the Calendar of State Papers, now available on the internet through British History Online.

- A record of a meeting of the Scottish Privy Council, at the Palace of Holyroodhouse, on 25 June 1574, that is held in the National Archives of Scotland.

- My own family history.

All but a few of the numerous characters in the novel were real people who were either engaged in the type of activities described, or likely to have been engaged in them.

K. C. Isted

1

The Hundred Place

It is Sunday the twelfth of April, in the year of our Lord fifteen seventy-four and the sixteenth year of the reign of our sovereign lady, Queen Elizabeth of England. But more significantly, it is the first Sunday after the feast of Hocktide[1] - the traditional date when annual elections are held for the governing body of the Cinque Port of Hastings.

As dawn breaks, I lie somewhere between sleep and wake with Hannah slumbering in my arms, in her bed at the White Hart Inn[2].

Clatter, clatter, clatter. The moment is shattered by the sound of small pebbles glancing off the window and a voice calling to me from the street below, 'Are you there, Rob?'

I get out of bed, stifle a yawn and rub the sleep from my eyes. I swing the window open and squint into the low light. I hang my head and naked torso over the sill, shudder in the cold early morning air, and in hushed tones call down, 'Aye, Dick, I'm here. What's to do?'

'Have you forgotten, we're due at the Hundred Place?' replies Dick.

---

1 Hocktide was an old English festival held on the third Monday and Tuesday following Easter Sunday that marked the victory over the Danes, in 1002, by King Ethelred II (the Unready).

2 The White Hart Inn, built 1547, (now the Stag Inn) is reputedly the oldest pub in Hastings.

'Damn! I'm sorry,' I exclaim, suddenly jolted into a greater level of consciousness by the realisation of my own stupidity. 'How could I…? Damn! Hannah has ways to make a man lose track of time. I'll be down in a minute.' I hurriedly pick up my clothes and tiptoe, boots in hand, across the rough-hewn floorboards of the room. 'Ouch,' I cry, as I stub my toes on a leg of the bed, failing miserably in my attempt not to disturb the sleeping Hannah, who pokes her sleepy head and tousled hair out from beneath the bedclothes. 'I'm sorry, Hannah, I have to attend the Hundred Place. Go back to sleep.'

Dressing carelessly, I leave the inn in haste. 'Ouch,' I cry again, as I bang my head on the low doorframe. 'Is nothing built with thought in mind for those of us whose head and feet are a greater distance apart than most men's?'

Dick laughs.

'You forgot this, sweetheart,' calls a yawning Hannah from the upper window of the inn. I look up. Hannah leans out and gently tosses me my sword.

'Thanks, Hannah,' I reply, catching the weapon by its plain leather scabbard. I continue to gaze up at her. Her long blond locks cascade over her soft white breasts where my head had lain only minutes earlier. Then, with thoughts of the tenderness and passion we have just shared, and might soon have shared again if we had not been interrupted, I add, playfully, 'Now get back to bed and keep it warm for me. I'll return as soon as I can and resume where we left off.'

At that moment, the sound of the brazen horn, calling the Communality of Hastings[3] to assemble at the Hundred Place, comes echoing through the narrow cobbled streets and alleyways between the half-timbered houses of the town.

---

3   The Communality: the governing body of the Cinque Port of Hastings, also know as the franchise.

A little mist hangs eerily about the town that stands couched in a small river valley with high hills on either side that project rocky cliffs towards the sea. At the lower end of the valley, between the two hills, stands the town's sturdy defensive wall with its three gates that breach the wall equal distance apart. On the West Hill stand the ruins of the old Norman Castle and a lighthouse to direct sailors into what remains of the small silted up haven into which the River Bourne flows.

Dick and I hurry away from the inn, running and laughing down the main street of the Parish of All Saints with its church standing at the northern end, high on a bank that makes its rough sandstone tower look taller than it really is. We cross the street, dart through an alley and emerge onto the banks of the Bourne, disturbing the local butcher Sam Tailor's squealing pigs that he allows to wallow in the river mud and wander the streets, much to the annoyance of the townsfolk.

We cross the small rickety wooden bridge that spans the Bourne, separating the parishes of All Saints and St Clements. The Bourne is little more than a poor rill at the moment, but there are tidemarks on the walls of houses backing onto it, marking the extent of the recent flood.

We run on, along the west bank, until we arrive at the Hundred Place - the traditional assembly area that is no more than a clearing - downstream of the brewery and to the rear of the courthouse.

There, gathered in a circle, are the thirty-five current members of the Communality that govern the town and the fifteen hundred souls that inhabit therein.

As I make my way into the circle, I am still struggling to tuck my shirt into my breeches and fasten my leather jerkin. This is greeted by disapproving frowns from some of the men who seem to be feeling the cold of the early morning air, and whom I suspect would regard my erstwhile activity and tardiness as typical of a wastrel's misspent youth. Others simply smile, possibly remembering their own youth, and regarding it as I do – a good time well spent.

'By command of the bailiff[4] and the sound of the brazen horn, in accordance with our ancient Royal Charter,' shouts the portly figure of the Sergeant of the Mace, bringing the assembly to order and introducing a touch of gravitas to the proceedings, 'I call upon the Communality of the Cinque Port of Hastings to enter two new permanent members; and elect a new bailiff and twelve jurats[5] from amongst your number, to serve for one year.'

The outgoing bailiff, Richard Liffe, a full bearded middle-aged man wrapped in a heavy and well-worn cloak, steps forward into the circle. 'Are there any here who would pray for the franchise?' he enquires, in a deep rasping voice. Dick and I step forward into the midst of the circle. 'Is there anyone here who will stand for them?' adds the bailiff.

'Aye,' says John Frank, the father of the assembly, with his long white hair and full white beard wafting gently in the on-shore breeze.

'Have they inhabited in Hastings, employed in some honest craft and been of good conversation, for a year and a day?' asks the bailiff.

'Aye,' replies John Frank, wearily, as if carrying the full weight of his years.

'All in favour?' shouts the sergeant.

'Aye,' up goes the cry from the gathering.

'Any opposed?'

There is silence.

---

4   The chief officer of a hundred: similar to a mayor, but with judicial responsibility.

5   A senior municipal officer of the Cinque Ports: an alderman and a magistrate combined.

'Swear them in,' orders the bailiff.

I place my hand on the bible held by the sergeant and swear the ancient oath: 'I, Robert Isted, from this day forward, will bear faith and loyalty to our gracious sovereign, Queen Elizabeth of England, her heirs, and the Communality of Hastings; the estate of the franchise, to my power I will maintain; and I will bear *scott and lot*[6] of my goods and chattels, so help me God.'

Dick follows suit. Then kissing the bailiff on his right cheek, as an act of allegiance, we receive copies of the Charter of the Freedom that list our privileges and obligations as freemen of Hastings and barons of the Cinque Ports.

I proudly examine the seal on the Charter that I am now entitled to use. It displays a ship on one side, with St Michael slaying a dragon on the reverse and *SIGILLVM : COMMVNE : BARONVM : DE HASTINGGIS* written around the edge – words that indicate it is the Common Seal of The Barons of Hastings.

I partially unfurl the document and read to myself a small part of the ancient charter: *'exemption from tax and tallage; the right of soc and sac,'* etc. Much of this archaic text is gibberish to me. But I know it grants members of the Communality of Hastings many privileges, including: the exemption from Crown taxes; the right to make our own laws; immunity from prosecution in Crown Courts; and rights at the Herring Fair, at Yarmouth, from which we make much money.

In exchange for this, we are required to provide fifteen ships, each with twenty-one men and a boy, for fifteen days each year, as required by the Sovereign.

'Who is nominated as my successor?' enquires the bailiff.

'I name James Brinham,' replies John Frank, pointing to the rotund, jolly, red faced, middle-aged Brinham.

'Aye,' says all the company in affirmation.

---

6   Scott and lot were local taxes.

'I can't afford to have my house knocked down for refusing the honour to serve as your bailiff,' quips the jovial Brinham, referring to the penalty for refusal contained in the ancient charter. He then places his hand on the Bible held by the sergeant and swears an oath similar to the one that Dick and I have just sworn.

'Who do you select as the twelve jurats to provide you with counsel and assist you with your duties?' asks the sergeant.

Bailiff Brinham announces the names of eleven established members of the Communality before adding, 'and Richard Isted,' as the twelfth and final jurat.

I'm surprised that Dick, as a new member of the franchise, has been selected as a jurat, although he is well worthy of the office. I suspect others are similarly surprised. But I doubt anyone is jealous or covets the job, because while a jurat is an important and honourable position, it takes time away from the even more important business of making money.

With the ceremony completed, there is much backslapping and handshaking. Then we all head off, in good humour and careless procession, to the Parish Church of St Clement for a short service and blessing of the freemen, jurats and bailiff.

I had been reluctant to commit to joining the Communality at this time. I had only agreed to it because of Dick's constant nagging about our taking this earliest of opportunities to exercise our birthright as heirs to both our late father and our elder brother, Barnard, who was recently taken by the plague. But now it is done, I feel a sense of deep anticipation and excitement.

'We're now men of position, if not yet of substance,' remarks Dick, as he and I leave the Hundred Place.

'I suppose we are,' I reply, cheerily.

'We need to start acting the part and plan for our futures, exploiting the opportunities the franchise provides.'

'I suppose so, Dick. What do you suggest?'

'For a start, now you've something worth bringing to the table, we should look to broker a wife for you: someone with a nice dowry, or an heiress of a good family without male issue. Or, perhaps, a young widow with her dead husband's fortune; anyone that will enhance your position, wealth and prospects and who'll provide you with heirs.'

'I didn't bargain for that,' I reply, with a shrug of my shoulders, taken somewhat aback by the suggestion. 'I'm still enjoying the carefree life of a single man to think of such things at present.'

'You live too much in the present, Brother.'

'Where else can we live?'

'But, Rob, you need to plan for the future – the present times yet to come.'

'There's time for that later.'

'Is there?' says Dick. 'Life is short and uncertain. Remember Barnard, and many of the companions of our youth, going along as we are now, only to be taken by sudden outbreaks of the plague or smallpox.'

'That's why I live for the moment.'

'But you need to strike a better balance,' says Dick, flapping his arms against his side in obvious exasperation at my reluctance to submit to his plans.

'I suppose you're right, as usual,' I sigh, trying to bring the matter to a close. 'But, I'm not sure how Hannah will take to that. She's certainly not the sort of person you've in mind for me,' I add, laughing, trying to lift the mood, before realising I have only provided Dick with another opportunity to continue the lecture.

'You should end that particular *affaire de coeur*, or at least be more discreet and disillusion her of any thoughts she may have of ensnaring you into marriage,' advises Dick. 'She's a mere innkeeper's daughter, and she's known other men before you,' he adds, disapprovingly.

'Hannah and I like to make merry, sleep and *swive* together. But we've little else in common and I realise there's no long term future in that.'

'But does she realise that, Rob?'

'I think so, although I've never discussed it with her.'

'I suggest you discuss it with her soon. You don't want to lead the poor girl on.'

The conversation ends, none too soon for my liking, as we enter the lichgate of St Clement's, with its squat square tower chequered with rough-hewn sandstone blocks and knapped flint. We pause in a customary show of respect at our father's grave: a simple sandstone memorial bearing a skull and crossbones, as a *memento mori*, above a simple inscription – *Here lieth the body of John Isted, died 1557.*

I feel little emotion as I remember him only as a distant father figure who had little hand in my upbringing, and who died when I was only a lad. But, I reflect on the circumstances of our kinship: a result of him satisfying his pent-up amorous frustration with my mother, while his wife was *hors de combat,* pregnant with Dick. This could easily have led to bitter and destructive half-sibling rivalry between Dick and me. But these feelings are completely absent in us, transcended by a genuine bond of friendship.

'Your father was my mentor and business partner,' says James Brinham, the new bailiff, as he joins Dick and I at the graveside. 'For his sake, I'm willing to help you lads make your way in the world. Come to my house, early tomorrow afternoon, at around the turn of the hour past the sound of the *sext* bell[7]. I've

---

7   The *sext* bell sounded at the sixth hour of the day after sunrise, as a part of the old canonical timekeeping system that persisted in many places in England until it was formally abolished in the 17th century.

some people I'd like you to meet, and a proposition to put to you that will help you meet your obligations to the franchise; and even better, to turn a tidy profit.'

2

The Proposition

I meet Dick at one of his small fish shops outside the Seagate, to go together to James Brinham's house.

'I've thought long and hard about what you said yesterday,' I say.

'And what did you decide?' asks Dick.

'Hannah's background and past matters not a jot to me. She's a lovely young woman and I'm not ashamed of her. And when it comes to marriage, I'll shun the conventions of our class. I won't make it a matter of business or dynastic ambition.'

'So, Rob, you're thinking of marrying?'

'Hold on. No! I'm not ready for that,' I hastily reply to correct any misunderstanding. 'It doesn't feature in my plans for the foreseeable future.'

'So you at least have some plans?'

'Nothing you'd recognise as such. But I agree with you about one thing, Dick.'

'What's that?'

'I'm not being fair to Hannah. I don't want her to miss the chance of making a suitable match through wasting her time on the likes of me.'

'I've heard you make that excuse before.'

'You may think it trite but it's nonetheless true and the right thing to do for all that,' I say, displaying my annoyance.

'I'm sorry, Rob. I know there's more depth to you than most people give you credit,' replies Dick, apologetically. 'And doing the right thing by Hannah is a start, at least. Now, as much as

I'd like to continue this conversation, we'd better be on our way to find out what this proposition of James Brinham's is all about.'

'It's probably him just wanting us to take on some job at the Herring Fair at Yarmouth, to defend our charter privileges there.'

'Maybe. But we won't find out tarrying here.'

Dick and I walk the short distance to James Brinham's house in the bright afternoon sunshine. We soon arrive at the house: a timber framed, wattle and daub building, with a tiled roof and leaded glass windows. It is a large house by the usual standards of Hastings, with a small garden and a stable to the rear.

We pause on the threshold and straighten ourselves up. I bang the heavy iron knocker on the black stained oak door, still wondering what this proposition might be.

A pretty young servant girl opens the door. I've not seen her before. She must have recently arrived in the town from the surrounding district, in search of work. She is a welcome addition to Hastings's adult females who are outnumbered by adult males, largely due to the high mortality rate in childbirth.

We are ushered through the dark narrow hallway into a lighter and airier room at the rear of the house, where James Brinham stands with our cousin, Tom, and another well dressed and prosperous looking gentleman.

'Greetings,' says James Brinham. 'You know your cousin, Thomas, but I'm not sure you know this other gentlemen, Sir John Pelham of Laughton. Now, Sir John, these hearty lads are Dick and Rob Isted, whom Thomas and I have spoken to you about.'

'How do you do, Sir John, I know of you, of course,' says Dick, as he shakes Sir John's hand.

'Greetings, coz',' I say, as I gently slap Tom on his back. 'What brings you here from Mayfield?'

'It's all to do with the reason I've asked you lads here,' interjects our host. 'Let's make ourselves comfortable at the table and I'll explain further.'

Dick and I glance at each other, with raised eyebrows, and sit together on one side of the polished oak table, with Sir John and Tom on the opposite side and James Brinham at its head.

'As you know, our charter requires us to provide ships to the service of the Crown,' adds James Brinham in a serious tone. 'We've been deficient in this for some time and it's putting our privileges at risk. So, I want you lads to provide a ship in fulfilment of your obligation as members of the franchise.'

'But that goes well beyond our share of the obligation, and we don't have the resources for it,' exclaims Dick.

'That's where these gentlemen can help,' says James Brinham, casually waving his right hand in the direction of Sir John and Tom. 'Perhaps it will be best if Sir John explains further.'

Sir John, a small dark-haired man in his late thirties, leans forward with hands clasped in front of him. 'As you may know,' he says, 'I'm Sheriff of the County and hold a number of other official appointments. I'm also well connected at Court, through my service in the last Parliament as the Member for Sussex. As a result, I'm in the position to arrange for you to purchase a ship of war that's surplus to the Queen's Navy's requirements, which Thomas and I secured an option on when we were in London last month.'

'For how much?' enquires Dick, who I am happy to let take the lead on such matters as he is more of a businessman than me.

'The bargain price of sixty-five pounds.[8]'

'That's still a great deal of money for us to find, especially after we've paid for our membership of the franchise,' says Dick, remarkably calmly in the face of such a sum having been mentioned.

'And why do we need a specialist ship of war?' I say. 'For as long as anyone can remember Hastings has only been asked to provide ships for transport services to the Crown.'

'If the money's a problem, I'll loan you a third of the price as a retainer for your services,' offers Sir John. 'You can repay me, with interest, from services rendered or your profits.'

'As your late father's business partner, I know you lads have the balance of the money,' states James Brinham. 'And a specialist ship of war will go some way to restore our relevance to the Crown and help protect our charter privileges from which you've recently sought to benefit.'

'That's all well and good, but what are these services you mention, Sir John?' asks Dick.

'A consortium of Wealden ironmasters[9], including your cousin and I, have a job for you,' replies Sir John.

'To do what?'

'The export of ordnance: cannon, shot and the like.'

'Why don't you just hire a merchant ship to do that?' I suggest.

'It's not quite that simple,' replies Sir John, with a sigh. 'We've an order to supply Dutch rebels to assist them in their revolt against their Spanish masters. Unfortunately, the Convention

---

8 It is difficult to determine the value of this in today's terms. However, the Labourers Act of 1563 established the maximum pay rates for skilled workers at 10d per day. In comparison with the earnings of a skilled worker in the UK in 2015, £65 in 1574 would represent approximately £220,000.

9 An ironmaster was the owner or operator of a large foundry or forge.

of Nijmegen,[10] recently entered into between England and Spain, prohibits the Crown from assisting the Dutch rebels. We are, therefore, unable to secure the necessary export licence from the Privy Council.'

'So you want us to break the law and risk the consequences?' says Dick.

'It isn't as clear cut as that and the risks are minimal.'

'How so?' I ask, excited by the prospect of such adventure, and wondering whether perhaps joining the stuffy Communality might not be quite so dull after all.

'What I tell you now mustn't leave this room,' replies Sir John, lowering his voice.

What could he be about to say, I wonder.

'I have it from Sir Francis Walsingham, the Queen's Principal Secretary,' adds Sir John, 'that Her Majesty wishes to continue to assist the Dutch in their rebellion against their papist oppressors, despite the treaty.'

'If the Queen wants this trade to continue, do you have anything in writing to that effect?' asks Dick.

Sir John gives out a nervous laugh before saying, 'I did ask Walsingham about this, but he regretted it would compromise the Crown's policy of engaging in certain activities while allowing it the possibility of denying them.'

'In other words, he wants us to do his dirty work for him without any possibility of any of the dirt sticking to him.'

'I see you have a firm grasp of politics, young man.'

'I don't like it,' says Dick, his right thumb and index finger holding his chin as if he is deep in thought. 'But if we agree to do it, how's it going to work in practice?'

---

10 The Convention of Nijmegen was signed between England and Spain, in 1573, in which England agreed to cease supporting Dutch rebels in the Spanish Netherlands.

'As the owners of this ship of war, you'll own the most potent of all Cinque Port ships,' explains Sir John. 'As such, I'll arrange for you to be the escort of the wool fleet to Sluis, in Flanders, which we're intending to use as cover to smuggle the ordnance.'

'What about inspection by the authorities?' I ask.

'They won't bother with such a fleet under the protection of a Cinque Port ship,' replies Sir John, dismissively.

'But that particular privilege is now more often observed in the breach,' explains Dick. 'We then have to defend the privilege and any consequences after the event.'

'That won't happen in this case.'

'How can you be so sure?'

'I'm the Commissioner for Piracy and Smuggling in these parts, so you'll have no trouble from my men.'

'Does that include the *searchers*[11]?' I ask.

'John Bode, the chief man at Newhaven and Meeching[12], from where we intend to ship the ordnance, is our man: bought and paid for.'

'What about the other side of the Channel?'

'We're working on that and we'll let you know the plan before you sail.'

'I don't like that either,' says Dick, scratching his head. 'But if we do this, how much money will we make?'

'Thirty pounds for escorting the wool fleet, of which two-thirds will be paid to you in advance,' states Sir John. 'You'll get another thirty pounds for your part in the smuggling, which you'll receive once the ordnance has reached its destination. So, you'll recoup most of the purchase price of the ship from these

---

11 Searchers: customs officers appointed to search ships and apply import and export tariffs.

12 Newhaven was created by a new outflow of the River Ouse being cut near Meeching, after the harbour at Seaford had silted up in the earlier part of 16th century.

two commissions. There may be similar commissions like this one in future. But given all I've told you, I can't guarantee it or know when the next one might occur.'

'But what are we going to do with this warship afterwards, if we decide to buy it, other than keep it to fulfil more than our share of Hastings's obligation to the Crown?' I ask.

'That's a good point, Rob,' adds Dick. 'Without any guaranteed work, it'll cost far too much for us to maintain.'

'Let's not play innocents, lads,' says James Brinham. 'You know as well as I do that men of Hastings have turned more than a little profit from confiscating goods from ships they stop and inspect in the Channel, under the protection and authority of our charter.'

'*Piracy*, you mean?' I exclaim.

'If we're going to call it anything, I'd prefer the term *privateering*.'

'I'm not sure there's much of a difference, or whether we ought to be involved in either,' states Dick, disapprovingly.

'Your father had no such scruples,' announces James Brinham.

'What!' exclaim Dick and I in unison. It's the first time I've heard of this.

'Yes, that's right. In fact, we were once summoned to appear before old King Henry's Privy Council, at Windsor Castle, accused by a couple of well-connected Spaniards of an act of piracy committed by a ship we owned.[13]'

'What happened?' I ask. It's revealing a side to Dad that I had not suspected before.

'We were filled with dread at the prospect,' says James Brinham. 'But Tom Cheyne, the old Lord Warden, who sat on the Privy Council, soon put our minds at rest. The hearing was

---

13 Dasent's Acts of the Privy Council, (1892) 264. Record of 28 Oct 1545 refers.

purely political to satisfy the Spanish, as the King needed them as allies against the French. Of course, it helped that our other shipping partner was Phillip Chute, the old Captain of Camber Castle, who'd saved the King's life at the Siege of Boulogne a year earlier. Nevertheless, someone had to take the blame.'

'Who?' I ask, eager to learn more.

'At Cheyne's suggestion, the finger fell on the captain of our ship, Will Woller. Your father, as bailiff, was tasked with seeing the goods were recovered and returned, of which I think he handed back some, and to hunt down Will Woller and put him on trial.'

'What happened to the scapegoat, Woller?' I ask, in case it becomes expedient to leave me to a similar fate.

'Nothing much. We told him to lay low for a while and then helped set him up with the White Hart Inn. I hear tell you know his granddaughter, Hannah Clarke.'

'Rob's known her quite often, in the Biblical sense,' jokes Dick.

Everyone laughs.

'There's little for you to worry about,' says James Brinham, attempting to reassure us. 'In accordance with our charter, you can't be tried in any court in England, other than the one in Hastings, without the consent of Lord Cobham, the Lord Warden, which I know he'll be reluctant to give. And at the Hundred Court, in Hastings, where I sit in judgement, you're guaranteed of being acquitted of any charges, simply by pleading *life and member*[14], to exercise your immunity from prosecution.'

---

14 A system whereby a member of the Communality charged with a crime could plead 'life and member' and be acquitted of the charge, without hearing any evidence, provided his fellow members agreed that his word was unimpeachable.

'On top of that, while the Crown bound itself, by the Treaty of Nijmegen, not to issue any new letters of marque, it hasn't cancelled the ones already in being,' states Sir John. 'Many of these merely refer to the bearer and have become tradable commodities. I've arranged for one to be yours, if you accept our proposition.'

'With all that, you're as well covered as anyone can be,' adds James Brinham.

'All you have to remember is not to get caught by the Spaniards, or some other power outside of the Queen's jurisdiction,' cautions Sir John. 'This is the only sin the Queen won't forgive, and I won't be able to help you under such circumstances.'

'I'm still not sure about this,' says Dick, with a worried frown. 'Rob and I'll have to think it over.'

'There's little time for that. Our option on the ship of war won't hold for ever, and the date of the assembly of this year's wool fleet is fast approaching.'

'Why don't you and Rob go into the garden to discuss it in private, then come back and give us your decision,' suggests James Brinham. 'It's a big opportunity for you lads to set yourselves on the road to fortune. And by the by, lads, it's an opportunity your father wouldn't have turned down.'

Dick and I leave the room, him looking anxious and me feeling excited by the prospect. We walk into the small herb garden at the rear of the house and stand amidst the gentle fragrance of the perennial herbs.

'I'm not sure about this Rob,' says Dick, with concern. 'I'm not much of a sailor and we don't have anyone else I'd trust with such an investment on matters such as this.'

'Well, I'm up for it,' I say, excitedly. 'I'm a good enough sailor and you can handle the business side of things ashore, which you'll be much better at than me.'

'I know you're a fair sailor, Rob, but you've never handled a vessel like this before, nor the number and type of men required to sail her on this sort of venture.'

'I've already thought about that. John Hills has the necessary experience from his past military service,' I say, referring to our sister Mary's husband. 'I'm sure he'll jump at the chance to sign on to serve as the master under my captaincy.'

'I'm still not sure.'

'You're always going on at me, Dick, about taking on responsibility. And now I'm willing to do so, you're suddenly not sure about it.'

'But this is irresponsible responsibility.'

'Then it's made for me!' I exclaim.

We both laugh. Then Dick pauses for thought, while it's my turn to be anxious.

3
The Decision

'You have your gunrunners and privateers, Sir John,' I announce, enthusiastically, as we re-enter the room where Sir John, James Brinham and Tom stand huddled in conversation.

'And you've got Hastings' ship service to the Queen covered as well,' adds Dick, in a more sober tone.

'Thank God for that,' says Tom, laughing. 'We've just been discussing how to dispose of your bodies had you turned us down.'

Dick and I laugh along with Tom, but I notice there isn't so much as a smile on Sir John's face.

'I'm pleased you've come to the right decision,' says Sir John, looking relieved, as he shakes Dick and I by the hand. 'I look forward to a long and profitable association between us.'

'Let's drink a toast to our venture,' invites James Brinham, filling and offering us some goblets of wine.

'To our venture,' we all say, clinking our goblets together.

Shortly afterwards Sir John announces, 'I'm afraid I've to return to Laughton on urgent business. Thomas will answer any further questions you may have. I'll see you at Newhaven before you sail.'

I return to the garden to make use of the privy. 'Phew, what a *fargo*[15],' I say to myself. 'It's about time the bailiff got the *gong*

---

15 *Fargo* is an old local word for a stink, presumably from wanting to go far to get away from it.

farmers[16] in.' But I linger longer than I wish, to overhear Sir John speaking privately to James Brinham, as he takes his leave.

'I hope you're right about these lads,' says Sir John. 'I've a great deal at stake in this. In particular, I've a lawsuit pending over some disputed property and several creditors pressing me for payment. If this doesn't come off, I may be bound for the Fleet Prison.'

'I knew things were a bit bleak, but I didn't realise they were that bad,' exclaims James Brinham, with concern in his voice. 'Won't your wife's family help?'

'I've already spent the dowry my wife brought to the marriage; and her father, Baron St John of Bletso, is none too pleased with me for that. I can't see him helping too readily without my suffering some humiliation, despite my having the continued love and devotion of his daughter.'

As Sir John mounts his horse and rides off, I slip back into the house unnoticed.

Back in the house, Tom, who sat there deferentially while Sir John held the stage, holds forth more confidently as he outlines the plans in more detail. 'As Sir John said, there isn't much time to lose. You've to raise your share of the money and be at the Tower of London by the end of next week. There you're to meet Mr Barons, one of the masters under the admiral, to buy the ship of war - the *Barque of Bulleyn*[17].

---

16 A *gong farmer* was the name given to those employed in emptying cesspits.

17 Records of the Navy of King Edward VI and Mary I, edited by C S Knighton and D M Loades, published by Ashgate for the Navy Records Society, shows that the *Barque of Bulleyn* was formerly known as the *Hoye Bark*. A contemporary painting of The *Hoye Bark* is Roll No. 18 of the Anthony Rolls held in the Pepys Library, Magdalene College, Cambridge. In contemporary sources, such as those contained in the Calendar of State Papers, Bulleyn is used as the spelling for the town of Boulogne in France, and the family name of Anne Boleyn.

'What type of warship is she,' I ask.

'She's a relatively small four-mast barque, formerly known as the *Hoye Bark* when she was taken a prize from the French during the Siege of Boulogne.'

'She's getting on a bit, then,' I remark, recalling the stories of some of the old timers who had provided services to the Crown in support of the siege.

'Yes, but she's recently been refitted and had some structural work done on her in the last few years.'

'We'll give her a good look over to make sure she's seaworthy, in any event.'

'She should be, but I don't know what we'll do if she's not,' says Tom, as if he has never considered the prospect. 'You're also to meet Mr Parker, the Admiral's Clerk, who'll give you the commission to escort the wool fleet, along with the letter of marque Sir John has acquired. I understand there are some conditions attached to it, but Parker will explain all that.'

'What about crew?' I ask.

'I understand you'll find plenty of beached sailors with the requisite experience, in and around the Pool of London. Parker will no doubt help you with this, for a small consideration.'

'Then what?'

'You must have the ship at Newhaven, by Meeching, by the end of the first week of May, in time for the shipment of the ordnance. I and Sir John will meet you there to give you, and the captains of the vessels carrying the ordnance, further instructions before you sail.'

'We'll have to be on the road by Sunday at the latest, to ensure we're in London on time,' states Dick. 'In the meantime, we've a lot to sort out.'

'We'll need to arrange to take John Hills with us, which I doubt will go down well with Mary, at such short notice,' I add, knowing that Mary has a nervous and protective nature.

'I'll leave that with you to sort out,' says Tom. 'In any event, you're to call on me, in Mayfield, on your way to London, to receive Sir John's contribution for the purchase of the ship. You can stay overnight at Moat House. From there, you can make your way to Tonbridge and then travel by river to Rochester.'

4

The Master

'We'd better go directly to John Hills's shop,' suggests Dick, as we leave James Brinham's house, with the sun hanging low in the soft, golden hued, western sky. 'We should catch him there before he packs up for the day.'

'I agree,' I say, as we set off in the direction of the Stade[18], down Market Street and along Courthouse Lane. There we see some children, by the Blackpool, dancing around in a circle singing the nursery rhyme about the old Queen - Bloody Mary - as Dick and I had done with our friends many years ago:

'Mary, Mary, Quite contrary,
How does your garden grow?
With silver bells and cockleshells.
And pretty maids all in a row.'

We quickly reach the Pulpit Gate. Passing through it, we emerge onto the Stade, with its distinctively tall, black stained, wooden clinker-built fishing huts, where the fishermen dry and repair their nets and tend to their small fishing boats beached on the shingle.

John Hills is at his fish shop when we arrive there.

'How's business, John?' asks Dick.

'And how's Mary, and our young niece and nephew?' I add.

---

18 Stade: Anglo-Saxon for landing place. It is the shingle beach in front of Hastings Old Town that has been used for beaching ships for over a thousand years. It is still the home of Europe's largest beach-launched fishing fleet.

'The family is fine and the fishing is good,' answers John. 'I landed a good catch today: mainly cod and some haddock. Unfortunately, so did many others, and that's kept prices low and left me with fresh fish I can't sell. So I'll probably smoke or salt what's left. But what brings you lads this way this fine afternoon? It's not to enquire about the family, nor the state of my business, I'll be bound.'

'It is sort of related,' replies Dick. 'We've a business proposition that might be of interest to you that will help you provide better for our sister and your children. Can you leave the shop with the lad while we go somewhere to talk?'

'Close things up for me, Sam, and then go home,' says John, to the young boy who works for him.

'Let's adjourn to the White Hart, where we can talk privately in the back room over a flagon of ale,' I say. Then I remember I was supposed to return there yesterday, to see Hannah after the meeting at the Hundred Place, before being distracted by Dick's scolding and James Brinham's mention of a proposition.

We enter the White Hart Inn: a timber framed building, with lathe and plaster walls and ceilings that have been discoloured by years of smoke from countless candles and fires lit in the large stone hearth.

'Robert Isted!' a familiar female voice says. 'You've got a nerve showing your face in here,' complains Hannah, poking me in my chest with her forefinger, almost as soon as we cross the threshold. 'If I'd listened to you, I'd still be alone in bed waiting for you to return.'

'I'll wager you wouldn't have been alone for long,' I quip.

'Now that's uncalled for,' says Hannah, looking hurt by the remark. 'You know I keep myself for you nowadays,' she adds, turning away, clearly upset.

'I didn't mean it, Hannah,' I say, putting my arm around her. 'I'll make it up to you later, I promise.'

Hannah looks up at me with tearful eyes, and I kiss her tenderly on her cheek. 'Now fetch us some ale, wench,' I add, giving her a playful pat on her *derriere*. She jumps playfully in response, looks back over her shoulder with a smile, and scurries off to draw the ale from the wooden casks behind the bar.

'I thought you were going to stop toying with that poor girl's affections?' says Dick, quietly.

'I'm going to break things off with her, before I set off on our venture,' I whisper.

'What venture might that be?' enquires John.

'We'll explain that once Hannah has brought us the ale and I'm sure we're alone,' replies Dick.

'It sounds intriguing,' says John, just as Hannah returns with three pewter tankards of ale.

'Now don't forget your promise,' says Hannah, with a telling wink, as she places a tankard in front of me, before leaving us alone.

Dick looks at me disapprovingly.

'All right, Dick, I know it has to be done,' I say. 'A long sea voyage will make it a bit easier to explain, and for Hannah to accept.'

'Now, you've really got me intrigued,' remarks John.

'Now we're alone, I'll get straight to the point,' says Dick. 'Rob and I are buying a ship of war from the Navy, arranged by Sir John Pelham of Laughton. Rob will be the captain and I'll look after the business side of things ashore.'

'So where do I fit into this?' interrupts John.

'I was getting to that.'

But before Dick can proceed further, I jump in, 'I'm a good sailor and can read the tides, winds and currents as well as any man. But I don't have the experience with this type of ship, or with leading the number and type of men needed to crew it on such a venture. So, we'd like you to sign on as master, under my captaincy.'

'I'll need to know more about this venture of yours,' says John. 'And why do you need a ship of war?'

'The ship will be our contribution to Hastings's obligation to provide ships for Crown service,' answers Dick. 'Hastings has been remiss in this for quite a long time and it might soon call into question our privileges, unless we do something about it.'

'We also have the commission to escort the wool fleet, assembling off Thanet, that's bound for Sluis next month,' I add. 'So, what do you think?'

'Of course, that's not all,' adds Dick. 'There are things about the commission we're not at liberty to tell you, just yet. But I can tell you there is more to it than meets the eye, for which we will be well paid.'

'That's interesting,' says John. 'But what will we do with this ship of war after the commission and the fifteen days we could be required for service to the Queen?'

'We intend to conduct a little privateering, by stopping and seizing the goods of foreign shipping under the protection of our charter and a letter of marque,' I reply. 'I know you've not been averse to such things in the past.'

'You know I'll do practically anything for your family,' says John, earnestly. 'Your mother was kind enough to persuade Barnard to allow your sister to marry a rough mariner like me, for love, instead of someone more befitting a gentlewoman. Although, Mary is still upset at not being allowed her full dowry,' he adds, with some feeling. 'But before we married, I promised Mary I'd given that sort of life up and would settle down. I won't go back on my word, especially now we've two young bairns.'

'Don't dismiss the idea just yet. Think on it, John,' I say, not wanting to give up on the proposition. 'I promise that out of your pay and share of any booty we take, you'll earn in six months more than you would in six years working as a fisherman. That's more than enough to cover any perceived shortfall in Mary's dowry. Then after six months, you can return ashore if you're still mindful. By that time I'll have gained the experience I lack at present.'

'That sounds fine to me, but I made Mary a promise. I doubt she'll release me from it, and I won't break it.'

'You know she loves us as well,' I say. 'I'm sure she'll want us to have someone whom we can trust. She'll also welcome the closer family ties this will entail, and the extra money to support your children. You might even make sufficient to buy your way into the franchise, with our support,' I add, knowing how to tempt John.

'Those arguments might work,' answers John, thoughtfully, 'especially with the limited time to help you lads out.' However, I know it is really only the possibility of becoming a member of the franchise that makes him warm to the prospect. The other things I mentioned were merely dressing it up to give him a reason he could more gracefully accept and sell to Mary.

'There is one thing we forgot to mention,' adds Dick. 'We'd like you to set off for London with us on Sunday, to take possession of the ship, crew her, and sail her to Newhaven where our commission starts in earnest.'

'You're not asking much, are you?'

'I'm sorry, but they're the constraints we're working with.'

'Never mind,' sighs John, shaking his head in mock despair. 'It'll probably be just as well to do this and get out of the way quickly, before Mary's doubts start to surface. It'll just give me enough time to make arrangements to leave my boat and shop.

I'll send a message around to your house later, once I've spoken with Mary.'

'I hope it all works out well,' says Dick, with sincerity in his tone. 'We're going to be busy making our own arrangements. But all being well, Rob and I will call on you within the hour after dawn on Sunday. We'll bring an extra horse with us for you to ride.'

'Bring an advance of money as well,' demands John. 'I'll need to leave some for Mary and the children to live on while I'm away.'

'Here's an *angel* now,' replies Dick, handing John a silver coin from his purse. 'And I'll make arrangements for Mary to receive a crown each week until your return.'

'That's very generous of you,' replies John, with all sincerity. 'We'd better make some good money out of this venture, otherwise I'll be owing you at the end,' he jokes with a chuckle in his voice.

'Let's drink to Mary, the children and our venture,' I suggest, raising my tankard.

'Mary, the children and the venture,' enjoins Dick.

'Hear, hear, and God help us all,' adds John, as we clink our tankards together before downing the remnants of our beer.

We leave the inn together. But before we get far, I stop in my tracks. 'I'll see you later this evening, Dick. First, I've a promise to keep,' I say, remembering what I had said to Hannah.

'There'll be no prizes for guessing what promise that is,' I hear Dick saying, disapprovingly to John, as they walk away.

5

The Last Swiving in Hastings

I walk along All Saints Street to the small house I had bought a couple of years ago, when the last of my half-sisters had got married and set up home with her husband. I could have continued to stay with Dick and his mother, as it is usually the case that both men and women remain in their parents' home until they are married. But instead, I decided it was time to put part of my inheritance to good use.

I had just been to pay the wages and an extra gratuity to the woman who comes in every day to keep house for me and prepare my meals. I have a little packing to do for the journey before going to the White Hart for my evening meal. After that I intend to break with Hannah, for her own sake, as I had told Dick I would. Then in the morning, I will shut up the house until I return to Hastings for the winter.

As I reach my house, I notice Hannah through the window. She has never been here before, despite my past encouragement. While she has no problem with me sleeping at the inn and my sneaking out of there in the morning, she does not think it seemly for her to do the same at my house. I have never understood why. When people see me leaving the inn early in the morning, they know exactly what we have been up to. At least I assume they do. Unless they think I've been *swiving* with Hannah's mother. Oh God! I hope not. I shudder at the thought and quickly expel it from my mind.

'What are you doing here, Hannah?' I ask, in surprise, as I cross the threshold.

'As you're leaving in the morning, I thought I'd prepare a meal for us here, so we can spend the entire evening alone together,' she says, nervously, with a sweet smile. 'I thought you'd be pleased.'

'I'm sorry. Of course I'm pleased. It's just that you took me by surprise; you never come here.'

'I know, but you've never been going away for so long before. Now you go through to your dining room and pour yourself a drink, while I finish cooking in the kitchen.'

I move through to my small dining room. The table is laid out with my best silver. On the table is a bottle of wine and two goblets. I pour some wine and look out of the window onto my small unkempt garden that rises steeply away from the back of the house.

Hannah enters the room with the first course: potage made largely of peas, cabbage, carrots and onions.

I seat her, moving the chair in behind her. 'Oops! I'm not used to this: being treated like a lady,' she says, as the chair moves against the back of her legs and she flops onto the seat.

'You should have been,' I say, softly, 'but we've never eaten together before; at least not outside of the inn where you work.'

I pour Hannah a goblet of wine, top up my own, and sit opposite her.

We eat the potage in virtual silence; in part because eating for Hannah has always been more a matter of physical sustenance than something to savour in conversation; and because I feel somewhat disarmed by this unexpected turn of events, in view of what I intend to do later.

Hannah brings in the second course: capon stuffed with oysters, accompanied by laver - seaweed - and pease-pudding.

'You have gone to a lot of trouble,' I say. 'This is really quite delicious.'

'I'm a good cook, when I puts my mind to it,' she replies.

'You'll make someone a good wife one day,' I say, without thinking.

She looks at me with her head bent down and her eyes looking up and says coyly, 'I hope so.' Then raising her head sharply and laughing, she adds, 'Do you have anyone in mind?'

I choke on a bit of the laver, partially in surprise at the question, and partially in an attempt to avoid answering it. Hannah gets up and pats me on my back. I cough a few more times. The moment is past and my ruse is successful.

After the main course, Hannah goes to the kitchen and returns with two puddings wrapped in pudding cloths. 'What is it?' I ask.

'You'll have to unwrap it to find out,' she replies. 'I know you like unwrapping sweet things,' she adds with a wry smile.

I undo the cloth to reveal a *quaking pudding*. 'It's my favourite.'

'I know. I made it especially for you.'

'You've done it very well. It has a perfect wobble to it; just like your lovely wobbly bits.'

We both laugh.

As Hannah takes her last spoonful of the quaking pudding, a little bit wobbles off her spoon onto her chin. She gets up, comes over to me, sits on my lap, removes the errant bit of pudding with her index finger and places it deep within my mouth. My lips grip her finger lightly, while she extracts it slowly, leaving the taste of the sweet pudding on my tongue. We stare deeply into each other's eyes, then kiss and kiss again with increasing passion.

Hannah unfastens my doublet. I lift her up and sit her on the table. I quickly extract my arms from the sleeves and cast the doublet to the floor. We kiss again, more passionately. Then, breathing heavily, Hannah lifts my shirt and puts her hands inside, against my chest, as I undo the tightly drawn leather belt from her waist. I pull my shirt over my head and toss the unwanted garment behind me. My hands move quickly to pull Hannah's simple off-white linen dress and under smock over her head. It catches her hair, revealing the exquisite curvature of her swanlike neck; and her soft white breasts wobbling like two quaking puddings as she makes an involuntary shiver of excitement.

With the dress and smock gone and her long hair falling carelessly about her shoulders, we are both left standing in nothing but our hose. I hold her close. We kiss again. She pushes me away a little and I feel her hands move slowly down, where her fingers move nimbly to undo the ties of my cod-piece that is now under considerable strain from within.

'The beast is free,' she says, with a giggle, tossing the codpiece aside.

'You'll have to find somewhere else to put it until it's tamed,' I quip.

'I know the very place,' she adds, shuffling back across the table, with arms outstretched in invitation to come with her.

As I move forward in close company with Hannah, I clear the table behind her with my arms, as if swimming, consigning plates and goblets to the floor, as her soft white back meets the dark hard wood.

With wandering hands and lips, and arms and legs entwined, it is difficult to tell where one ends and the other begins. We consume each other with a hunger that had never been so sated by anything served upon this table before.

We lay exhausted, with mutually intermingled beads of sweat.

'You have ten minutes,' says Hannah, suddenly. 'Then, I want you again; at least twice more before the night is done,' she adds, as she rises from the table, takes me by the hand and leads me up the narrow stairs.

6

Into the Weald

As the April sun emerges from the sea to the east, Dick and I make our way to All Saints Church, to put in an appearance at early Morning Prayers before we embark on our journey. I am not normally one for praying but, like everyone, I attend church as required by law[19]. But on this occasion I make a special effort to seek divine help in our venture.

We collect John from his home and set off on our journey in the morning sunlight, but with the ground still showing signs of the overnight rain. We ride north over Senlac Hill, near Battle, where we make our first stop to rest and water the horses.

'So did you break with Hannah?' asks Dick.

'I meant to. But every time I saw her with the intention of doing so, I couldn't bring myself to do it and ended up taking her in my arms,' I reply, somewhat bewildered by my failure.

'It sounds like bewitchment to me,' interjects John. 'She and her mother have a reputation with spells and potions.'

'That's superstitious nonsense. The potions are only garlic, herbs and honey, for minor ailments,' I exclaim, as I remount my horse and we resume our journey in welcome silence.

We work our way along the Wealden forest roads. We pass through a number of small villages - Netherfield, Dallington and Heathfield. But outside of these we see few people and

---

19 The Act of Uniformity (1559) required everyone to attend church once a week or be subject to a fine of twelve pence – more than a day's pay for a skilled worker.

little sign of their activity, apart from occasional evidence of coppicing and the odd sight of smouldering charcoal pits in forest clearings.

When we reach Cross In Hand, we turn right at the junction with the Mayfield road. Just north of there, the road turns into thick, cloying, mud. With no alternative, we dismount and lead our horses slowly through the quagmire. While I recover my left boot from the vice-like grip of the mud, I notice a sign to 'The Isted' where smoke rises from a chimney of a house largely concealed by the fall of the ground. 'Does Thomas own this property?' I ask.

'No, but I understand the family had once owned it for an age,' replies Dick, as he also stands out of a mud bound boot, 'until our great-grandfather sold it when he acquired greater and better property, in Framfield, as a dowry on marrying.'

This is the first I have heard of it. No wonder Dick thinks I should marry as a means of enhancing my prospects.

We struggle for more than fifty yards, until we reach higher ground, where some attempt has been made to metal the road with slag and ash: the waste products of the local iron industry.

Finally, nine hours after we had set off on our journey of some twenty miles, we arrive at Moat House muddy and tired.

We dismount in the courtyard as Tom emerges from the large timber framed, part wattle and daub, and part brick built house, with a thatched roof and leaded glass windows.

'Welcome,' says Tom, warmly. 'You made good time.'

'Thanks, Tom,' replies Dick. 'The roads weren't good, but we left very early and made fair progress. The worst bit was at the bottom of the hill, between here and Cross In Hand.'

It's a good job you weren't attempting the journey six weeks ago. Until then, the roads had been impassable for a couple of months.'

'Never mind, we're here now, safe and sound,' I add.

'I'm not sure you've met our brother-in-law, John Hills, Mary's husband, whom we mentioned to you in Hastings,' says Dick, gesturing towards John.

'I don't think I've had the pleasure,' says Tom, shaking John warmly by the hand. 'You're lucky to find me here,' he adds, 'I was just going to visit a retainer of mine who was injured at my forge. I'll get you settled first and then go. We'll meet later and talk over supper.'

'That's fine,' says Dick. 'We don't want to detain you unnecessarily.'

'Leave your horses with young Jim. He'll water them, clean them up and bed them down in the stable with some feed,' says Tom, gesturing to a scruffy young lad lurking at a respectful distance.

Young Jim leads the three horses away as Tom ushers us to the house. We remove as much of the mud from our boots as we can on the iron boot scraper at the porch, before entering the house via a heavy oak door with a horseshoe nailed to its front.

'Molly will provide you with some light refreshments, show you to your rooms, bring you some hot water and see that your boots are properly cleaned,' says Tom, gesturing to a young servant girl waiting in the vestibule. 'I'll see you at supper in the dining hall this evening. Molly will call you when it's time. Until then, you have the run of the house.'

The plain and homely looking Molly ushers us across the floor covered with fresh rushes, into an anteroom, then scuttles off to fetch some food and beer.

Early that evening, Molly summons us to the wood panelled, candle lit, dining hall where Tom is waiting, standing by the hearth.

'I regret my wife, Dorothy, won't be joining us,' says Tom. 'She's taken our children to visit my sister, Elizabeth, and her family, in Withyham. I say regret, but it's actually a blessing, as I don't like to bother her with such business as ours. And so we can talk more freely.'

Molly brings in a cauldron of broth and ladles out a good measure, into pewter bowls, for each of us. 'It's only broth and bread, followed by a haunch of venison with some pease-pudding,' says Tom.

For some unknown reason the old nursery rhyme about this staple food being readily available in most households, in some form or other, pops into my head:

'Pease-pudding hot,
Pease-pudding cold,
Pease-pudding in the pot,
Nine days old.'

7

Business

Tom serves the venison to each of us on silver plate. We help ourselves to the ubiquitous pease-pudding and commence eating, using the usual combination of a knife, spoon and fingers.

A little way into the main course, Tom says, 'Do you mind if we get business out of the way over supper?'

'Of course not,' replies Dick.

'Good! Do you have your share of the purchase price for the ship?'

'Yes.'

'Excellent! Do you have any questions about the mission?'

'No! Everything seems to be clear,' says Dick, 'although we'll no doubt have more questions when we're given our final instructions before we sail.'

'Good! But, I think I ought to tell you a little more of the background to our business,' says Tom, with a detectable touch of reticence in his voice. 'As you know, I'm a member of a group of Wealden ironmasters who've been selling ordnance into the cross-Channel trade at Lewes, and directly to agents on the continent. The partners were my brothers-in-law, and Sir Thomas Gresham[20] who also owns a furnace, in Mayfield.'

'Were?' I ask.

---

20 Sir Thomas Gresham, 1519 – 1579, merchant, diplomat, ironmaster; and financial wizard who virtually wiped out Edward VI's national debt by raising the value of sterling through his dealings on the Antwerp Bourse; and who founded the London Royal Exchange.

'Gresham was involved until recently,' sighs Tom, in a way that indicates some regret and frustration. 'He obtained commissions for us through his contacts abroad, from his time as England's ambassador in Antwerp. Unfortunately, he's distanced himself from us and Sir John Pelham has taken his place. Pelham's in desperate need of the money, and we need his political contacts to replace Gresham's.'

'Why did Gresham distance himself from you?'

'Largely as a result of Ralph Hogge's actions, and complaints from the Navy Royal about our use of timber to produce charcoal for burning in our furnaces.'

'Who's Ralph Hogge?'

'He's a pioneer in the technique of casting cannon who has the monopoly of government ordnance contracts,' explains Tom. 'We've not tried to compete with him in this, but directed ourselves towards overseas markets.'

'What did he do to upset your consortium?' asks Dick.

'Despite his monopoly of government contracts, I think he cast a jealous eye on our business,' replies Tom, with a pained expression. 'But there could be more to it than that, which I'll explain later. In any event, he wrote to the Board of Ordnance, at the Tower of London, suggesting we've been infringing his patents and that the unregulated cross-Channel trade could result in English ordnance ending up in the hands of our enemies.'

'And could it help England's enemies?' I ask.

'He has a point regarding some of this trade, where we can't be certain who the end users will be,' explains Tom. 'This is particularly true with what's sold on through Lewes. John Harman controls much of that trade and has commissioned some Kent and Sussex ironmasters to manufacture cannon to French and Spanish specifications for export. This is clearly against our national interest, and our consortium will play no part in it.'

'So what's the problem for you?' asks Dick.

'Hogge named a few ironmasters engaged in the cross-Channel ordnance trade, including my brother-in-law and partner, Nicholas Fowle, and Sir Thomas Gresham.'

'Is that why Gresham left?' I ask.

'That was the start of it,' says Tom, with a heavy sigh. 'As a result of the complaints of Hogge and the Navy Royal, a survey was conducted of all the Wealden furnaces and forges to determine those that were capable of manufacturing ordnance. I, Gresham, Fowle and other ironmasters have had to sign a bond for the sum of two thousand pounds, promising not to produce cannon without a licence from the Privy Council.'[21]

'That's an enormous amount of money,' I say in surprise.

'Yes! And in light of all this, Gresham has broken from us and is using his political contacts to secure Privy Council licences for the more limited approved trade. I understand he's being awarded a commission to supply a hundred culverins to Denmark; possibly as compensation for withdrawing from the illegal trade, as he's still a royal favourite.'

'You can't blame him for taking advantage of that,' states Dick.

'I don't,' says Tom, as if surprised by the suggestion. 'In any event, we've continued to manufacture ordnance. And now we wish to clear our stocks. We'll do so as soon as the roads are passable for moving things of such weight to a point on the Ouse where we can send them by river to Newhaven. It'll be temporarily stored there in Bean's warehouse below Bishopstone. It's a little earlier in the year to move it than we'd

---

21 Thomas Isted signed the bond, at Greenwich, on 4 March 1574 – Calendar of State Papers Domestic, Queen Elizabeth – Volume 95: March 1574 refers.

wish, but needs must. We'll just have to pray for a period of continued dry weather to ensure the roads are passable.'

'But why the unseemly haste as we've the Crown's tacit approval, despite the licensing regime,' asks Dick, with a puzzled look.

'The departure of the wool fleet is a constraint,' replies Tom, seemingly frustrated by all our questions. 'And, as it says in the Bible: Psalm 146 verse 3: "Put not your trust in princes, nor in the son of man, in whom there is no help". That applies to queens and their servants as well,' he adds.

'I take it you mean Queen Elizabeth and Walsingham.'

'Aye! I met with Walsingham when I signed the bond at Greenwich last month,' states Tom with a heavy sigh. 'I was left in no doubt that he was behind the complaints from Hogge and the Navy Royal. This was just the excuse he needed to bend us to his will and at the same time be better able to deny any involvement in his own machinations. And I've no doubt he'd deny us if it were expedient for him to do so. So, keep a wary eye open, and don't take anything at face value that anyone tells you.'

'Thanks for the warning, Tom,' says Dick, angrily. 'I think we should've been party to all this before we committed ourselves.'

'It makes no difference to me,' I say.

'If you lads are in, I'll be there for you,' adds John.

After a thoughtful pause, Dick says, 'All right, we're still all in. It's too late to back out now. But I'd like our fee in advance,' he adds, forcefully.

'That's not unreasonable, given the circumstances,' replies Tom, with a sigh. 'I can't promise the full amount, but I should be able to pay you something at Newhaven.'

There is a stony silence following this unfortunate exchange of words between Dick and Tom. To break it, I ask, 'Why is the Weald the centre of the iron and ordnance industry, Tom.'

'We've abundant raw materials, in the Weald, necessary for the process,' he replies.

'Such as?'

'Easily accessible iron bearing rock - clay ironstone; trees to produce charcoal, to burn to provide the sort of temperatures required for separating the iron from the rock; and suitable material to build and insulate a furnace to maintain the heat required for the process,' explains Tom. 'They've been making iron in these parts since pre Roman times, in bloomeries – small kilns made of brick and clay. The process remained virtually unchanged until the introduction of the blast furnace.'

With the stoniness of the silence sufficiently broken, Tom adds, 'Now let's adjourn to a more comfortable room, and talk of more pleasant things over some smuggled brandy I procured from a portsman when I was in Hastings.'

We move to another oak panelled room carrying candelabra to light our way. A heavy tapestry, depicting a hunting scene, hangs on one wall. In the opposite wall there is a large stone hearth in which burns a warm and welcoming fire.

'By the way, Dick, I hear a marriage might be in offing with the Warnett girl from Framfield,' says Tom, pouring a large measure of the brandy he had obtained in Hastings, into small silver goblets for everyone.

This is the first I've heard of it, but I hide my surprise.

'I've met Ann Warnett a few times,' replies Dick. 'She's the makings of a lovely young woman: intelligent, good-natured, and from good stock that should bring forth healthy children of the right stuff. The Warnetts are an old family and more importantly she'll come with a good dowry including some prime land. This will fit very nicely with some of the old family lands, in Framfield, that passed to me from Pa via Barnard.'

I'm still a little shocked and disappointed in Dick, despite our previous conversations on the subject of marriage, especially as he's often criticised me regarding my treatment of women. But I'd never treat a woman like that: like a prize heifer for breeding purposes, a source of income, and a means of complementing and enlarging an existing estate. At least with me, they know I'm with them because I like them for themselves and not for what they own.

'It sounds like a good match to me. In light of this news, I'd like to propose a toast,' says Tom, topping up our goblets with more brandy. 'To Dick, Ann Warnett, and a profitable and productive union.'

We join him in the toast and down the brandy.

'I always think it tastes so much better knowing it's been illegally obtained,' adds Tom.

We all agree, in good humour, as we huddle around the fire.

'I've fired cannon when I was aboard an armed merchant ship in service of the Queen,' says John. 'They were mostly brass. Although some were made of wrought iron, with the barrels made of banded fused iron bars. What sort of cannon do you make?'

'I manufacture cast iron cannon,' replies Tom, pouring us all another good measure of the illicit brandy.

'And what are the best: brass, wrought iron or cast iron?' I ask.

'That's a matter of opinion, and where and how you're intending to use them.'

'What do you mean?'

'For a start, I don't think anyone would choose to use wrought iron cannon, made of fused bars,' says Tom, dismissively. 'They're old-fashioned and too many things can go wrong with their structural weakness; not least of all, explode without warning.'

'What's the best between brass and cast-iron?'

'That's where it becomes more of a matter of opinion, depending on the circumstances.'

'How so?'

'Where weight is no problem, in defending a fixed fortified position, cast iron cannon are the best option,' says Tom, proudly. 'But where weight is a consideration, particularly in ships, it becomes a bit more complex. Indeed, the Navy Royal has a preference for brass cannon, although they have a mixture of both and I suspect the balance will eventually change towards cast iron.'

'Why's that?'

'Cost, reliability and the changing nature of ships and warfare at sea,' says Tom, thoughtfully, as he tops up our goblets with more brandy. 'Cast iron cannon are cheaper than brass, as England has an abundant supply of iron. But copper has to be imported. And with improvements in casting iron cannon they are becoming increasingly more reliable. Indeed, the more one of our cast iron cannon is used the better it seems to preform; whereas brass ones can only fire four shots or so in succession, before they have to cease firing to cool down. Then after being used on a number of occasions, their barrels warp and they have to be scrapped or recast.'

'Can you tell us how you make the cannon,' asks John.

'I can do better than that. Rather than give you a long description of the process, why don't I show you in the morning, before you set off.'

'That would be very interesting, but we've deadlines to meet and I'm anxious to get on our way as soon as possible,' says Dick.

'That's not a problem. My furnace and forge are very close to here,' states Tom. 'And as well as knowing something of the political importance of your mission, I'd like you to understand something of the process, time, effort and the sheer scale of the investment the consortium have in the shipment we've engaged you to protect. The imperatives aren't just political, religious and military, you know. There are important personal imperatives as well. There are a lot of people depending on you,' he adds, forcefully.

'If you put it like that, we'll make the time, of course,' replies Dick

Tom tries to pour us another brandy, but even with shaking the bottle only a few drips emerge. 'Gadzooks, all the brandy's gone,' he declares, with surprise and disappointment. 'I suggest we retire for the night and meet at first light.'

We make our way by candlelight, up the wooden stairs and along the upper corridor to our rooms. A few moments later, I hear the snores of tired and replete men echoing through the house, before I also surrender to sleep.

8

Furnace and Forge

'Good morning gentlemen,' says Tom, brightly, as we emerge from our slumber and gather out in the courtyard in the dampness of the early morning forest air. 'I think we'll start off by visiting my furnace. It's a little further on from my forge, but it's the start of the process.[22] Anyway, we have to come back here, past the forge, before you resume your journey.'

We mount our horses, which Jim has brought from the stable, and ride less than a mile to Old Mill Furnace. I had not seen anything quite like it before. I am, of course, familiar with similar millponds, floodgates, water wheels, and toothed gears for powering flourmills. But here they power two huge bellows that blow air into pipes connected to a wall of an arch in a twenty foot tall stone tower with wooden supports at each corner. There is another arch in an adjacent wall, in front of which is a large pit. In the surrounding area, there are also a number of wooden outbuildings, a large A-frame for lifting heavy loads, piles of charcoal and limestone, and piles of small brownish stones that I assume are clay-ironstone. The noise from the huge bellows is loud and unnatural to our ears, and the air hangs thick with foul fumes emitting from the tower.

'It's very impressive, Tom,' exclaims Dick.

---

22 Old Mill Furnace: TQ 588245. Moat Mill Forge: TQ 592251

'It is that,' says Tom. 'The introduction of this blast furnace, in my father's time, enabled us to produce iron on a different magnitude of scale to the old bloomery process. Here we have a large furnace; waterpower to operate large bellows to attain the right temperature; and a slightly different process, with the addition of limestone as a flux to help separate and remove impurities. All this gives us the ability to cast straight from the furnace, into moulds we make in the mould shop onsite. It is, altogether, a bigger, better and more integrated process.'

'Can we see how it works, Tom?' I ask.

'Yes, you're in luck. They're just about to cast the last cannon for shipment. If you come this way, you'll get a better view.'

We move around to an adjacent side of the tower and take up a position looking towards the arch on the other side of the pit.

'We've already run off some molten iron to form *pigs* ready for delivery to the forge for further processing, and another quantity into moulds for shot, nails et cetera,' states Tom. 'But this batch will be of the highest quality. It'll go straight into a mould to produce a cannon - in this case a saker - cast in one piece. If you look closely, you can just see the top of the mould in the casting pit where it's plumbed upright. Sand has been shovelled around it to secure it into position.'

We watch, intently, as the white-hot molten metal is carefully poured into the mould.

'What happens next now the cannon's been cast?' I ask.

'It's allowed to cool. Then the mould is dug out and lifted from the pit by means of the A-frame. It's then broken out of the mould and taken to the conversion forge and boring mill.'

'What happens there?'

'I'll be better able to explain that process to you, if not show you something of it, when we go to my forge,' says Tom,

52

looking at the height of the rising morning sun. 'I think we'd better do that now, mindful of your long journey ahead.'

We mount our horses and ride along a track less than half a mile long that connects Old Mill Furnace with Moat Mill Forge. The track has been metalled in places with slag and ash from the furnace to better enable carts carrying heavy material between the furnace and forge.

We arrive at Moat Mill Forge: a large rectangular stone building with a tiled roof. It has a wide-open barn door, tall sturdy chimneys and water wheels on each of its long sides. We dismount and enter the forge. Inside it is hot, noisy, and full of bad air despite the open door and windows.

'As you can see, we have two hearths,' says Tom. 'This is the finery and this is the chafrey,' he adds, pointing to each of the hearths on opposite sides of the building, close to the entrance.

'Why two hearths and what's the difference between them?' I ask.

'We use the finery to get rid of the slag and make the metal more malleable.'

'How?'

'The hearth is filled with charcoal, quite a bit above the top, and the fire is blown hotter by means of the water-powered bellows,' says Tom, pointing to the mighty bellows making a loud puffing sound. 'At the right time and temperature the finer lays a block of pig iron on the top and covers it with a further layer of charcoal. The metal sinks lower as it gets hotter and the charcoal burns. More charcoal is added as required. Eventually, the metal sinks through the fire and grows cooler. Then at the right moment, the finer retrieves the metal by means of an iron crow.'

'You say at the required time and temperature, and as necessary. But how does the finer know that?' asks Dick.

'He's no way of measuring it exactly, other than a trained eye and experience. That's why a good man is much sought after.'

'What happens next?'

'Shingling the loop.'

'Shingling the loop?

'If you watch, I think the finer is just about to do it,' says Tom.

We watch the finer - a muscular man, stripped to the waist, apart from a full-length leather apron - as he pulls a crusty mass of iron from the hearth. 'That's the loop that he's about to shingle,' adds Tom.

We watch as the finer bashes the loop on the iron plates between the two hearths, removing the external crust of charcoal and cinder.

'Why's it called shingling the loop?' I ask.

'Like a lot of the terms we use, it's derived from Flemish or French used by the foreign workers we used to employ when blast furnaces were first introduced from the continent. Shingling the loop was the closest any of the locals could get to pronounce it.'

We then watch the finer drag the loop along a paved area to the great water-powered hammer to the rear of the hearth.

'What will he do now?' I ask.

'He's going to give it a few strikes with the water-powered hammer to remove the remainder of the cinder.' *Clang, clang, clang* sounds the great hammer bearing down on the loop, spewing out more cinder with each blow.

'Then what?'

'He'll return it to the finery for reheating. Then when it's at the right temperature, it's taken back to the hammer to produce an ancony.'

'An ancony?

'It's another Flemish word. You can see a number of them over there,' says Tom, pointing towards the chafery hearth.

We look over and see a number of flat wrought iron bars, with knobs on each end, in a heap by the side of the chafery hearth.

'What happens to them?' asks Dick.

'The anconies are heated in the chafery hearth for about fifteen minutes at a time, and then hammered out into malleable wrought iron bars from which we in the forge, and blacksmiths elsewhere, make sundry items.'

'It's more complicated than I'd imagined,' I say.

'Now let me show you my favourite toy,' adds Tom, leading us past the great hammer, out through the back door of the forge and into a long narrow wooden building. 'This is it,' he announces with pride, pointing to a wooden trolley about fifteen feet long with its wheels in a wooden guided rutted track of a bit more than twice its length; above which is an iron bar extending through the wall.

Dick, John and I look at each other somewhat bemused at Tom's delight. 'It's very nice, Tom,' says Dick, pausing momentarily, before asking the obvious questions, 'But what is it, and what does it do?'

'Of course, it isn't obvious, because it isn't working at the moment,' replies Tom, with a little laugh. 'This is my boring mill. When it's operating, a cannon cast at the furnace, like the one we saw earlier, is fixed securely to the trolley by ropes. It's then pulled up the track onto the revolving bar, which is powered by the water wheel on the other side of the wall. This then reams out the bore of the cannon.'

'But how can it cut cast iron?' asks Dick, with surprise.

'It only cuts out any roughness left by casting around the core of the mould. It can do this because the bit is made from tempered steel that's much harder than cast iron.'

'How do you produce steel?' I ask.

'It's produced in relatively small quantities in a bloomery process, using a higher proportion of charcoal to ore,' explains Tom. 'In this state it's very hard but brittle and will even break if you hit it with a hammer. The brittleness of the steel is reduced by tempering it - heating it and cooling it rapidly by plunging it into water. The man doing this has to carefully judge when it's hot enough. If it's only just a little bit cooler, it has no effect on reducing the brittleness.'

'That's quite fascinating,' says Dick, 'I'd like to see all this in operation.'

'Next time you're here, I'll be pleased to give you a full demonstration of everything,' says Tom. 'However, we really need to make a move now.'

9

To Tonbridge

Back at Moat House we eat a welcome breakfast in preparation for the journey ahead.

'I've decided to come with you as far as Tonbridge,' announces Tom. 'I'll return via Withyham where I'll spend a day or two visiting Elizabeth, before returning here with Dorothy and the children. I can also take your horses with me and return them to you at Hastings, sometime.'

'We'll be pleased to have your company,' replies Dick, warmly, now the unpleasantness of yesterday evening is well behind them.

'But before we go, let me give you Sir John's share of the money for the ship,' says Tom, handing Dick a bag of money and a letter. 'There's also a letter of introduction to a friend and business acquaintance in Rochester, Richard Watts, who I'm sure will provide you with a night's hospitality and assist you with your onward journey to London.'

'Thanks Tom,' say Dick, tucking the money into his doublet before glancing at the address on the letter. 'Satis: Latin for adequate, is an odd sort of name for a house,' he adds, showing off his knowledge of Latin that he'd learnt as part of his study of the law.

'Yes, it's a bit of self-deprecating humour.'

'How so?'

'When the Queen was in Rochester last year, she imposed herself and her retinue on Richard as he owns the best house in the city,' reports Tom, with a smile. 'Richard royally entertained her. Then when the Queen departed, he said he hoped she enjoyed her stay. To which the Queen merely replied, "satis", in a dismissive and condescending manner, indicating it was only just adequate. She then got in her carriage and drove off without further ado. So Richard, having a greater sense of humour than the Queen had gratitude, renamed his house Satis House.'[23]

We all laugh.

'I hope that hasn't put him off entertaining,' I add.

'You'll find him very hospitable. But if he's away on business, I suggest you seek accommodation at the Cooper's Arms, in nearby St Margaret's Street. Mention my name to the Landlord – Septimus Dymus,' suggests Tom. 'Now we really must be on our way. I've got Jim to put some skins of water on your horses. It's safe to drink, as it's come straight from my spring.'

'Thanks Tom, it'll make a pleasant change to drink undiluted water from a clean and secure source, as we dare not take water to drink from the Bourne in Hastings.'

As we leave the house to mount our horses, I notice that Jim has replaced Tom's rouncey with a small palfrey[24]. Tom looks a little foolish with his large frame atop such a small steed. But it sets off with a smooth ambling gait, of four equal beats, with three legs on the ground at any one time. Our rounceys can neither match it for speed nor smoothness in any of the two and three beat gaits they are capable of, and I'm filled with envy. 'When we get back from our venture, the first thing I'm going to spend some of our profits on is one of those racy little horses,' I say to John, as we attempt to keep up.

---

23 Satis House still exists. Charles Dickens used its name in his novel Great Expectations as the name of Miss Haversham's house, although according to Dickens's biographer, John Forster, he modelled the house on the nearby Restoration House.

24 A rouncey was a general purpose horse for riding and the carriage of goods. A palfrey was a small fast riding horse, with an unusually smooth gait of four beats, used for travelling – the little sports car of its day.

We ride up the hill onto the high road, past St Dunstan's Church with its graveyard containing a number of ancient yew trees with their craggy, peeling bark of reddish-brown and purple tones. Then quickly passing by the adjacent Archbishop's Palace we take the road towards Frant and Tonbridge.

After about four miles, just past the crossroads at the march of the three Parishes of Mayfield, Rotherfield and Wadhurst, the road is blocked by a cart that has shed a wheel. I suspect this is not an uncommon sight given the heavily rutted roads in the area. We dismount and lead our horses toward the obstruction, to see if we can render any assistance. As we approach, several hooded men, armed with hammers, cudgels and knives, leap out of the undergrowth and from behind the cart. Tom is quickly bundled into the ditch at the side of the road, while after a short struggle Dick is felled by a blow to the head and stabbed in his left shoulder. John and I, walking a distance behind them, draw our swords and rush to their aid. In face of this threat, the assailants flee in some disorder.

As I kneel down to attend to Dick, I spot two men at our rear taking hold of our horses.

'The horses!' I yell.

The two thieves, in a panic, are unable to mount the steeds but lead them off at a trot: one along the road towards Rotherfield and the other in the opposite direction towards Wadhurst.

'Quickly! You take the one on the right and I'll take the one on the left,' shouts John as he and I set off in pursuit.

I close quickly on my man. He lets go of the horses. And after he has felt the weight of my boot up his backside, I leave him to continue running off along the road. I gather the horses by the reins and as I turn to go, I see the other thief also let go of the horses. But instead of letting him escape, as I had done, John cuts him down with a slash of his sword to the back of his legs, runs him through where he falls and unceremoniously kicks his body into the drainage ditch by the side of the road.

When John and I arrive back, Dick is sitting up, dazed and bleeding, being attended to by Tom.

'I see you recovered the horses,' says Tom. 'What about the men?'

'Mine got away,' I say.

'Mine's dead in a ditch,' reports John, without displaying any sign of emotion, regret, guilt, triumph, or pleasure.

'Was that really necessary?' asks a shocked Tom.

'The man was a thief,' replies John, still without any flicker of emotion. 'He might have got away otherwise. But had we taken him, he'd have hanged. I just administered summary justice, and saved the magistrate and the hangman the trouble.'

'I hope you never have to face such arbitrary and summary justice for the sins of your chosen trade,' says Tom, disapprovingly.

'I just do what I can for me and my own. There's no sin in that. There'd be no sin in what that poor devil was doing either had he not been doing it to us.'

'So sins are what other people do which offend you, your family, friends and associates.'

'Exactly! And, in that descending order of priority.'

'You're quite the philosopher, John. It's not a philosophy I subscribe to, but I fear it's one more widely practised than I'd like to think.'

'Do you think the ambush was an attempt to confound our plans, Tom, or just chance?' I ask.

'I suspect they were just robbers,' replies Tom. 'It's not the first time this sort of thing has happened hereabouts. It was probably just our bad luck to be in the wrong place at the wrong time. But you never know these days. It would be as well to be extra vigilant from now on.'

'Can Dick ride?' enquires John.

Dick tries, but fails to get to his feet.

'I'm afraid Dick won't be able to travel anywhere for the next few days,' says Tom, with concern. 'I'll take him back to Moat House where his injuries can be better tended. I'll also inform the Constable of Loxfield Hundred of the incident, and he can sort out any question of jurisdiction with the Constable of Rotherfield. They can make arrangements to recover the body, if it hasn't been collected by the fellow's confederates by then.'

'Will we need to remain to see the Constable,' I ask, concerned by the delay this would cause.

'John should really stay to provide a statement,' states Tom, giving John a disapproving glance. 'But I think it best if you both go on. I'm sure the Constable will take my word of what happened as a man of standing in the community, and by looking at Dick's wound.'

We get Dick into his saddle, with Tom behind him to prevent him falling. I take the money and letter of introduction from Dick's doublet. As I do so he whispers, 'Be careful, Rob, in handling John. I've seen a side to him today that I've not seen before.'

'I will, don't you worry,' I reply. 'Just concentrate on getting better.'

'Now, don't forget, Rob, you're to contact Walter the boatman at the Chequers Inn, near the bridge in Tonbridge. He's expecting you and will take you by river to Rochester. He has been promised a florin to cover his fee, food and lodging,' instructs Tom. 'And when you get to Rochester…'

I interrupt him before he has a chance to finish, 'Don't worry, Tom. John and I know exactly what to do in Tonbridge, Rochester and London. You take care of Dick and we'll see you both at Newhaven.'

'I know, but there's a lot riding on this. There is just one final thing, though. Leave the horses at the inn. I'll arrange for young Jim to collect them after he's taken a message to Dorothy to remain at Withyham a little longer, until I'm able to come for her and the children.'

We bid our final farewells and go our separate ways: Tom and Dick back to Moat House, and John and I in the opposite direction along the road towards Frant and Tonbridge.

We arrive at the Chequers Inn, later than expected but without further incident.

'Two pints of your best ale, landlord,' I order. 'Can you tell us where to find Walter the boatman, please? We were supposed to meet him here but were delayed on the road.'

Before the landlord can reply, a small tough looking man of indeterminable years interrupts, 'If you buy me a pint, I'll take you to him.'

'You have a deal,' I say.

'Is that your usual cider, Walter?' asks the landlord with a chuckle.

'Aye, it is, Will,' replies the man.

We all laugh and introduce ourselves properly as the landlord serves the beer and cider.

'You're much later than I'd expected,' says Walter. 'We won't make it to Rochester before dark. So, I suggest we stay overnight in Maidstone.'

'I'm afraid we'd a little trouble on the road that delayed us,' I say, without further explanation, not wanting to cause any alarm with the details of the event. 'But we're anxious to get to Rochester and beyond as soon as possible.'

'We can set off from Maidstone at first light tomorrow and I'll have you in Rochester within a couple of hours. It'll be a lot quicker and easier than it is from here to Maidstone.'

'Well, I suppose we ought to get underway now,' suggests John, downing the remnants of his pint.

'Right you are, sirs, my boat is on the river just downstream of the bridge.'

I finish my pint, and as I place the empty flagon on the bar I ask, 'Can you stable our horses, landlord? They'll be collected in a day or so by a retainer of Mr Thomas Isted of Mayfield.'

'That's no problem, sir. I'll get my lad to put them in the stable.'

'Thank you. Here's sixpence for your trouble,' I add, handing him the small silver coin.

The landlord bites the coin to ensure it has not been debased by lead. Then with a sucking of his teeth says, 'That will do nicely, sir.'

We collect our saddlebags, food and skins of water, and follow Walter to his boat, which is moored on the opposite side of the nearby, five-arched, sandstone bridge that spans the Medway.

'There's just one thing before we go, sir, the matter of,' says Walter, clearing his throat, holding out his calloused and grubby hand.

'Of course. I think a florin was the agreed price,' I reply, handing Walter a silver coin.

Walter bites the coin, as the landlord had done and says, 'It's a pleasure doing business with you, sir.'

10

To London

John and I board Walter's boat: a relatively narrow, lightweight, shallow-draft vessel of no more than eight feet long. We set off immediately, with Walter at the oars in the middle, John in the bow and me in the stern.

The bridge at Tonbridge; and the imposing castle with its massive sandstone curtain walls, high keep and impressive gatehouse, quickly diminish in size and disappear as we make steady progress down river. We pass through some flash-gates across some weirs; swap boats at one particularly difficult weir, through a local arrangement between a number of boatmen who work the river; and alight to porter the boat for a short distance at Yalding and Teston. Then some four hours later, as we round a bend in the river, Maidstone comes into view.

We moor the boat at a landing on the east side of the river by the Collegiate Church of All Saints that is built of ragstone, in the Gothic perpendicular style, with buttressed walls and a crenellated parapet. A little further downstream, I notice the old Archbishop's Palace, with its central two-storey section built of ashlar stonework, and timber framed wings at either side.

'Maidstone looks like a big and prosperous place,' I remark, looking around.

'It is that,' replies Walter. 'There be more than two and a half thousand souls living in the town nowadays. But you should see the crowds here at the weekly market, at Lockmeadow[25], on the other side of the river.'

'I suppose you must come here a lot.'

'Aye, sir. I live here; born and bred a Man of Kent[26],' replies Walter. 'My home is just off Knightrider Street, not far from here. It'll make a nice change for me to sleep with the wife tonight. She knows I may be coming, so there shouldn't be any nasty surprises,' he adds with a chuckle.

John and I spend a quiet night at the inn. I sleep well despite the sound of scurrying mice within the plaster and lathe walls, and the unfortunate events of the day and my concern about Dick.

Walter collects us half an hour after the sounding of the prime bell.

We board the boat just as the tide has turned and we make steady progress downstream, with hardly any need to use the oars other than to maintain course.

We pass by the fire damaged Allington Castle, Aylesford Priory and a host of small villages. Then as we round a bend in the river, we are greeted with the sight of the imposing Rochester Castle and the equally impressive cathedral, surrounded by the sturdy city walls. As we get closer, we can also clearly see Rochester Bridge[27] spanning the Medway, with its eleven stone

---

25 Maidstone was awarded a charter to hold a market at Lockmeadow, by King Henry III, in 1261. Markets are still held there every Tuesday and Saturday.

26 Men and Maids of Kent live east of the River Medway, an area that was traditionally settled by the Jutes. Kentish Men and Maids live to the west of the river an area that was traditionally settled by Saxons.

27 A bridge crossing the Medway at Rochester has existed since Roman Times. In 1391, Sir Robert Knollys and Sir John de Cobham built a stone bridge. They also instituted the Wardens and Communality of Rochester Bridge that is still responsible for the current bridge's maintenance.

built arches, and a drawbridge and winding house between the sixth and seventh piers. The drawbridge is up and a ship with a tall mast is passing through it on its way downstream.

We alight from the boat, downstream of the bridge on the east bank.

John and I set off along the busy black cobbled, cartwheel rutted, high street. Turning through the arch of the Cemetery Gate, made of patterned stone and flint, we are greeted with the impressive façade of the Norman cathedral. It has fine ornate carvings around the tympanum above the main door; and many gargoyles in the form of animals, people and mythical beasts.

Opposite the cathedral stands the castle, with its curtain wall enclosing the tallest keep in England, made largely of irregular Kentish ragstone. Curiously, at the southwest corner of the curtain wall and keep stand round towers, in contrast to all the others that are square[28]. Then in front of us at the top of Boley Hill, at the left hand corner of the castle ditch, I notice a melee going on beneath an elm tree. A man is being forcibly led away, followed by an unruly crowd shouting insults at him.

'What's going on?' I ask of a stranger.

'Simon the butcher has been short selling meat in the market, by altering his weights. He's just been convicted at summary trial, at the Pie Powder Court[29] held under yonder Justice Tree,' replies the stranger, pointing to the elm tree.

'What's going to happen to him now?'

---

28 The round towers were built to replace the square ones that were destroyed by King John, during the great siege of 1215, during the First Baron's War that was caused by the King's refusal to abide by the Magna Carta.

29 Pie Powder Courts were established by boroughs during markets to deal with disputes between merchants, acts of theft and violence. Their use declined over the years, but they were not formally abolished until the Administration of Justice Act of 1977.

'He's going to be put in the stocks near the High Street,' he adds with obvious delight, as he runs off in pursuit of the hapless butcher.

John and I walk on past the Justice Tree and spot a small sign on a gate, saying Satis House. I knock on the door of the impressively large house, which is opened by a pretty and neat young servant girl. 'Is Mr Watts at home?' I enquire. 'I have a letter of introduction for him.'

'I'll go and see,' replies the girl, taking the letter and scuttling off, leaving us on the threshold. She reappears a few minutes later. 'Will you come this way, gentlemen, please?'

John and I follow her to a room at the back of the house. An elderly gentleman with long white locks of thinning hair and a full white beard is sitting at a desk. A middle-aged lady wearing a white cap and a black dress sits embroidering in a nearby window.

'I'm Richard Watts and this is my wife, Miriam,' says the old man by way of introduction.

'How do you do, sir? I'm Robert Isted and this is my brother-in-law, John Hills,' I reply. 'Ma'am,' I add, nodding in the direction of Mrs Watts. She looks up, smiles back and continues to sew in silence.

'I see from Thomas's letter, you're on your way to London. He asks if I'll assist you while you're here and help you on your way,' says Mr Watts, glancing at the letter and putting it down on his polished desk.

'We'd be most grateful if you would.'

'You're in luck,' says Mr Watts, with a smile. 'There's a coastal sailing barge leaving Town Quay for London, on this afternoon's tide. It's carrying some goods for me. I'll send a message to the master, William Weekes, to let him know you'll be sailing with him. Then, I'll get my man to escort you there once you've had some refreshment.'

There is only one vessel on the quay – the *River Queen*: a small two-mast, fore and aft spritsail rigged barge, shallow in draft, broad in the beam, with a degree of flair at the sides and almost plumb ends.

'Ahoy there,' I shout to a sturdy man with a tanned weather-beaten face. 'Are you Captain Weekes?'

'I am,' replies the man. 'You must be Mr Isted and Mr Hills who want passage to London.'

'Yes.'

'Come aboard, gentlemen, we'll be ready to sail shortly, at the stand of the tide.'

As we cast off, the south-westerly breeze fills the rust red, flaxen sails and we are quickly off on a run in the stream.

We sail past Chatham Dockyard's new repair facility, at Sunne Hard, where John and I look out and see shipwrights working on the hull of a three-mast galleon breached on the muddy riverbank.

A little further on we spot a whole host of ships of war moored in a long line athwart the stream, flying the Navy ensign of green and white stripes, with the Cross of St George in the canton. Amongst these are the navy's latest ships, the *Dreadnought* and *Swiftsure,* with no forecastle to speak of compared to the older vessels.

Beyond them, on the opposite bank stands the recently completed Upnor Castle – an artillery fort protecting Chatham Dockyard and the fleet at anchor.

When we reach more open water in Long Reach, we put up full sail and make swifter progress towards the Isle of Sheppey. Then rounding Grain Spit and Roas Bank, we sail out of the Medway and into the Thames. A little while later, we put into the docks at Cliffe where we stay overnight.

John and I sleep well in the cramped, dark, aft cabin. We emerge on deck later than we had intended.

'Good morning, gentlemen,' says Captain Weekes. 'It's a fine morning.

'Good morning,' I reply, stifling a yawn. 'When do you think we'll arrive at our destination?'

'It won't be long before we've finished loading our cargo of salt from the local saltpans and be ready to cast off,' replies the captain. 'We'll catch the tide at exactly the right time. With luck we should make London by the time it turns again, in six hours. In the meantime, there're some biscuits, cheese and beer for breakfast.'

'That's excellent, thank you.'

'I could eat a horse,' says John, as we try to soften the hard tack biscuits in our beer.

'The horse would've been preferable,' I quip, as I try to bite a small piece from the edge of the soaked biscuit.

'Aye. But you'd better get used to it,' warns John. 'Biscuits like these will be a staple part of your diet from now on.'

The *River Queen* sets sail close-hauled against the prevailing wind, past Higham Saltings and along the Saxon Shore.

Where the river narrows between Gravesend and Tilbury, we see the large water bastions of the Hermitage Bulwark at Tilbury and the Gravesend fort jutting out into the river that protect London from a naval attack.

We sail on meandering with the river. As we turn into Galleon's Reach, by Woolwich Dockyard, we see the remains of a large burnt out carrack beached on the mud – the *Harry Grace a Dieu*. It seems a sad end for any vessel and a salutary reminder of the dangers of fire aboard ship.

We meander on through Woolwich and Blackwall Reaches and into Greenwich Reach, where we see the Palace of

Placentia:[30] a magnificent red brick built palace that runs an enormous length of the riverfront. At the eastern end there appears to be a forge, not dissimilar to Tom's, surrounded by outbuildings. Beyond that lies a stable and what appears to be a tiltyard for jousting.

We round the next bend, past Deptford Creek, and see Deptford Dockyard[31] on our larboard side that stretches along the Thames for more than two hundred yards. There is a graving dock with wooden floodgates, in which there is a galleon that I assume is undergoing graving: the cleaning and removal of barnacles from its hull. Just beyond the docks there are some large tidal basins accessed from the river by open narrow watergates. There are a number of ships of war in the basins, but not as many as we had seen at Chatham.

Then as we round the bend at Wapping, we see the full magnificence of the Tower of London: the imposing fortress that is the gateway to London and Westminster beyond. Its parallelepiped keep – the White Tower – made of Kentish ragstone, is not quite as tall as Rochester's. But with its ashlars of Caen stone laid around the corners, windows and arrow-slits, it gives it the impression of greater sturdiness and symmetrical beauty.

As Captain Weekes brings the River Queen alongside Tower Wharf, just upstream of the Water Gate[32], I notice there are four ships at anchor in the stream.

---

30 The Palace of Placentia was the principal royal palace during the Tudor Period. However, it fell into disrepair during the Stuart and Commonwealth periods. Charles II had it demolished and replaced with what is now the Old Royal Naval College, Greenwich.

31 Deptford Dockyard was founded in 1519 and closed in 1869, although a naval victualing depot continued there until 1960.

32 The Water Gate is now commonly known as Traitors Gate, as many Tudor prisoners entered the Tower of London through the gate.

John and I go ashore. 'Goodbye, Captain Weekes. Fair winds and following seas,' I say in farewell.

'And long may your big jibs draw,' replies the captain, as we make our way along the wharf eager to take possession of our ship.

11

The Tower of London

John and I walk along the wharf towards the main gate at the southwest corner of the Tower. As we do so, we finally see the *Barque of Bulleyn*, with its distinctive black bull figurehead below its bowsprit, which is the furthest of the ships at anchor in the stream.

'She's not quite as I'd envisaged; not at all typical of any of our ships,' says John.

'What do you mean?' I ask.

'For a start, she's carvel-built[33]; not clinker-built like most of ours.'

'I suppose that's because she was originally a Frenchie.'

'It also looks like she's had some extensive refit work done on her to reduce the height of the forecastle, along the lines of the Dreadnought design,' remarks John, pointing out the alterations. 'Her mizzen mast is also lateen rigged like her bonaventure, and not square rigged like her main and foremasts.'[34]

---

33 Carvel-built ships have their hull planking flush and smooth, with their edges laid close to each other; as opposed to clinker-built ships, where the planking overlaps.

34 Nowadays barks or barques are classified as ships with three or more masts, with all but the mizzen being square rigged. However, that was not the case in the 16th century. It is not totally clear how the *Barque of Bulleyn* was rigged, but taking into account the ships in the Anthony Rolls, and the archeology of the *Mary Rose* the assumption is the fore and main masts were square rigged and the mizzen and bonaventure masts were lateen rigged.

'It does look a little odd.'

'But it may give her greater manoeuvrability and ability to sail close to the wind, without unduly affecting her downwind speed,' adds John, thoughtfully. 'But we won't know that for sure, until we take her out and put her through her paces.'

'I can also make out four weatherproof gun ports on the starboard side and two in the bow,' I say, excitedly. 'If that's mirrored on the larboard side she's got ten guns. That's as many as we have defending Hastings' wall; more than enough for our purposes.'

'We should be able to work out some nice tactics for taking merchant ships at sea.'

'Let's see Barons, and then go aboard to give her a good look over,' I add, eagerly.

We cross the bridge over the moat towards the Byward Tower entrance with its cylindrical towers on either side. There we are greeted by a Yeoman Warder wearing a red jacket with black stripes and gold patterning on the breast, overlaid on the left side with a badge consisting of a red, white and green rose below a golden crown. Around his neck he wears a white ruff made of starched linen cambric, and perched on his head is a cap with a grey feather in it. He bars our way with a halberd about one and a half times as tall as him. 'Can I help you, gentlemen?' he asks.

'Can you tell us where we can find Mr Barons, one of the masters under the admiral?' I ask in reply.

'Is he expecting you gentlemen?'

'Yes, but we don't have a specific appointment.'

'I'll get someone to escort you.'

'That won't be necessary. If you just explain where he is, I'm sure we can find him.'

'No! That won't do at all, gentlemen,' states the Yeoman, looking aghast at our suggestion we should be allowed in unattended. 'We can't let all and sundry in here. This is a Royal palace. Although the Queen doesn't stay here, we have a number of guests detained at Her Majesty's pleasure; and we don't want any of them going missing, now do we. So you'll be escorted whether you think it necessary or not. Jack, take these two gentlemen to Mr Barons in the Wakefield Tower,' he adds, calling to a young messenger boy squatting just inside the gate.

The young messenger escorts us along the inside of the curtain wall, past the Bloody Tower, to Wakefield Tower that stands just behind the Water Gate. As we enter the building, I cannot help but notice the immense thickness of its walls: some fifteen feet thick.

We walk past a number of rooms filled with shelves crammed full of rolls of parchment, until we arrive at a closed door with Mr Barons's name on it. The messenger knocks on the door and we enter the office. 'I have two gentlemen to see you, sir,' he says.

Mr Barons, a large man with a woeful countenance, looks up from behind his chart-strewn desk. 'Who might they be?' he asks.

'I'm Robert Isted and this is John Hills,' I reply.

'Ah, the gentlemen I've been expecting about the *Barque of Bulleyn*. Do you have the money with you?'

'Yes, but we'd like to inspect her first,' I say.

'You're welcome to,' says Barons in a disagreeable manner. 'She's old but has had some rebuilding work done on her. You'll find her ship shape, if not exactly Bristol fashion. If you decide you don't want her, there're others who'll buy her for more than the price agreed with Sir John Pelham.'

'Nevertheless, we'd like to inspect her first.'

'She's ahead of the line anchored in the stream. Come back and see me when you're done and ready to pay me the money.'

'Will someone escort us?' I ask.

'No! You can find your own way there,' says the disagreeable Barons. 'It's easy enough. Just help yourself to a boat at the Water Gate.'

'So much for security,' remarks John, as we leave Barons's office.

We take a boat from the Water Gate, unchallenged by the Yeoman Warder on duty there, and row out to the ship. We climb the ladder, amidships on the larboard side, and disturb the ship-keeper asleep on watch. 'What can I do for you, gentlemen?' he says, yawning.

'We're the prospective owners, come to have a look around before we take possession of her,' I answer.

'She's a fine ship, sir. Would you like me to show you around?'

'No, that's all right. We can see ourselves around,' replies John, who seems to be relishing having a deck of such a ship beneath his feet. 'But first, can you provide us with a lantern to light our way below?'

'Aye, I've a whale oil lantern somewhere,' replies the ship-keeper, who duly goes off to fetch it. As he does so, I survey the river from our elevated position and get a good view of London Bridge, a little further upstream. I count eighteen stone arches, with a drawbridge and winding house in the centre of the bridge. It is quite unlike any other bridge I've seen anywhere else, with countless stone buildings standing on it. Some are several stories high that overhang the river by several feet, with many of them forming an enclosed tunnel above its road. At either end of the bridge are two brick gatehouses. On top of the gatehouse on the southern side, there are more than twenty severed and tarred heads of traitors displayed on pikes. Some of them must have been there for years.

My sightseeing is interrupted by the ship-keeper returning with the lantern.

'Where shall we start, John?' I ask.

'I think we should start from the bottom upwards,' replies John, taking the lantern from the ship-keeper. 'Although she looks a fine ship at first sight, if the keel isn't sound and there're problems below the waterline she may not be seaworthy.'

We go down the ladder onto the gun deck and stop suddenly in our tracks. 'There aren't any guns,' says John, with some surprise.

'Maybe they've been taken ashore while the ship was laid up,' I say, hopefully.

'Possibly. But if so, they may have been reissued to other ships, or we'll have a devil of a job getting them back from the Board of Ordnance,' states John, dampening my spirits. 'By the way, how much are you paying for her?' he adds.

'Sixty-five pounds.'

'For that price you're unlikely to get her fitted out with cannon, or much else, and she's still a bargain at that. I only hope you've brought more money with you to pay for the things we're going to need.'

'I haven't brought much,' I reply, somewhat downhearted. 'But, I'll get an advance of the fee for escorting the wool fleet, when I see the Admiral's Clerk, Mr Parker,' I add, more cheerily.

'How much is that?'

'Twenty pounds in advance of the thirty we're due for the commission.'

'Let's see what else we need. But I've a feeling that may barely cover everything, and that doesn't include cannon.'

We move below onto the orlop deck, where we crouch beneath its low deckhead. 'As I suspected, there's no spare cable, nor any other spare gear, nor stores of any kind,' remarks John, as we survey the empty space.

We move further below and make our way carefully around the dark cramped space surveying the keel and planking below the waterline.

'The good news is the keel is sound, the masts are all well seated, and she's watertight,' says John, with some delight and some relief to me. 'She's had some furring done at some stage that's made her slightly wider in the beam.'

'Furring?'

'Yes, you can see they've added a second layer of tapered framing timbers to the futtocks,' says John, banging his palm on one of the ships' ribs. 'This has added a bit to her beam. But, she's still fairly narrow there: not unduly broad for a ship of her length. It could've been done to improve her stability: possibly to correct a design flaw, or allow her to take a better sail, or accommodate the change to its current configuration. Some people don't like this sort of thing, but when it's done properly it can enhance performance. The shipwright work looks first rate,' he adds, tapping the timbers once again.

'I see,' I reply, without really understanding the naval architectural implications.

'Let's have a look what we've got above deck and then discuss where we go from there.'

Back on the main deck, we enter the captain's cabin below the quarterdeck and discover there is no furniture. 'Why am I not surprised,' exclaims John.

'It looks like we'll have a pretty long list of requirements,' I say, disappointedly. 'I only hope the money I have will stretch that far. In any event, we won't recover most of the purchase price from our first two commissions, as we'd thought.'

'We'll see if anything has been put in a lay apart store and what else we might be able to squeeze out of Barons and the naval storehouse, gratis. Then we can put things in priority order and start spending your money,' says John, with quiet purpose.

We disembark, row ashore and pass through the Water Gate unchallenged by the Yeoman Warder; then walk the short distance back to Barons's office, a little subdued but not downhearted.

'Well, gentlemen, what do you think of her?' enquires Barons, as we enter his office.

'She's a bit long in the tooth but has nice lines. She might suit our purpose. But when are you going to put back the cannon, furniture, spare gear, and navigation equipment?' demands John.

Barons laughs, in complete contrast to his previously miserable demeanour. 'I'm sorry, gentlemen, I haven't had cause to laugh so much since I saw Nicholas Udall's "Ralph Roister Doister", at the Red Lion theatre, before it closed due to the plague,' he says, still chortling.

John and I laugh as well, partially as a nervous reaction, but mainly at the spectacle of the erstwhile miserable Barons laughing.

Barons regains his composure, returning to his previously gruff self. 'You can forget about the cannon for a start. The brass falcon was removed and sent to the Board of Ordnance in the White Tower, for melting down and recasting. The wrought iron portes piece[35], fowlers[36] and quarter slings[37] were extremely old and might well have shattered if they'd been fired much more. They were all sent for scrap. As for everything else, it went back into the naval storehouse and was either condemned, sold on, or reissued long ago.'

---

35 A portes piece was a large wrought iron breech-loading gun with a ten-inch bore.

36 A fowler was a wrought iron breech-loading gun that fired stone shot.

37 A quarter sling was a wrought iron small bore breech-loading gun.

'That's unexpected and disappointing,' I remark.

'What do you expect for the money you're paying? Do you want her or not? I haven't got all day.'

'We'll take her. Here's the money,' I say, slamming the leather purse containing the sixty-five pounds on the table in front of Barons. 'I'd like a receipt for it,' I add, forcefully.

'All right, gentlemen,' replies Barons, counting the money, before writing out a receipt on a scrap of paper and handing it to me. 'You've got yourself a fine ship at a bargain price. But if you don't get her out of here within a week, I'll charge you mooring fees.'

'We'll be gone by then, don't you worry,' I reply, irritated by the lack of common courtesy.

Barons ignores us and resumes looking at the charts on his desk. We leave his office, slamming the door on the disagreeable encounter.

'We've got a lot to do in a week: get the ship fitted out, stored and crewed, and then get the hell out of here,' states John, still annoyed by Barons.

'We'd better start by seeing Parker,' I say, 'to receive the commission and the money, and see what help we might be able to get from him.'

12

The Admiral's Clerk

'Do I have the pleasure of addressing Mr Parker?' I ask, entering the office with Mr Parker's name on the door, next to the office of the Lord High Admiral of England, The Earl of Lincoln.

'Aye,' comes the reply, 'but it remains to be seen whether it's a pleasure or not.'

'I hope it will be,' I say, more in hope than expectation after the encounter with the peevish Barons. 'My name is Robert Isted and this is my brother-in-law, John Hills.'

'It's a pleasure gentleman,' says Parker, extending his hand. 'I've been expecting you. Please excuse my rather rude greeting. The admiral's gout is playing him up, and he's leading Mr Barons and me a merry dance about his plans to standardise the ensigns and review the cipher flags. But that's not your concern. You're here about your commission.'

'I also believe you have a certain letter for us as well?'

'You mean the letter of marque. I have everything right here,' states Parker, as he reaches into his desk draw and pulls out two documents containing official seals, and a bag of money. 'I think you'll find everything in order.'

'I'm sure it is,' I say, taking hold of the documents and the money. 'But I understand there's a condition attached to the letter.'

'Only the standard one: any brass cannon you take are to be surrendered to the Board of Ordnance for Crown use.'

'That's no problem. I was also wondering whether you could render us some assistance in taking on crew? I'll be happy to pay you for your time and effort.'

'I'm sure I can help you out there,' replies Parker. 'I'll get my assistants Jasper Swift, Fox and Pope to put the word out. I'll also be happy to be in attendance, if you wish. I know many of the men and can help you sort the wheat from the chaff.'

'I'd appreciate that. I could also do with your advice about fitting her out and storing her - she's a completely empty vessel,' I say, hoping this run of co-operation will hold.

'I'll give you a letter for Mr Christopher Epps, a Storekeeper of the Navy, at Deptford, asking him to give you whatever assistance he can,' replies the helpful Parker. 'I'll also have a word with Richard Bowland, Storekeeper of the Ordnance, to see what he might be able to do regarding ordnance and habiliments.'

'How much will all that cost, do you think?'

'I don't know,' says Parker, scratching his head. 'But you'll only be charged cost price, plus some small gratuities. Let's say a crown for me and Mr Epps and a shilling a piece for Fox, Pope and Swift. However, I can't speak for Mr Bowland's people, or even whether he'll be prepared to help.'

'That seems fair. The only problem is, we've little more with us than the advance of our commission,' I add with a little embarrassment.

'Hmmm,' murmurs Parker, thoughtfully. 'I've only a little discretion regarding the advance payment for your commission. I can advance you twenty-three pounds, which is only three pounds more than I've already given you. However, I'll take the fees for my men, Mr Epps and me, and anything Mr Bowland and his people require, from the balance we owe you. Anything left over will be paid to you on your return, or to your representative when we've word that you've completed your commission.'

'That's kind of you, Mr Parker. I'm in your debt.'

'Don't mention it. I'll even arrange to get your ship alongside the Tower Wharf, rather than leave her moored in the stream. It'll make things a lot easier for seeing potential crew and loading provisions.'

'But Mr Barons was talking about charging us mooring fees in the river,' I reply, concerned about the rising cost.

'Don't worry about Mr Barons,' says Parker, reassuringly. 'He's obviously having a bad day. I'll make arrangements to move the ship tomorrow. It won't cost you a penny and you can stay a day or two longer if need be.'

'I'm most grateful.'

'Now where're you thinking of taking your ship after you've escorted the wool fleet to Sluis?'

'John and I've discussed it briefly,' I reply. 'I haven't entirely made up my mind, but we thought we'd work up the ship and crew in the narrow seas; perhaps intercepting foreign ships in the Channel, or maybe even coming out of the Baltic.'

'And then?'

'We'll probably lay the ship up in Hastings over the worst of the winter months, and then plan a new campaign next spring.' I add. 'If I could afford to acquire another ship, or work in concert with someone else, I'd like to consider branching out further - looking to intercept Spanish treasure ships en route from the Americas.'

'A worthy and ambitious plan,' replies Parker, seemingly impressed by our aims. 'Come and see me next winter and I'll see if the admiral will be prepared to part with another of the ships we've more or less permanently laid up. In the meantime, we can look to take on crew with the requisite knowledge and experience for your immediate plans.'

'That would be most helpful.'

'Jasper,' shouts Parker. A young man quickly appears at the door. 'Jasper, these gentlemen require a crew for the *Barque of Bulleyn*. I'd like you, Fox and Pope to put the word out and direct suitable seamen to attend aboard the ship, on Tuesday, at one bell on the afternoon watch. Oh, and see if the Scotsmen Fisher and Johnston, and the Frenchman Fontane, are still around.' Jasper turns to go. 'Oh and while I remember, get John Gulecht, the Dutchman, to put the word around in his tavern.' Jasper turns to go again, 'Oh, and Jasper, arrange for the ship to be brought alongside the wharf by noon tomorrow.' Jasper hesitates to go. 'That's all, Jasper. Now make it so.'

'That's excellent,' I say, grateful for the arrangements. 'Now, when can we arrange to obtain the stores and fittings from Deptford.'

'That reminds me,' says Parker, taking another paper from his desk and handing it to me. 'I'd forget my head if it wasn't fastened on. I was given this invitation for you to dine with Henry Knollys, in his apartments in the Palace of Placentia at Greenwich, on Monday evening. If you decide to accept, I'll write a letter of introduction for you to give to Mr Epps at Deptford, along with your list of requirements, on your way to or from Greenwich.'

'I'd prefer to get things underway with the stores before then, if possible.'

'That's not a problem either. I'll arrange for you to go to Deptford tomorrow. But what are your intentions regarding Knollys's invitation?'

'I don't know Henry Knollys, or anything about him, so why has he invited me to dine with him, Mr Parker?'

'It could be any number of reasons,' says Parker, pausing for thought. 'He'd his eye on the *Barque of Bulleyn* at one time. He owns a privateer ship the *Elephant*. Perhaps he wanted it for a similar purpose. In any event, you should be aware he's the Queen's second cousin, on her maternal side, although there're rumours he may be related even more closely than that.'

'What do you mean?'

'The Queen's aunt, Mary Boleyn, was King Henry's mistress. Her daughter, Catherine Carey, Knollys's late mother, had something of the old King's looks and colouring; as does Knollys,' says Parker, with a wink. 'Royal descent has never been acknowledged, nor claimed. But given recent history, that would be a dangerous thing. Nevertheless, if Her Majesty remains unmarried and without issue, and the Roman Catholic Mary Queen of Scots remains the official heir to the throne, you never know what might happen if there is need to cast around for an English Protestant successor.'

'But he'd be excluded because he's from a bastard line,' I say, reflecting on some limitations of inheritance placed on me by my birth.

'But it's happened before,' explains Parker. 'William the Conqueror was a bastard, and the Tudors are from an illegitimate Lancastrian line. Although the line was retrospectively legitimised, it was still specifically excluded from succession. Henry Knollys is the eldest male of his line, if we exclude his mother's younger brother Baron Hunsdon who is every inch a Carey. There are, of course, other suspected royal bastard lines, but none surviving that are so well believed and none that are also maternally related to Queen Elizabeth.'

'I had no clue about any of that,' I say, with surprise.

'I probably shouldn't have told you all that. So please be discreet with the information.'

'I will.'

'You should also be aware that Knollys is something of a favourite of the Queen, as was his mother, despite neither being shown favour in the form of titles,' adds Parker. 'But, he's recently been made an Esquire to the Body of the Queen, which is why we see him occasionally at the Tower and why he has apartments at the palace at Greenwich.'

'Thank you for the information,' I say. 'John and I will certainly be interested to hear what he wants, and to dine in apartments in a Royal palace.'

'I don't think I'd better go,' says John. 'I'll be a bit out of place dining with the likes of such folk at a palace. I can find plenty of other things to do.'

'All right, John, if you're sure. Now, I suppose we'd better go and find somewhere to stay tonight.'

'I'll be going home shortly,' says Parker. 'I take a wherryboat from here to the stairs at the Pelican Inn[38], close to where I live in Wapping. I'm sure the inn will have room for you. You can then travel back here with me in the morning.'

Mr Parker clears his desk and we make our way onto Tower Wharf.

'Eastward ho,' shouts Parker, to a passing wherry: a bright red, wide beamed, clinker-built water taxi, about ten feet long with an extremely pointed bow.

'Where to?' asks the wherryman, who wears the green jacket bearing the badge of the Company of Watermen[39] that licenses and regulates watermen and wherrymen working on the Thames.

'The Pelican at Wapping.'

'That'll be a penny each, gentlemen.'

We step into the boat and Parker duly pays the money.

---

38 The Pelican Inn is now called the Prospect of Whitby.

39 The Company of Watermen licensed and regulated wherrys operating between Hampton Court and Gravesend under an Act of Parliament dated 1555.

The wherryman rows eastward along the north bank of the Thames. As we pass Wapping Stairs, John and I can't help noticing a man hanging from a simple gallows consisting of two upright posts and a crosspiece, on the shoreline just east of the stairs.

'I see you've noticed the Admiralty gallows at Execution Dock,'[40] observes Parker. 'It's for the exclusive use of the Admiralty. That's one of Jack Callis's men who was captured ashore recently and convicted of piracy in the High Court of the Admiralty. He was hanged two days ago and did a pretty Marshall's dance that drew great cheers from the crowd.'

'A Marshall's dance?' I ask.

'Yes. You'll notice we hang them on a short rope so their necks aren't broken and they slowly choke to death,' says Parker, in a detached manner. 'This causes their limbs to twitch in a strange sort of dance, which we call the Marshall's dance after the Admiralty and City Marshalls who preside over the executions. We usually leave the bodies there until they've been covered by at least three tides. This one will be cut down tomorrow, tarred and hung in chains at Cuckold's Point near Rotherhithe, as a warning to others.'

John and I look on uncomfortably and in silence.

'There's no need for you gentlemen to worry,' says Parker, sensing our unease. 'You have a letter of marque, and as long as you operate within its bounds, you have nothing to worry about from the Admiralty.'

Shortly afterwards we reach the Pelican, a relatively new waterside tavern. The wherryman puts ashore bow first, so the long pointed bow provides a bridge for us over the worst of the mud. Nevertheless, we take care in alighting to avoid stepping in the sewage washed up on the shore and a couple of large

---

40 Execution Dock was exclusively used for the execution of pirates, smugglers and mutineers. It was last used in 1830.

black rats that seem unconcerned by our arrival. We then climb the Pelican Stairs leading to the tavern.

John and I spend the evening at the Pelican Inn, making out four lists of our requirements: habiliments; victuals; navigation equipment and charts; and ordnance, weapons and munitions. We then retire and spend a peaceful night, despite the inn being frequented by some dubious characters that jokingly refer to it as the Devil's tavern. At least we assume they were joking.

13

Cannon

Parker calls for John and me, about an hour after dawn, and we make the reverse journey back to the Tower through the early morning mist blanketing the river.

'Did you make out your list of requirements?' enquires Parker, as we enter his office.

'Yes and I'm ready to go to Deptford to see what we can obtain from the naval stores,' I reply.

'We have a boat going to Woolwich Dockyard at noon. I'll arrange for it to drop you off at Deptford and then to call at Greenwich to let Knollys know you'll be accepting his invitation.'

'That's very kind.'

'It's no bother. Can I have a look at the lists you've prepared?'

'Certainly,' I reply, handing the lists to Parker.

'They seem quite comprehensive. But I suspect other things will occur to you later,' says Parker, carefully perusing the lists. 'I suggest you see Mr Epps about the victuals, as well as the naval stores. Fresher food can be had at a cheaper price in Deptford than we can get in London. I'd also ask him about the navigation equipment. I'm sure he'll have some of the basic things like a traverse board, log and lead lines, sand clocks and a cross-staff.'

'What about charts?'

'Hmm. The Board of Ordnance has received sample copies of some of Sexton's maps of parts of England. I suspect he will get the contract to produce maps for the entire country. I obviously can't let you have any of them, but you're welcome to see them and make copies of the coastlines of any. I can also let you have a copy of Lily's *Britanniæ Insulæ;* along with the latest map of the Western Scheldt, produced by Abraham Ortelius of Antwerp, that will be useful for your commission.'

'That's excellent,' interjects John. 'Could I have a look at them while Rob's away at Deptford?'

'I think that can be arranged,' says the helpful Parker. 'As for the ordnance, weapons and munitions, I'll see what I can get through Mr Bowland of the Board of Ordnance. But, I'm not hopeful we'll achieve very much.'

'I only wish I could get a message to my cousin, Thomas Isted of Mayfield,' I say. 'He could arrange to fit the ship out with cannon when we arrive at Newhaven.'

'That can be arranged.'

'How so?'

'You can use the Queen's post,' offers Parker. 'We've riders leaving from here every day, on all the main roads radiating from London. There're post stations every ten miles or so, where the riders change horses or the post is handed on to other riders. It used to be specifically for government business, but more recently it's been opened up to certain private individuals. Indeed, it's hard to stop people using it unofficially.'

'I'll write Thomas a short letter, if you would be kind enough to arrange for it to be sent.'

'I'll be pleased to do that. But you should be aware, I suspect the postal service is also part of the government spy network,' cautions Parker. 'Anything of interest sent by private individuals is almost certainly reported to Sir Francis Walsingham, the Queen's Principal Secretary and spymaster. Indeed, Thomas Randolph, Master of the Post, is related to the Walsinghams through marriage. I don't suppose that's coincidental.'

'We've nothing to hide,' I reply. 'Nevertheless, I wouldn't want to be too explicit about our business in a letter to be delivered by the hand of a stranger. I'll make it a little cryptic but something that will be clear to Tom.'

'There's paper and ink on my desk which you can use.'

'You'd better ask him to supply some pig iron, as well,' says John, 'as we'll need to ballast and trim the ship differently with the extra weight of cannon on the gun deck.'

I sit at the desk and think for a moment. Then, putting quill to paper, I write:

Cousin,

Arriving in London, I find we are completely deficient in the product you showed us at Old Mill. For our venture's sake, I pray you will help put this right when I see you next. We have room for ten of such that you showed us, or the like. Could you also supply equal weight of pigs to balance things?

Your loving cousin and servant,

Robert.

I fold the letter carefully and write on the outside:

Mr Thomas Isted,
Moat House,
Mayfield,
Sussex.

I seal the edge with wax into which I impress my signet ring.

Parker takes the letter, looks at the address and says, 'That shouldn't be a problem. Regular correspondence goes to Mayfield from the Board of Ordnance, to Ralph Hogge and Sir Thomas Gresham.'

'Thank you, Mr Parker, that'll be of great help.'

'I've the letter for you, for Mr Epps,' adds Parker, handing me the letter. 'The boat for Woolwich departs at noon from the wharf. I'll get Jasper to let the master know you'll be travelling on it to Deptford; and give him a note to drop off at Greenwich, to let Knollys know you're accepting his invitation. Now you really must excuse me, I've a lot to do today. If I don't see you before, I'll see you both aboard the ship on Tuesday, at one bell on the afternoon watch.'

John and I take our leave from Parker's office with a renewed sense of optimism.

14

Deptford

The admiralty barge pulls in alongside the wharf in front of the impressive naval storehouse at Deptford Dockyard, just long enough for me to step ashore. I make my way to the office of Mr Epps clutching Parker's letter bearing the new admiralty seal consisting of an anchor.

'Do I have the pleasure of speaking to Mr Epps?' I ask, on entering the office.

'You do,' replies Mr Epps. 'Have you had your midday meal?'

'No,' I answer, somewhat bemused.

'Neither have I. You can join me if you wish, or wait here until I return?'

'I'll come with you.'

I follow Mr Epps out of the office, along a short corridor, and into a stone-built storehouse with a wide door opening onto the wharf.

'Take a seat,' invites Mr Epps, pointing to a small barrel.

'I thought we'd be going to a tavern,' I exclaim, still bemused by the invitation.

'Oh, no,' says Mr Epps, laughing, as we sit on adjacent barrels. 'We've a delivery into the victualing store, and it's part of my job to ensure it's fit to supply to the Queen's Navy. I like to think of it as quality control. You'll be doing me a favour in joining me today. I'd value a second opinion, as I'm trying out a new supplier of beer.'

'Well, if I can be of any service to you and the Queen,' I reply, happy to have a beer at Her Majesty's expense.

'By the way, who are you and what do you want?' asks Mr Epps, somewhat belatedly.

'I'm sorry. I'm Robert Isted, the new owner and captain of the *Barque of Bulleyn*. I've a letter of introduction from Mr Parker, the Admiral's Clerk, which explains everything,' I say, handing over the letter.

As Mr Epps takes a look at the letter, a huge black man rolls a kilderkin of beer through the door. I'm startled by the sight, stand quickly and reach for my sword.

'Hold on, Mr Isted,' calls Mr Epps. 'Haven't you seen a blackamoor before?'

'No, I haven't, although I've heard of them. I'm most heartily sorry,' I add, addressing the equally startled black man.

'There are quite a few of them in London nowadays,' explains Mr Epps. 'Isekeri was brought here by Sir John Hawkins[41], several years ago. He's a slave at one of the Southwark brew houses we do business with.'

'A slave!' I exclaim.

'I know. I don't hold with it myself,' says Mr Epps, shaking his head in disapproval. 'Sir John Hawkins is a great naval man. It was his idea behind the design of the *Dreadnaught*. In many respects, you couldn't wish to meet a more congenial gentleman. But I can't help thinking there's a flaw in someone who makes a fortune out of the enslavement and suffering of his fellow men.'

'We're all sinners, I suppose, but there are some sins much worse than others.'

---

41 Sir John Hawkins first entered the slave trade after he captured a Portuguese ship, in 1562, that was carrying over three hundred slaves that he subsequently sold in San Domingo.

'Let's set aside such unpleasantness and get on with the business at hand. We're going to do a blind tasting of our two main suppliers, Leakes of Southwark, St Katherine's Brew House near Tower Hill, and a new one: the Red Lion Brew House of Lower East Smithfield. Draw off the beer, Andrew, and let's have some of the recent delivery of ship's biscuits and cheese as well,' adds Mr Epps, beckoning to a small man in ragged working clothes.

Andrew draws off two tankards of beer from three different firkins and brings one from each to Mr Epps and me. I take a couple of large gulps from the first.

'What do you think?' asks Mr Epps.

'Not bad,' I reply. 'It has a pleasant nutty flavour.'

'Now, try the second one.'

I take a couple of gulps. 'Now, I really like this one. It has much more of a bitter aftertaste that I'm used to from where I'm from.'

'Now, the third.'

'That's not bad either, although it's a little thinner than the other two,' I remark. I take another gulp of the second beer. 'I prefer the second one, but all three are very acceptable.'

'Thank you. I've been drinking the beer of our usual suppliers for years, so I know which is which.'

'Which one did I prefer?'

'You chose the one from the Red Lion Brew House,' reports Mr Epps, before taking a swig of his pint of the same beer. 'They claim to take their water from an extremely deep well and pride themselves in its purity. They also say they use more hops that are now widely grown in Kent, rather than importing them from the Low Countries or using other flavourings. You and I have slightly different tastes, but I like it as well and will add the Red Lion Brew House to our list of suppliers. Now let me have a look at your list of requirements?'

'Here they are,' I reply, pulling the lists from my doublet and handing them over. 'I need to completely store my ship, which is basically an empty vessel.'

Mr Epps spends a few moments perusing the lists before saying, 'I think we can do most of this. When do you want it?'

'We need to depart by Monday week, at the latest. Can you supply it all by then?'

'That shouldn't be a problem. I suggest you berth alongside here, whenever you're ready. It'll be easier and cheaper to load here than take it up river to the Tower.'

'How much will it cost?'

'I can't cost it now,' says Mr Epps, running his eyes over the lists again. 'Some of the things I'll need to buy in especially for you. I notice from Mr Parker's letter that you've received some money from him for a commission, but that you need to restrict costs. I'll see what I can salvage from the things we are going to sell or scrap that might suit your purpose. A lot of it's perfectly fine. It's just that some naval captains insist on new, especially when they're off on a long voyage; not that many of the Queen's ships go all that far for very long.'

'I'm most grateful.'

'That's no problem. However, I'll need payment in advance for the things I'll need to buy in for you, and payment on delivery for the rest.'

'I can give you five pounds now,' I say, handing over the money.

'That should be sufficient for now. If there's nothing further I can do for you, I have to see the pusser off the Bonaventure.'

'No, that's all. I'll hail a passing wherry and be on my way. I'll send you a message to let you know when we'll be ready to come here to store.'

'Farewell, Mr Isted. And, if things don't work out for you at sea, there could be a job for you here as a victualler,' quips Mr Epps, with a chuckle.

15

The Royal Palace at Greenwich

I alight from the wherry at Greenwich, and climb the stone
stairs leading from the river to the palace grounds, still
wondering why Henry Knollys has invited me to dine with
him. At the gate at the top of the stairs stand two Yeoman of
the Guard, dressed and armed similarly to the Yeoman Warders
at the Tower.

'Who goes there?' demands one of the yeomen in an
authoritative manner.

'I'm Robert Isted; here at the invitation of Mr Henry
Knollys,' I reply.

'Tom, escort this gentleman to Mr Knollys's apartments,
while I remain on watch,' says the yeoman to his fellow guard.

I'm led straight ahead through a large stone archway in the
centre of the palace, just a few yards back from the Watergate.
From there, we enter into an enclosed courtyard. On the
opposite side, we climb a few steps, enter a doorway and ascend
three flights of stairs. At the top the yeoman knocks loudly on
a bare oak door. A servant opens it.

'This gentleman has an appointment with Mr Knollys,'
announces the yeoman.

'What's the gentleman's name?' enquires the servant.

'I'm Robert Isted,' I say.

'Come this way, sir. You're expected.'

We walk along a short corridor and enter a room with a
vaulted ceiling that is well lit by a number of wrought iron,
floor standing, multiple candlestick holders. On the far side

of the room, in front of a large stone hearth containing a warm and welcoming fire, stand two gentlemen and two ladies drinking from silver goblets.

'Mr Isted,' announces the servant, standing to attention by the door.

'Welcome, Mr Isted,' says one of the men, who is tall, with thick red wavy hair and a neatly trimmed beard, whom I estimate is about ten years my senior. 'I'm Henry Knollys, but you can call me Harry, as all my friends do. This is my wife, Margaret; my ward, Anne; and George Downing. George is from the Low Countries but now resides up river at Ratcliff.'

'How do you do?' I say, giving a courteous bow of my head. 'I'd appreciate it if you'd call me Rob.'

'With pleasure, Rob,' says Harry. 'I hope you'll excuse us for a moment. George and I have a little business to attend to. Margaret and Anne will entertain you in our absence,' he adds, as he and George Downing depart, leaving me alone with the ladies.

'Would you like some wine?' asks Margaret, a slight, fair-haired woman, wearing a high-necked gown with a small ruff, whom I estimate is about the same age as me.

'That would be very agreeable,' I reply.

'Harry tells us you're a baron of the five ports and the captain of a ship of war,' says Anne, a tall slim woman of about twenty years of age, wearing a dress displaying an expanse of bare bosom - a fashionable custom of unmarried highborn ladies that is also gaining currency among the lower order. This is thought to be a suitable way of indicating a lady's unmarried status, and for her to display her charms to potential suitors.

'That's correct, but I'm very new to both,' I reply, trying not to stare at her breasts.

'Nevertheless, it must be very exciting being the captain of a ship of war.'

'I'll let you know when I get back from my first voyage.'

'When will that be?' interjects Margaret, handing me a goblet of red wine.

'I'm due to escort the wool fleet from the headland of Thanet to Sluis, in the Low Countries, very shortly,' I reply, taking the goblet. 'But I'm not certain where I'll be headed after that, nor exactly when I'll return.'

'I do hope you'll come back soon and enrich our lives with tales of derring-do,' says Anne, taking a deep intake of breath that draws my attention towards her *décolletage*.

Harry and George re-enter the room. 'I'm sorry about that,' says Harry. 'I hope the ladies have kept you entertained while we've been away.'

'They have, most charmingly,' I reply, with a smile.

'Let's dine now,' says Harry, gesturing the way, as Margaret takes my arm. 'I hope you like venison. I killed a deer in Greenwich Park a little while ago, but I'm not sure it's been hung long enough.' Then leaning over towards Anne, Harry whispers something in her ear and she giggles.

Following a very congenial dinner, the ladies retire and leave us men alone to talk over a glass of malmsey.

'I've a confession, Rob,' says Harry, in a more sober tone. 'I've made some enquiries about you. I understand there's more to your commission, to escort the wool fleet, than meets the eye. I also hear you are in possession of a letter of marque.'

'It's true I've a letter of marque,' I reply, wondering what and how much he knows. 'But as for my commission, I've no idea what you mean,' I add, hoping I might either draw him out or bring the conversation to an end.

'I admire your discretion and will mention it no more, other than to say I wish you well in that endeavour.'

'As do I,' adds George. 'I'm a Watergeuzen, or a Sea Beggar as you English call us. I stayed behind in England to represent our interests with our friends at court, when the Queen expelled our ships from her shores.'

'I'm sorry about the expulsion,' I say. 'I met a number of your fellows who operated out of Dover.'

'It seemed a tragedy at the time. But as it turned out, it was the best thing to happen for our cause. Without a refuge, it spurred us into action. Our fleet, under Willem de La Marck and Admiral de Treslong, took the port of Den Briel. This encouraged others to rise up in rebellion against our Spanish oppressors, and we can now operate from a number of ports in our homeland.'

'It's an ill wind that bloweth no man to good,[42]' I say, quoting the old sailor's proverb I hear a lot in Hastings.

'Indeed,' says George, taking a sip of his malmsey. 'But what I was getting around to is, I know your mission, probably better than you do at the moment. And I want to impress on you its importance to our cause, and express our gratitude to you for undertaking it. In recognition of that, I'm in a position to arrange for you to acquire a *kaperbrief*, issued by the Prince of Orange.'

'A kaperbrief?'

'It's a Dutch letter of marque, authorising you to take ships and furnishers of the Duke of Alba,' explains George. 'The Duke of Alba was replaced last year and the Prince withdrew the letters as a consequence, in accordance with an agreement with the Spanish. But things have moved on since then; and I assure you it will be honoured by the Prince, regarding ships and furnishers of the new Spanish Governor - Luis de Requessens.'

---

42 An old sailor's proverb, listed in John Heywoods Book of Proverbs, compiled in 1546, forty-five years before Shakespeare included it in his play Henry IV Part II.

'I'll be pleased to accept and use it in help of your cause.'

'You should also note this covers you for stopping and searching Dutch ships at sea, and confiscating their ships and cargo if they're serving the interests of Spain,' adds George. 'The Spanish, for such a great power, are overstretched at sea. They rely on the parts of the Low Countries loyal to them for maritime support in the Netherlands and beyond.'

'Now you're well covered by letters of marque, there's another matter I'd like to discuss with you,' states Harry. 'You're probably not aware that I was, at one time, thinking of purchasing the *Barque of Bulleyn*. I was intending to operate it with the *Elephant*, my privateer ship, to enable me to go after more valuable prizes. But you got her first, at a bargain price.'

'I'm sorry, Harry. I was unaware of that,' I say, despite having been told by Mr Parker.

'There's no need to apologise, Rob. I like the cut of your jib,' replies Harry, warmly. 'I was, therefore, wondering whether you might consider a partnership, working in concert with Fernando Fielding: the captain of the *Elephant*. I think there could be considerable mutual benefit, realising greater returns for us both. If all goes well, we might be able to put together a band of privateers to rival John Hawkins's band of *Sea Dogs* and help relieve some Spanish and Portuguese treasure ships of their ill gotten gains from the Americas.'

'Hmm, that sounds an intriguing proposition,' I say, somewhat surprised by this turn of events. 'But I'll first have to discuss it with my partner - my brother, Dick. Then discuss the terms more fully and meet with Fielding to determine whether we can work successfully together,' I add, cautiously.

'Quite right! I'd expect nothing less,' says Harry, a little too positively, which makes me think he's a little disappointed I didn't jump at the chance. 'I'm travelling north shortly and have arranged to meet with Fernando at the Holy Island of

Lindisfarne, at the beginning of June,' he adds. 'If you've no firm plans, you could rendezvous with us there after you've escorted the wool fleet to Sluis. If you take some prizes en route you might be able to dispose of some of the booty at the Queen's Storehouse on the island, or at Berwick-upon-Tweed.'

'I'll speak with my brother when I get to Newhaven. All being well, I'll see you on Holy Island,' I say, hopefully, as I suspect Dick will see the benefits of this.

'I'll be writing to the captain of the garrison on Holy Island, Sir William Read, to let him know I'll be coming,' says Harry. 'I'll also let him know you might be joining me there and ask him to offer you every facility, as he provides what support he can to visiting ships of our trade.'

'That would be very kind. Now I'd better take my leave if I'm to get back to London tonight.'

'It's far too late to get a wherry south of the river and this far east of London. You should stay the night and return in the morning. Have another malmsey?'

'That's very kind, but I don't want to put you to any inconvenience.'

'It's no inconvenience,' says Harry, pouring us another drink. 'The Queen is holding Court here in the morning, prior to her going on to Eltham Palace for a while. Why don't you stay for that and I'll see if I can arrange to present you at Court?'

'I'm sure Her Majesty won't want to be presented with the likes of me,' I remark, as I am totally unprepared. 'Besides, I came to London with little more than I stand up in. It's hardly befitting my coming here, let alone to be presented at Court.'

'Nonsense!' exclaims Harry. 'You're a baron of the five ports. I know they're not held in very high esteem nowadays, but the Queen is fully aware of them and their status.'

'I'd be honoured, if you're sure it will be all right.'

'Of course it will be all right. It's just one of a number of fringe benefits of our potential partnership. Unfortunately, I'm part of the procession, but George will take you to the presence chamber in the morning and I'll join you there.'

After another malmsey, I am shown to a guest room where I quickly settle in bed for the night. About half an hour later, while in a very light sleep, I sense the door opening and the flicker of candlelight. But I fail to stir until a soft warm body slips under the covers and snuggles up behind me.

'Huh,' I murmur, with a sharp twitch of my naked body. 'Who's that?'

'It's Anne.'

'What're you doing here?'

'I couldn't help you noticing me, noticing you, noticing me, over dinner,' says Anne, 'and I was wondering whether you were thinking what I was thinking. But, if you weren't and aren't interested I can go.'

'No, no, I'm sorry. You just startled me,' I reply. 'I know what I was thinking, and your being here seems to indicate we were thinking along the same lines.'

We both laugh.

'And I think you can tell I'm interested,' I add, as I draw Anne towards me to hold her in a close embrace.

'Ooh, yes, so you are,' says Anne, softly, looking down.

Anne pulls her nightgown over her head and sits astride me, as I gaze at her beautiful sylph-like body in the flickering candlelight. 'You'd better put this on,' she adds, suddenly, holding up an oiled linen sheath with a blue ribbon threaded though one end.

'What on earth is that? And what am I supposed to do with it?' I exclaim, somewhat puzzled, slipping it on my raised index finger.

'It's a Falloppio sheath[43] and you put it on your *pistol*, you ninny.'

'Why would I want to do such a thing?'

'It's a way of preventing pregnancy and avoiding catching the *French disease*. I don't want to risk getting the disease; or of being with child, without a betrothal at the very least.'

'I've never heard of such a thing.'

'Falloppio sheaths are widely used at Court, ever since a certain very high born lady, whose name I won't mention, who doesn't wish to get married, pregnant or diseased, insisted her lovers use them,' explains Anne. 'There's nothing to be worried about,' she adds, reassuringly.

'All right! I'll use it. But I'm afraid the thought of it has had a rather subduing effect.'

'Oh, I'm sure I can encourage the *stallion's yard* to rise again,' says Anne, confidently. And, she is quickly proved right. The opportunity soon presents itself for her to slide on the Falloppio sheath and secure it by tying the ribbon in a neat bow on the dorsal side, with a giggle.

I reach up and gently caress Anne's soft round breasts. She rises up as high as she can on her knees; and my hands, involuntarily, slip down her tapered sides towards her hips. She lowers herself, a little at first, giving out a quiet gasp of air and a murmur of pleasure. Closing her eyes, she tips her head gently backwards and shakes her flowing auburn hair. Then arching her supple back she sinks lower still, giving out a louder gasp. She leans forward with a pleasurable wriggle as we start to move together as one: at first slowly and gently, and then with increasing passion and intensity, until a mutually and coinciding crescendo of pleasure overwhelms us both.

---

43 Gabrielle Falloppio, 1523 to 1562, invented a condom, made of oiled linen, to prevent syphilis. He conducted a trial of over 1000 men, none of whom contracted the disease.

I sleep as only the just do - the just after – and awake to find Anne is gone. Had it all been a dream, or was that one of the fringe benefits Harry had referred to.

I get dressed, pick up the three spent Falloppio sheaths and drop them down the privy in the garderobe, where clothes are stored for the smell to ward off the unwanted attention of moths. It works but, unfortunately, this often leaves those wearing the clothes with something of the air of the privy about them.

I meet George Downing at the appointed time and place. We proceed to the vast presence chamber, adjacent to the Queen's chapel, with its walls hung with rich tapestry and its floor strewn with freshly dried rushes. We take our place on the right side of the chamber, towards the rear.

A number of clerics and gentlemen enter the room. They include the moustachioed Archbishop of Canterbury – Matthew 'nosy' Parker[44] – dressed in his full regalia, along with a number of counsellors and officers of state. Then in procession come the gentlemen and nobility of the Court, richly dressed in furs and velvet, with bright red and blue silks, and a few wearing cloth of gold and silver. I look at myself in my plain doublet and breeches and think what I must look like to them: a bumpkin straight up from the country.

Following closely behind the nobility is the Lord Keeper of the Great Seal, bearing the Great Seal of England in a red silk purse. He is flanked on either side by two soldiers: one carrying the Royal Sceptre; and the other carrying the Sword of State sheathed in a red scabbard and held point upward.

---

44 Matthew Parker, is believed to be the original 'nosy Parker', gaining the epithet for his prying into the qualifications and activities of the clergy, which was extremely unpopular with them.

The Queen enters to a fanfare of trumpets, closely followed by her ladies in waiting dressed mostly in white: a sign of purity. As the Queen passes, everyone drops to one knee and bows their head. Guarding her and her ladies, on each side, are a large number of gentlemen of the Honourable Band of Gentlemen Pensioners. I notice Anne amongst the ladies, but she passes me by without giving me so much as a glance.

The Queen takes her place on the throne, on a raised dais at the end of the hall. She is wearing a red coloured wig on which is perched a small golden crown. Her oval face is painted with a white lead preparation and her cheekbones highlighted with rouge. While this has created something of a fashion, I understand it is really to hide the hair loss and pock marks resulting from her having suffered smallpox some eleven years earlier. She is of average height, slim and appropriately of regal bearing. She has a slightly hooked nose, small dark eyes, and thin red painted lips that when she smiles reveals discoloured teeth caused, I am told, by an over fondness for sugar. She wears a white dress bordered with pearls, revealing an expanse of bare bosom belying her forty years of age. I understand this is intended more as a political statement, regarding her contentious unmarried status, than it is an attempt to be in tune with the fashion for younger single women. She also wears around her shoulders, a black silk mantel decorated with silver threads.

After a short while a gentleman dressed in velvet and wearing a gold chain calls out the names of those presenting petitions to the Queen, whom she receives graciously. He then calls out the names of those receiving letters of patent.

When that business is concluded, he announces in a loud voice, 'Mr Robert Isted, a baron of the Cinque Ports.' I'm startled, having not been informed of the correct protocol and do not quite know what to do, until Harry appears and ushers me forward.

'Your Majesty, I have the honour and privilege to present Mr Robert Isted, a baron of the Cinque Port of Hastings, who is visiting your Court,' says Harry, bowing before the Queen. I follow his lead and bow as well.

'Hmm,' murmurs the Queen, looking me up and down. 'You're one of those scruffy rough sort who got into a fight with the Heralds over the silk canopy and staves[45], in the Abbey, at my coronation. If they fought for the realm as fiercely as they fought for the silk and they fight for their charter privileges, I could dispense with the entire Army and Navy.' The Court laughs. 'Why should I bother with you churlish knaves, with your courtesy titles? Come on, young man, give me an answer.'

'Er, er, I have absolutely no idea Your Majesty,' I reply, somewhat taken aback by the Queen's disdain. 'But we're extremely grateful that you do, and pray that Your Majesty will long continue to do so,' I quickly add, before thinking, what on earth am I saying.

There is a moment's silence, which is broken by the Queen laughing loudly with the rest of the Court following suit. 'An honest answer young man that I get little enough of around here; if not somewhat impertinent. What are you doing here and what do you want from me?'

'I'm here at Mr Knollys's invitation. I'm not here to ask you for anything, Ma'am.'

'Do you hear that? He doesn't want anything. Well, that's certainly a refreshing change,' says the Queen in a loud voice,

---

45 Barons of the Cinque Ports had the right to carry a canopy of silk or cloth of gold, supported by silver staves and bells, above the monarch at their coronation and to claim this as their fee. The earliest record of this is at Richard I's coronation in 1189. The practice was abolished following George III's coronation in 1761.

so all her courtiers can hear. 'Take a good look around here at the great and the good, young man,' she adds, leaning forward to address me quietly. 'Most of them are as rich as Croesus, and yet hardly a word comes out of their mouths when they don't want something or other to add to their wealth. Are you sure there is nothing you want to ask of me? Not that I'm likely to grant it.'

'No, I have everything I came for. I bought a ship of war from the Navy Royal, at a fair price, to help Hastings meet its obligations to Your Majesty and to turn a little profit for myself.'

'Will wonders never cease: a Cinque Port prepared to pay its dues for its privileges,' laughs the Queen, loudly. She removes her glove and extends her right hand towards me. Again, I'm unsure what to do. But at Harry's unspoken gesture, I take her small hand with its long delicate fingers sparkling with jewelled rings and, bowing, gently kiss it. 'Now be off with you,' she adds, abruptly, waving me away with that very hand. But I sense there may be a little flush of the cheeks behind the white lead preparation.

I back away still bowing, in company with Harry, as I had seen the great men of state do before me. The Queen arises and all the assembled lords and gentlemen shout loudly, 'Long live Queen Elizabeth!'

'I thank you my good people,' replies the Queen, graciously. She then leaves the room into her private chapel, followed by her ladies in waiting, the archbishop and some other clerical gentlemen, leaving the rest of the assembled crowd behind.

'Forsooth!' I exclaim. 'Her Majesty is certainly ill disposed towards the five ports.'

'Maybe so,' replies Harry. 'But she certainly took a fancy to you.'

'It seemed not to me.'

'She removed her glove and gave you her bare hand to kiss. This is a sign of particular favour,' says Harry, putting a friendly arm about my shoulder. 'You may recall she didn't do this for any of the ambassadors or other petitioners, nor for any of the great men to whom she gave letters of patent.'

I felt both honoured and bemused. 'Well, I'd better take my leave before she thinks better of it. I've to return to the Tower to sign on crew this afternoon.'

16

Signing on Crew

I alight from the wherry on Tower Wharf, just downstream of where the *Barque of Bulleyn* is now berthed, more than half an hour late for the signing on of crew. I climb the ship's brow to find a host of men gathered on the weather-deck. John is overlooking them from the quarterdeck and looks as if he is about to address them. I catch his eye and he stops. I beckon him to continue.

'Avast there,' shouts John. Everyone stops what they are doing and gives him their full attention. 'I'm John Hills, master of the *Barque of Bulleyn*, sailing under Captain Robert Isted, a gentleman of Hastings. We'll be sailing to Newhaven, in Sussex, at high tide on Monday. From there we sail to forgather with the wool fleet, at the headland of Thanet, which we'll escort to Sluis in Flanders. We have no commission after that, but we'll be looking to ply our trade in the *narrow seas*. We're a Cinque Port ship, so we're required to provide service to the Crown for a certain number of days a year and in times of strife. For this you'll get three square meals a day, pay according to your rate and our commissions, and be subject to the rules and punishments laid down in the Black Book[46]. If you sign on, you can bring your things aboard whenever you wish, but there'll be no victuals provided until we've stored at Deptford on Monday. If that doesn't suit, you can save us all time and depart now. That's all.'

---

46 The Black Book was a collection of naval laws and customs that dated from the 14th century.

John returns to the weather-deck and I join him and Parker at a table set up just forward of the aftcastle.

'I'm sorry we started without you,' says Parker. 'We waited half an hour but with no sign or word of you we thought we'd better get things underway.'

'That's quite all right,' I reply. 'I'm sorry I'm late. I was detained at Greenwich.'

'Would you like to take the lead?'

'Why don't you carry on? I'll just observe and join in as necessary.'

'As you wish. Let's be having the first one, Jasper,' orders Parker.

Jasper escorts the first man to the table.

'Johnston, isn't it?' asks Parker.

'Aye, Mr Parker, we met last week,' he replies.

'What are you and what's your experience?' asks John.

'I'm a bosun of many years experience,' replies Johnston. 'My last ship was the *Greyhound* out of Leith. Walter Bartane was the master.'

'What are you doing here?'

'Bartane and I didn't see eye to eye and we parted company by mutual agreement, at Sandwich,' says Johnston, a little sheepishly. 'I made my way here to seek a berth on another ship. I've been offered a berth by Mr Gulecht to sail to Barbary. But hearing about this from Mr Pope, I thought it might suit me better.'

'As bosun, you and I'll have to work closely together,' says John, with concern. 'So why did you and Bartane fail to get along, and why should I have confidence that you'll work well to my orders?'

'Bartane is my brother-in-law. There were old family and personal issues between us. I thought they'd been forgotten, but they resurfaced at sea. So we agreed to part at Sandwich. I'm being straight with you Mr Hills.'

'Make your mark here and don't make me regret it,' says John, sliding the ship's articles across the table for Johnston, who makes his mark by drawing a bowline. 'Next.'

I think John's made the correct decision. The man has an honest face, and he'd no need to mention the disagreement with the master on his previous ship if he were intent on lying.

'This is Peter Fisher of Leith,' says Parker, as the next man approaches.

'What are you?' asks John.

'I'm a pilot of many years experience in English, Scottish, French and Dutch waters,' says the small, tough-looking man, who is wearing good quality clothing that has quite clearly seen better days.

'All right, pilot, how will you determine our position when we're out of sight of land?' asks John, by way of testing him.

'I'll calculate our latitude and longitude and plot it on whatever portolan charts we have.'

'How will you do that, exactly?'

'I'll determine the latitude by measuring the height of the noon sun from the horizon, or at night the height of the Pole Star, by means of a cross-staff. Then I'll check it against my copy of the Portuguese astronomical tables, which I've here,' replies Fisher, pulling some papers from his kit bag.

'How about the longitude?'

'I'll do that by dead reckoning, provided you've got someone to take logs every half hour and peg it on a traverse board. Then I'll transfer that information, along with the latitude, onto the portolan chart to give you as accurate an estimate of our position as possible.'

'Welcome aboard, Mr Fisher,' invites John. 'Make your mark here.' Fisher signs his name. 'Next.'

Fisher seems to know his trade but there's something about him that doesn't seem quite right, although I cannot put my finger on what it is.

'I don't think I've seen you before,' says Parker, to the next man ushered forward.

'My name's Adam Sawyer, a surgeon of Penzance, now residing in Southwark,' replies the tall, clean and smartly dressed middle-aged man.

'What's your experience?' enquires John.

'I've not been to sea for twenty-six years, but more recently I served as a soldier under Captain Brickwell, at the garrison at Berwick. I can set bones, stitch up gashes, amputate limbs, bleed and apply leeches, undertake trepanation and more complex surgical procedures besides,' answers Sawyer.

'Hmm, a proper ship's surgeon may be a bit of a luxury for the likes of us, but you might prove useful if you're prepared to do other things.'

'I'm happy to do a bit of soldiering. I can shoot and fight as good as any; better than most. Then, afterwards, I can stitch up those who are unfortunate enough to come against me.'

'But why does a man like you want to go back to sea after such a long time?' I ask.

'The twenty marks standing fee I receive from the Exchequer isn't enough for me to live on; even if it were regularly paid, which it isn't,' replies Sawyer, indignantly.

'But surely, you could make more practising medicine ashore.'

'Maybe. But to be frank, I miss the excitement. And sailors get so many more interesting injuries and diseases,' adds Sawyer, with a wry smile.

I look at John and give him a nod.

'Welcome aboard, Sawyer. Make your mark here,' says John.

Sawyer seems a man who has led an interesting life and is out for one last hurrah. I suspect we'll be able to provide him with that. In any event, it'll be good to have a surgeon aboard; and a proper one at that, rather than one of the barber types.

Parker, John and I see a steady stream of men until five bells and take on thirty-five covering all branches, including an experienced master gunner-cum-blacksmith who I think shall prove very useful when we get our cannon. I only hope that Tom received my letter and has been able to help in that regard.

'Thank you, Mr Parker,' I say, after we see the last man. 'That's more than sufficient to man all the watches and cover any contingencies that might arise on our way to Newhaven. We can take on the rest: another dozen or so, and a couple of boys, when we get there.'

17

Setting Sail

I board the *Barque of Bulleyn,* in the light of the early dawn, just before the stand of the tide when we are due to sail.

Mr Parker greets me as he is making his way ashore. 'We've just finished loading what the Board of Ordnance has been able to supply,' he says. 'I'm afraid this is all there is,' he adds, with an expression of disappointment, as he hands me a list.

I read through the list:

Guns:
6 bases[47]
6 hail-shot pieces
4 muzzle loading matchlocks
2 snaphance

Gunpowder:
8 demi-barrels of serpentine powder[48]
16lb fine corn powde

---

47 Bases and hail-shot pieces were small breech-loading iron guns, that fired lead shot or dices of iron, that could be mounted on a ship's rail.

48 Serpentine powder and corn powder were gunpowder mixtures of saltpetre, sulphur and charcoal. Serpentine was finely ground and usually used for priming handheld guns. Corn powder was hydrated and forced through a sieve to form pieces of a certain size, which made it more reliable and less susceptible to damp due to the comparatively smaller surface area ratio, and was used for heavy ordnance.

Shot:
  200 dice of iron for hail shot pieces
  100 shot of lead for bases
  120 shot of lead for matchlocks and snaphance.

Munitions:
  4 pickhammers
  2 sledgehammers
  2 crowbars
  2 commanders
  200 tampions
  2 canvas bags and 1 form for cartouches.

Weapons:
  40 bows
  1 gross of bowstrings
  85 liveries of arrows
  40 morris pikes
  40 bills
  36 assorted darts for tops
  24 pots holding lime[49]

'But this is much more than I'd asked for, let alone expected,' I say, with astonishment, to the now grinning Parker. 'Were you making sport of me, Mr Parker?'

'I'm sorry, Captain Isted, I couldn't help myself. Mr Bowland has done you proud,' says Parker, still smiling at the success of his own pretence of disappointment. 'It's almost the full outfitting of a navy ship of your size, with the exception of cannon and shot.'

---

49 Lime was used as a chemical weapon, by it being thrown in the air to blind sailors on downwind ships prior to boarding.

'How much do I owe for all this? I doubt I've sufficient money left to pay for it.'

'You owe absolutely nothing.'

'How so?'

'Mr Bowland said he knows of your other mission, of which we've not spoken. He says it's in England's national interest. So, he's signed them out to you, on permanent loan, as if you were still a ship of the Navy Royal, or a ship taken up from trade during a national emergency.'

'Please express my profound gratitude to Mr Bowland,' I say, sincerely. 'I only hope my cousin has received my letter and will be as generous with the supply of cannon.'

'I hope so as well,' says Parker, warmly. 'Have a safe and profitable voyage. I look forward to seeing you here before too long. In the meantime, I'll speak to the admiral about selling you one of our other surplus ships, next spring. I think I might be able to persuade him to part with the *Falcon*.'

'I've seen it at anchor in the stream.'

'It was built a little less than thirty years ago, but has been extensively rebuilt and refitted since,' adds Parker. 'It's probably a little greater tonnage than the *Barque of Bulleyn*, but slightly less well armed. Operating the two together should be more than a match for most.'

'I agree. I'll take a closer look at her on my return.'

'I'd better depart, otherwise I'll be sailing with you,' jokes Parker. 'The Thames is a busy place nowadays, but you should have no trouble with the Trinity House pilot I've engaged to see you safely down river,' he adds. 'If you put him ashore at Gravesend, he'll either pick up another commission there or return to Trinity House at Deptford.[50]'

---

50 Trinity House was founded, in 1514, by a Royal Charter of Henry VIII, and located at Deptford. In 1796 it moved its headquarters to its present location, on Tower Hill, London.

'Get her underway, John, I order. The Trinity House pilot has the ship.'

'Aye, aye, sir,' replies John. 'Let's get her underway, Mr Johnston.'

'What's with calling me sir, John?' I ask somewhat bemused.

'I think it'll be best for good order and discipline if we establish a clear chain of command by me calling you captain or sir; and you calling me Mr Hills, or master, in front of the crew.'

'I understand. But, it's not what I'm used to.'

The bosun and bosun's mate, with a whistle, a few barked words and hand signals, set working parties to their various tasks. The brow is quickly removed and the mooring ropes cast off fore and aft. Staffs are inserted into the capstan and a working party turns it to weigh anchor, to the sound and beat of a work chant led by the bosun's mate.

'We're a ship of war with a bully's head,
Heave away bully-boys, heave away,
We're still alive while others are dead,
Heave away bully-boys, heave away.
We're bully-boys with a bully's heart,
Heave away bully-boys, heave away,
We'll hang together or be hung apart,
Heave away bully-boys, heave away.
We're . . . '

'My compliments, Mr Johnston,' I say. 'That's a fine working chant for our ship; very apt given our figurehead.'

'Thank you, cap'n. The bosun's mate and I thought it up,' replies Johnston.

'The words in the second verse seem a bit out of place though, don't you think.'

'Maybe, or maybe not, given the weapons and supplies we've just loaded and the number of specialist soldiers you've signed on; not to mention the gunners. You must be intending to acquire some cannon and completely fit her out like the ship of war she is. At least that's the scuttlebutt on the lower deck.'

'What else do the lower deck have to say on the subject.'

'The crew realise you couldn't say much while we're alongside the Navy headquarters at the Tower. But, as you might have guessed, most of us aren't strangers to war, nor *the trade*. Indeed, Mr Fisher is a man of particular experience in these matters.'

'Thank you, Mr Johnston. That will be all.'

'Aye, aye, sir.'

Then with second thoughts, I add, 'Oh! And, Mr Johnston, whatever we may or may not be up to, the Admiralty and the Board of Ordnance are fully aware of it. Otherwise they wouldn't have sold us such a ship, or provided those supplies you mentioned and helped in signing on the sort of crew we have. Nor would they have given us this first commission that will help us work up the ship and shake down the crew, for whatever our later purpose. You can add that to the scuttlebutt, if you wish, but without attribution. Do you understand?'

'Aye, aye, cap'n, fully understood.'

We make our way slowly but safely downstream under the guidance of the Trinity House pilot, in a light but favourable breeze, and arrive at Deptford nearly two hours later.

As the ship comes alongside the wharf, Mr Epps is waiting along with the required stores and provisions.

'Get it aboard, Mr Hills. I'd like to make further progress today while we still have the tide and a favourable wind,' I say, in as an authoritative manner as I can muster.

'You heard the captain. Make it so bosun,' orders John, giving me a wink, which I assume is an indication of satisfaction at my having heeded his words.

By means of a whistle and a few barked words, the bosun gets working parties opening up the hatches in the main and gun decks, through to the orlop deck and the hold where most of the provisions and gear will be stowed. They rig up a block and tackle to a boom, wrap the line around the capstan, and load the stores into grappling nets in accordance with a prearranged loading and storage plan. Two small working parties man separate lines carefully controlling the swing of the boom from the dockside to a position over the hatch, while another controls the height by working the capstan to the sound and beat of the ship's new capstan work chant. Another party guides the loads through the hatch, while yet another breaks open the nets and stows the cargo in its appropriate place.

We are half way through loading when an open carriage, of the lightweight Hungarian style, comes along the wharf and stops next to the brow. Out get Harry, Margaret and Anne who then proceed up the brow. I'm surprised by their arrival and hasten to the top of the brow where John and I greet them.

'This is a surprise,' I say, 'I wasn't expecting to see you here.'

'A pleasant one, I hope?' replies Anne.

'Of course, a most pleasant one.'

'We couldn't let you sail without wishing you bon voyage,' says Harry. 'Besides, Anne was most insistent. Perhaps you could get someone to show Margaret and me around the ship while you two talk, or whatever?'

'Of course! This is my brother-in-law, John Hills,' I say by way of introduction. 'My sister Mary's husband,' I add, quickly, to avoid any confusion regarding my own marital status. 'John, will you be good enough to show Mr and Mrs Knollys around? I'm sure Johnston can handle the remainder of the loading.'

'Aye, aye, captain,' says John, smartly. 'It'll be a pleasure. If you'd like to come this way.'

'Can you show me your cabin, Rob?' asks Anne.

'Of course.'

We enter the great cabin, only to find it full of men moving furniture around. 'Leave that for now. You can finish it later,' I order.

'Aye, aye, cap'n,' they reply, as they file out giving me a salute, as if touching their non-existent caps between thumb and forefinger.

'I'm sorry about the mess but until now I'd no furniture, apart from a canvas hammock.'

'There's no need to apologise. I came to see you, not your furniture,' says Anne, extending her arms toward me.

'I'm very pleased but surprised to see you, Anne,' I say, taking her arms and drawing her near. 'When I awoke early at Greenwich and you were gone, I almost convinced myself that it was a dream: a delightful dream, but just a dream, nonetheless; or that you may have simply regretted the night before.'

'It was no dream. It was a reality I'll always cherish, and hope it's one we can share again.'

'I hope so as well,' I say, as I draw Anne closer and kiss her tenderly in a warm embrace.

The door opens and John enters. 'I beg your pardon captain. We've completed loading and battened down the hatches. Mr Epps provided everything, except the Falloppio sheaths that you added to the order; whatever they are.'

Anne looks hard at me.

'I ordered them for the crew. Honestly!' I plead. 'I've no, no…,' I add stuttering with embarrassment.

Anne bursts out laughing at my awkwardness. 'I'll pretend to believe you,' she says, playfully punching me on my arm.

Before I can say anything else, a bemused John interrupts, 'Excuse me, captain, Mr Epps is waiting for payment. And you said you wanted to make as much progress as we can while we still have the tide and a favourable wind.'

I look into Anne's eyes, wondering whether to go or delay until the next morning tide. 'We can't stay much longer,' says Anne. 'I have duties to attend to at the palace. So you'd be as well to go now.'

'Make ready to sail, Mr Hills,' I order, with a sad heart. 'My compliments to Mr Epps, I'll be out to settle with him shortly.'

'Aye, aye, captain,' replies John, shutting the door behind him as he leaves the cabin.

Anne and I kiss more passionately. 'I really do regret we have to go,' I say, before kissing her gently one final time.

I pay and thank Mr Epps and then bid my final fond farewells to Harry, Margaret and Anne, who wait on the quayside to see us off.

As the working party on the capstan raise the anchor they sing loudly, led by the bosun's mate, so those on the quayside can hear:

'Cap'n Rob Isted's a gentleman bold,
Heave away bully-boys, heave away,

We've plenty of victuals and beer in the hold,
Heave away bully-boys, heave away.

The cap'n's lady is fair and fine,
Heave away bully-boys, heave away,

I wouldn't be sailing if she were mine,
Heave away bully-boys, heave away.'

Anne smiles, blushes a little and then waves more fervently, while Harry roars with laughter.

We make steady progress while we still have the tide, but make slow progress once it starts to turn, despite the light favourable breeze. So we drop anchor until the next stand of the tide. When we reach Gravesend, in fading light and with little sea room, I decide to stay there at anchor overnight.

'Drop anchor, Mr Hills, and put the pilot ashore,' I order. 'We'll stay at anchor overnight. But tomorrow, when we've plenty of sea room, I'd like to put each watch through their paces,' I add, in accordance with John's earlier private suggestion.

'Aye, aye, captain,' replies John. 'Make note of that, Mr Johnston; give the men fair warning.' Then whispering to me he says, 'Now you're getting the hang of it.'

There is a commotion below deck and three frightened sailors emerge onto the weather-deck.

'What in damnation's going on?' I shout.

'Damnation is right,' says one of the sailors. 'The Devil is hiding in the cable locker.'

'Nonsense! If the Devil were aboard, he'd hardly be cowering in the cable locker from the likes of you,' says John, angrily. 'You're with me, Mr Johnston,' he adds, as he and a more reticent Johnston make their way below to investigate.

Some minutes later, they emerge with John holding a large black man by the scruff of the neck. 'It's a blackamoor stowaway, captain,' he says. 'We could keep him until we return and claim a reward, or sell him on, or simply toss him overboard.'

'I know this man. You're Isekeri, aren't you?' I say, looking down on them from the quarterdeck.

'Yes, master,' replies Isekeri.

'What're you doing stowing away aboard my ship?'

'I was delivering beer to the storehouse while the ship was loading cargo. And remembering your words about slavery to Mr Epps, I thought you might help me escape and return home.'

'We're not going anywhere near Africa, but I won't turn you in or sell you on either. If you work hard you'll receive fair pay and you can leave a free man whenever you wish, which I suggest you do before we return to London.'

'*Assalamu Alalikum Wa Rahmatullahi Wa Barakatuh,*' says Isekeri, giving a dignified bow.

'Hmm, quite so,' I reply, slightly embarrassed. 'Sign him on, Mr Hills, and set him to work,' I order. 'And Isekeri, you don't call anybody master from now on; except for Mr Hills of course,' I add, awkwardly, as an afterthought. Isekeri looks at me somewhat confused. 'I think you'd better explain it to him, Mr Hills.'

18
Sea Trials

In the light of day, with fair winds and plenty of sea room, we progress along the north Kent coast. John and I test the ship and crew with the *whole nine yards* and various other combinations of sail. We run downwind, and gybe on various beam and broad reaches. We could make better progress to our destination, but John and I want to get well acquainted with how the ship handles and to see how the crew perform.

Having worked the crew hard and now with a contrary wind, I decide to anchor overnight at the northern end of Pegwell Bay, just south of the headland of Thanet where we are due to rendezvous with the wool fleet in a little over a week's time.

'Drop anchor, Mr Hills. We'll stay at anchor overnight. There'll be no shore leave,' I order, although it is John's private recommendation I am again following. 'But give the men an extra half ration of beer for all their hard work this day,' I add, as my own idea.

My orders are carried out, before John speaks to me privately, 'You handled the seamanship very well today, Rob, and you're giving orders with a real sense of authority,' he says, encouragingly. But, I was sensing a but. 'But, you shouldn't be issuing extra half rations of beer for the sort of effort the men have put in today. It'll make you popular initially, but you can't keep it up and it makes it difficult to know what to do when they've really done something to deserve it.'

'I hear what you say, John, and I'll try not to make a habit of it.'

We set sail with the dawn sun and clouds casting ripples of light along the white face of the western cliffs to our stern.

I take the first watch, and as we are sailing more windward I test the ship out on various larboard and starboard tacks, with various combinations of sail to see how close-hauled we can sail without getting *in irons*.

The wind strengthens and we make less progress than I would like, although better than many a good ship would have made. And when it starts to blow a gale, John and I decide to drop anchor for the night in the lee of Dungeness.

The gale eases overnight, before we set sail, but a strong south-south-westerly wind arises during the late afternoon, which makes going very difficult as we head west along the Sussex coast towards our destination. Rain then starts to lash in on the wind in the early evening, further reducing our visibility, as we approach the outflow of the Ouse between Seaford and Meeching.

As three bells sounds on the first dog watch, the lookout calls out, 'Lights off the starboard bow.'

I join John on the quarterdeck where he is standing with Fisher the pilot, and Cornish with a man whose name I haven't yet learned on the tiller.

'What do you reckon, pilot?' asks John.

'The static lights must be the harbour at Seaford, and the moving ones are the lights of ships safely at anchor,' replies Fisher. 'I suggest we move closer to them, anchor there and then make our way through the channel to Newhaven in the morning.'

'Maintain this heading and take soundings.'

The leadsman, standing in the chains up against the shrouds on the starboard side of the foremast, swings the lead and casts it forward. Then shortly afterwards calls out, 'By the mark three fathoms deep.'

'What's the tallow show?' shouts John.

'Sand,' replies the leadsman, examining the material stuck to the tallow wad on the end of the lead.

'We'll run *off and on* until morning. We'll turn seaward when we mark three fathoms, then turn landward every half hour thereafter,' orders John.

'But, cap'n, the men are tired,' complains Cornish at the tiller. 'We only need to line up the higher and lower beacons to make our way safely into the shelter of the harbour.'

'They're false lights, Cornish,' I say. 'The Seaford Shags[51] are out and we don't want to be their pickings. Do as the master orders.'

'Aye, aye, cap'n.'

'Cornish, don't question my orders with the captain again,' says John, sternly, without so much as a glance at Cornish that makes it seem even more menacing.

'Aye, aye, Mr Hills,' replies a chastened Cornish.

'Ship ahoy, aft of starboard,' calls the lookout.

'The ship's heading for the false lights. Shall we hail them to warn them off?' asks Cornish.

'We'll do no such thing,' says John.

Cornish motions as if to question the order, but holds his tongue.

'Since the harbour at Seaford silted up, the only living many of the Shags can make is by claiming flotsam and jetsam in accordance with their charter privileges as a limb of Hastings,' I say, as means of explanation. 'I don't approve of them bringing this about by wrecking ships through the rigging of false lights. But Mr Hills and I are known hereabouts, and we've to put in

---

51 In the 16th century, the people of Seaford engaged in wrecking were nicknamed the Shags, after the seabird.

at Newhaven in the morning. The Shags wouldn't take kindly to any interference on our part. In any event, it's too late to be able to stop them.'

We watch in silence as the other ship runs aground, lured there by the false lights. Then with the force of the waves pounding into it broadside, it turns onto its side with half seas over.

As we continue to run off and on the shore, we see the lights on the Shags' boats rowing to and fro the capsized ship.

I spend a restless night imagining the shipwrecked sailors swimming towards their hoped for rescuers' boats only to be ignored, or pushed away or clubbed with the oars; and any who make it to the shore being cudgelled and stripped of their clothes. Should we have tried to warn them? Would it really have been too late, had we tried? We shall never know now.

19

Newhaven

As the sun rises and casts its skirts along the shore, those of us safely aboard the *Barque of Bulleyn* clearly see the broken wreck of the ship on the sandbank. Ashore, the Shags - men, women and children - are hauling away their ill-gotten gains on mules and in handcarts, leaving the sailors' bodies lifeless on the beach or bobbing up and down in the water.

'Steer a course for the channel,' orders John.

As we make our approach, we pass the broken ship run aground by the false lights. As we get closer to the shore we see the vicar of St Leonard's, with help from some of his parishioners who may or may not have been party to the wrecking, taking away the dead bodies from the beach and tending to two survivors.

Turning a blind eye to this devastation, as best I can, we make our way safely through the channel cut by the great storm some years earlier. We pass the Bishopstone tide-mills, make a careful turn to larboard and proceed on towards the dock at Newhaven.

To my surprise, Tom is waiting on the dockside as we berth and comes aboard as soon as we are tied up alongside.

'Greetings, coz. This is a pleasant surprise,' I say.

'I was told there was a ship of war approaching the channel and assumed it must be you,' replies Tom, as we clasp hands in greeting.

'Where's Dick?' I ask, anxiously. 'I was hoping to see him with you. How is he?'

'He's fine,' says Tom, in a reassuringly nonchalant manner. 'I had to come on a couple of days early with the last of the cannon. I left Dick at the Moat, being nursed by Dorothy and the Warnett girl. He's going to break his journey and stay overnight at Laughton with Sir John Pelham. They should both be here later tomorrow.'

'That's good,' I say, with some relief. 'Did you get my letter?'

'Yes, I did. It caused a little bit of a stir, as we'd come up short on a recently increased order. But to cut a long story short, there's been a rapprochement with Sir Thomas Gresham, following some intelligence he received from his contacts in Antwerp about the importance and urgency of this shipment.'

'I had an inkling of this in London, from a representative of the Watergeuzen.'

'Anyway, the good news is, with Gresham back in the fold, albeit temporarily, we can meet the entire order and supply you with six pieces of ordnance: four minions and two sakers, along with a good supply of shot.'

'Those six guns will be more than enough for our purposes, especially as the Board of Ordnance gifted us some bases, hail-shot pieces and sundry other stuff. When can we get them aboard?'

'Very shortly. When I saw it was you coming in, I sent my man to have them brought here straightaway. I think that's them coming along the dockside in the wagons now.'

'Mr Hills,' I call.

'Aye, cap'n,' replies John, hastening to the brow. 'Good morning, Thomas.'

'Good morning, John,' replies Tom.

'Mr Hills, will you get Johnston to arrange to load the ordnance and pig iron from yonder wagons under the supervision of the Master Gunner.'

'Mr Johnston, fetch Mr Norris and the slinger, I've a job for you,' shouts John, as he takes his leave.

'What's with all this Mr Hills and cap'n?' enquires Tom. 'Have you and John had a falling out?'

'No! It's John's idea to establish my authority, a clear chain of command, and engender good order and discipline,' I reply, still feeling rather awkward about it.

'How's it going?'

'It's working well, I suppose. But, it's not as much fun as being one of the lads.'

'It's our duty to take up the responsibility we are born to at some stage, and regrettably that sets us apart from some companions of our youth,' replies Tom, sagely. 'Now, let's go ashore and look at your guns before they're swung aboard.'

Tom lifts the cover from the wagon. 'See, they're Gresham guns,' he says. 'They have his trademark initials and grasshopper symbol on each of the barrels. They've all been test fired at the proving banks at Mayfield and given a thorough inspection afterwards. I doubt you'll find better guns anywhere. The bad news is, it's eaten up all your fee.'

'I wasn't expecting you to make a gift of them,' I say convincingly, although I had hoped there would be some money coming to us now. 'Unfortunately, with the fitting out and storing of the ship, practically all the money we were to receive from you and escorting the wool fleet has already been spent. We'll have to make more money soon by other means, otherwise we'll have little or nothing to pay the crew.'

'Pelham's not too happy about it either,' confides Tom. 'He was counting on claiming the greater portion of your fee to recover the loan he made for you to buy the ship.'

John, Johnston and Norris join us on the dockside. 'What do you think of them Master Gunner?' I ask.

'They're fine looking minions and sakers, cap'n,' answers Norris.

'How do you think they'll perform?'

'The four minions have barrels about eight feet long and the calibre looks about three and a quarter inches. It'll fire iron shot of about three inches in diameter of near on four pounds.'

'You've got a good eye,' remarks Tom.

'So with a full charge and thirty degrees of elevation on an upward roll, I expect we could put one across a ship's bows at a range of more than five hundred yards. The sakers are more substantial guns. They'll fire a heavier shot with a larger charge, and as a result can cause more damage at greater range than the minions.'

'That should do us very nicely,' I say.

'Of course, if you want me to dismast a ship, cap'n, you'd better get us in close. And if you want me to sink her, I'll need to fire the sakers on the downward roll, skim the shot off the surface of the water and hit her below or near the water line,' adds Norris, seemingly excited by the prospect. 'But if you want to do some real damage, I'd like to be in real close and personal, preferably across her stern. I can then use a smaller charge.'

'But a larger charge will give the shot a greater velocity and more impact to cause a breach,' says Tom, beating me to making the same point.

'Aye. That's all well and good when you're trying to make a breach in a stone wall, but against a wooden ship a slower moving shot will cause much more damage: splintering and deflecting around the ship, rather than punching a nice neat hole from one side to the other.'

'Quite!' I say, pleased that Tom spoke before me, preventing me from displaying my ignorance in front of Norris.

'Of course, it would be very useful if we could have one larger gun, like the portes piece the ship used to carry, if we were ever to go to war,' adds Norris.

'I'll bear that in mind Norris,' I say, thoughtfully. 'But for now, I'd like you to start training up gun crew and then come to talk tactics with Mr Hills and me. Then when you think the gun crews are ready, we'll do a live firing to test them out. I want to make sure we get their range more exactly and are properly prepared when we're called upon to use them in anger.'

'Aye, aye, cap'n,' acknowledges Norris, enthusiastically. 'With your permission, as they've come without gun carriages, can I set the carpenter to work to make them? It's a simple enough job. I can give him a sketch of what's required.'

'Aye, make it so Mr Norris.'

'He seems a very able man,' remarks Tom, as we walk away to let them organise the slinger to get the cannon aboard.

'Yes, we managed to recruit some experienced hands with the help of the Admiral's Clerk and his men. Norris, who's also a blacksmith, is a particularly good find.'

'Well, I'd better get going now,' announces Tom. 'I've other business to attend to. I'll return late tomorrow afternoon, with Sir John, Dick and the three captains of the ships carrying our ordnance. Can we hold our meeting in your cabin?'

'Of course, but there's not a lot of room for a conference.'

'Nevertheless, we'd like to meet aboard your ship for security reasons. It's better to be cramped than risk having our plans overheard ashore in a tavern.'

20

The Plan Comes Together

Sir John Pelham and party make their way up the brow of the *Barque of Bulleyn*, shortly after two bells on the first dogwatch.

'Welcome aboard Sir John; gentlemen,' I say, greeting them at the top of the brow. 'Dick, you're certainly looking a lot better than when we parted,' I add, giving him a warm embrace.

'Ouch!' cries Dick, physically recoiling from the touch.

'I'm sorry Dick. I wasn't thinking.'

'It's all right, Rob. I'm a lot better, but it's going to take quite some time before it's properly healed. I've got to be careful not to reopen the wound.'

'It's good to see you well, Dick,' says John, motioning as if to clasp his shoulders, before thinking better of it. 'How are Mary and the children?'

'I hear they're well and looking forward to seeing you while you're here.'

'Good! I'm hoping to go to Hastings tomorrow to spend two or three days with them before we sail.'

'Anyway, Dick, tell me how you've been?' I enquire. 'I hear Margaret Warnett has been looking after you,' I add, with a wink.

'You can catch up with all that later,' interrupts Sir John. 'We've business to attend to first. I think you know these other gentlemen,' he adds, referring to John Pykerden of Meeching, Captain of the *James*; John Brodie of Meeching, Captain of the *Pelican*; and John Conny of Hastings, Captain of the *Anne Bonnaventure*[52].

'Aye. I suppose I shouldn't be surprised you three would be involved in this venture.'

'Nor I, you Rob,' replies John Conny, slapping me on my back.

'Shall we adjourn to your cabin?' interjects Sir John, impatiently, 'We've a lot to get through.'

Sir John, Tom, Dick, the three merchant captains, along with John and I, stand cramped around the table in the centre of the great cabin.

Sir John unfurls a map and spreads it across the table. 'This is the latest map of the area around the Western Scheldt estuary, produced by Abraham Ortelius of Antwerp,' he announces. 'The Watergeuzen use the exact same map. You're going into Sluis, here; and the commercial centre in Bruges, where the Merchants of the Staple[53] are based is here,' he adds, pointing to places on the map on the southern side of the Western Scheldt. 'Bruges and Sluis are under the control of the Spanish, although it's a complex and fluid political, religious and military picture that cuts across all regions. The Watergeuzen control the Scheldt with their ships based at Vlissingen here,' says Sir John, pointing to a spot on the opposite side of the Scheldt. 'It is in the interest of all parties to leave you genuinely unmolested, although the Spanish who regard the Watergeuzen

---

52 The *Anne Bonnaventure*, captained by John Conny, was the only ship that Hastings sent to join the English Fleet to meet the Spanish Armada in 1588.

53 The Company of the Merchants of the Staple of England, to give it its full title, was incorporated by Royal Charter in 1319, and is the oldest mercantile corporation in England. All English exports of wool were controlled by the Freemen of the Company who, in return for their monopoly, paid a levy back to the Crown.

as no more than pirates would not be surprised if they sought to disrupt the trade controlled from Bruges. This may work to our advantage in getting the three ships safely to the Dutch rebels, without alerting the Spanish to our deception.'

'The easiest thing to do will be to foregather with the Watergeuzen on the open sea out of sight of the Spaniards. Or the three ordnance ships could just disengage from the fleet, when they have no need of our protection, and enter Vlissingen or another port under rebel control,' I suggest.

'If it were only that simple,' replies Sir John, exhaling deeply. 'The Spaniards have spies everywhere, including in Vlissingen. And believe it or not, even aboard Watergeuzen ships, and possibly amongst Catholic sympathisers aboard the wool fleet. So we need to be very careful, as it's imperative we preserve English neutrality in the eyes of the Dons.'

'So what do you want us to do?'

'After long discussions with Watergeuzen representatives in London, we've decided the best thing will be for them to take the ships by force in a mock sea engagement. Only their captains and first officers will know of this plan. I'd be obliged if you would keep it similarly secret on a strictly need to know basis.'

'If you'll forgive me,' interjects John. 'I don't like it. There are far too many unpredictable matters: winds, tides, currents, sea state, visibility, co-ordination of time and position. Then there are the number of ships involved, and the inevitably erratic behaviour of fighting men unaware of what's really going on. Too many things can go wrong.'

The three merchant captains frown and make murmurings of concern.

'I share your concerns, gentlemen. But let's hear the full plan first and see if we can make it work,' I say, in a conciliatory tone.

'Thank you,' replies Sir John. 'From next Tuesday and for as long as it takes until you arrive, a small squadron of three or four Watergeuzen ships from Admiral Boisot's fleet will be on patrol here,' he adds, pointing to an X which marks the spot off the Western Scheldt estuary, a few miles southeast of the Westkapelle Lighthouse.

'It's approaching the estuary a little further north than we would normally plan to do, but it's not that far north to cause any real suspicion.'

'Good! The three ordnance ships are to hoist the *bandiera della sanitaria* as means of identification,' explains Sir John. 'None of the ships will need to have it hoisted, but neither will it draw any suspicion if these three are flying it. The Watergeuzen will then cut these ships out of the wool fleet and take them a prize into Vlissingen. In any event, you are to engage the Watergeuzen and exchange fire with them. Put on as good a show as you can but allow them to succeed without getting sunk or sinking anyone else. All being well, the Watergeuzen will get the guns, the wool will get through to Sluis, England's uneasy peace with Spain will not be in jeopardy, and you may even end up heroes to all sides.'

'It sounds simple enough when you say it like that, but there is still plenty of scope for mishap,' I say, thoughtfully, considering John's earlier reservations. 'But I suppose we have no alternative but to make it work, as there's no chance of getting a revised plan to the Watergeuzen before we get there.'

'Regrettably, that's the truth of it. With the constraints placed upon us, we had to take some decisions and we're now stuck with them.'

'Any immediate thoughts, John?' I ask.

'Assuming we hit our mark and the Watergeuzen are where we expect them to be, we could assist the plan by making sure the three ships are in loose formation on the larboard side of the fleet,' replies John. 'And if we can get Captains Pykerden, Brodie and Conny to forget their seamanship and act rather lubberly at the crucial moment, we might be able to pull it off.'

'That sounds promising.'

'If you'll allow me to talk it through with the three of them, I'm sure we can come up with a workable plan for your approval, Rob.'

'Aye, it might work at that,' says Captain Conny, with nods of approval from Captains Brodie and Pykerden.

'Make it so, John,' I order.

'If there's nothing else, perhaps the four of us can withdraw to my ship to do that,' suggests Captain Conny.

'I'm happy to leave the detail to you,' says Sir John, in agreement. 'But before you go, I need to impress upon you the increased importance of this mission. I've recently received a report that the Dutch have had a significant setback in the South,' he adds, sombrely. 'Their army of almost nine thousand men was badly defeated by a larger Spanish army under the command of Sancho de Avila, at a battle at Mookerhyde[54]. Over four thousand Dutch were slain and the rest fled in disarray in all directions.'

There is shocked silence around the table at such a devastating defeat and loss of life.

'What's more, William of Orange's two younger brothers, Lodewick and Henry van Nassau, were killed in battle,' adds Sir John, sadly. 'Lodewick who provided key political and military leadership to the cause will be particularly missed.'

'How decisive is all this to the rebellion?' I ask.

'The struggle still goes on. But with this defeat, the siege of Leyden will probably be resumed. The Dons are also expected to attempt to reinforce Antwerp, and there are rumours of a fleet preparing to come out of Spain. So I emphasis, this

---

54 The Battle of Mookerhyde took place on 14 April 1574.

138

shipment of ordnance has renewed importance, for England as well as the Dutch.'

'What's so important to it for England,' asks Captain Conny.

'It's in our interest for the Protestant Dutch to succeed, or at least to keep the conflict going and oppose a resurgent militant Catholicism on the continent,' explains Sir John. 'Victory for Spain in the Netherlands will leave her free to turn her attention to England and a renewed attempt to place the Catholic Mary Queen of Scots on the throne. On top of that, if our part in this is discovered, there'll be the devil for us to pay with Queen Elizabeth as well, in an attempt to preserve the precarious diplomatic relations with Spain.'

'Perhaps we'd all better stay clear of the country for awhile, until we're sure all is well,' I suggest.

'Arrangements have already been made for Captains Pykerden, Brodie and Conny to ply their trade between the Hansiatic states in the Baltic this summer, after they have been released by the Watergeuzen,' says Sir John, with smiles and nods of satisfaction from the three captains. 'Perhaps we can discuss what you're to do, in private, after this meeting,' he adds, looking at me.

'Certainly. There're also things that occurred, in London, of which you and Dick should be made aware.'

'Unless there are any questions, I suggest we bring the meeting to a close and allow Mr Hills and the merchant captains to retire and set about the detailed planning,' states Sir John.

Captains Pykerden, Brodie and Conny, and John, take their leave while I pour four glasses of brandy for Sir John, Tom, Dick and myself.

'What happened in London that you wanted to tell us about, Robert?' asks Sir John.

'I dined with Henry Knollys at his apartments in Greenwich. There was also a Dutchman present, named George Downing.

He and Knollys seemed to know quite a lot about our plans, although nothing explicit was mentioned and I was careful not to confirm anything.'

'That doesn't surprise me. Knollys is well connected and a champion of the Dutch cause. Downing is ex-Watergeuzen and I've had some dealings with him regarding our export of ordnance.'

'It's a relief you're able to confirm that. Downing also impressed on me the importance of the mission and offered me a letter of marque issued by the Prince of Orange. He only asked five shillings for it to cover his costs, so I readily accepted.'

'That's a very good deal,' says Sir John, with a satisfied smile. 'You can't have too many of these things. Was there anything else of interest?'

'Yes. Knollys also said he'd thoughts of buying the *Barque of Bulleyn*, before you got the option for us to buy it from under his nose. However, he didn't seem upset by it. Instead, he proposed we work in partnership with a privateer ship he owns, captained by Fernando Fielding.'

'What did you tell him, Rob?' asks an anxious Dick.

'I said I'd have to speak with you first. Then if you were in agreement, I'd need to meet with Fielding to determine whether we could successfully work together and work out the detailed terms.'

'When and where are you going to do that?'

'Subject to your concurrence, at Holy Island, in early June when Knollys is due to rendezvous with Fielding.'

'Holy Island has become a haven for pirates and privateers operating in the North Sea, since the dissolution of the monastery,' states Sir John. 'The Queen has a garrison and storehouse there, which helps support these ships to a certain extent and where they can dispose of certain items of booty.'

'What do you think of the idea, Sir John?' asks Dick. 'I'd value your advice.'

'Although Knollys can sometimes be a bit of a hothead, he and I are politically of the same mind; and being the Queen's cousin, he's extremely well connected,' replies Sir John. 'It's entirely up to you lads, but a partnership with someone as well connected as Knollys could well work to your advantage. I don't know much about Fielding, but I understand he's a privateer of some experience and you might learn a trick or two from him.'

'I don't know, Rob,' says Dick, unexpectedly cautiously. 'In many ways it seems too good to be true. But things are moving very fast. I only wish I could accompany you to the meeting on Holy Island.'

'It's a pity you're not able to make such a sea journey,' adds Sir John. 'But I think Rob has handled himself very well up to now. Perhaps it's best left up to his discretion.'

'All right, Rob,' says Dick, giving me a nod of approval. 'You have my agreement to enter into a partnership with Knollys and Fielding, if you're happy we can work with them and the terms are agreeable.'

'Thanks, Dick and Sir John, for your show of confidence,' I reply. 'I'm still learning the ropes, but I'm sure I can handle it.'

'If there's nothing further, Thomas and I will have to take our leave. We've some other business to attend to,' says Sir John, finishing off his brandy.

'If you have a further moment, I forgot to tell you the best bit, or maybe it's the second best bit.'

'What's that?' asks Tom.

'Knollys arranged for me to be presented at Court,' I say to everyone's surprise. 'When I was presented to the Queen she was rather uncomplimentary about the five ports. I'm not quite sure what I said in reply, but it seemed to amuse her. Anyway, she removed her glove and allowed me to kiss her hand, which I understand is quite an honour.'

'It is indeed,' comments an impressed Sir John. 'I can see I may have underestimated you somewhat. If you keep on like this, Robert, I predict a big future ahead of you.'

'Well done, Rob. I always knew that taking on responsibility would be the making of you,' adds Tom. 'But, if that was the second best bit, what was the best bit.'

'I met a lady of the Court, Harry's ward, who showed me particular favour,' I reply, a little coyly.

'I'm pleased,' says Dick, with a smile. 'She sounds like the sort of person I've been trying to encourage you to meet.'

'I'd like to stay and learn more about your adventures in London,' interrupts Sir John, arising from his chair. 'But Thomas and I really do have some urgent business to attend to. And I suspect you've a lot to do as well.'

'Regrettably, I'll have to go as well,' adds Dick. 'I'm quite fatigued after the journey here and my shoulder is throbbing. Sir John, Tom and I are staying in Seaford tonight and I'll sail onto Hastings first thing in the morning. Perhaps, John might like to accompany me, if he can get away early. Will we be seeing you in Hastings before you sail?'

'I'm afraid not. John wants to spend time with Mary and the children, and one of us has to stay here to make preparations for sailing.' Although, part of my not going is to avoid seeing Hannah until I've got it clear in my mind what my feelings and intentions are for her and Anne. 'But if you see Hannah, give her my apologies and let her know why I haven't come to visit her.'

'I will,' says Dick. 'And you be very careful, Rob,' he adds, in a whisper. 'The more I hear about this gun running, the more complicated it gets and the less I like it.'

21

The Dream

I finish dinner alone in my cabin, pour myself a large brandy and recap on the things we have achieved over the last few days since arriving at Newhaven. Everything has gone very well, notwithstanding the complicated plan and Dick's caution. Nevertheless, since I woke this morning, I've had a strange feeling of foreboding. Trying to set this aside, I take to my cot and attempt to sleep.

I come to in a daze. To my surprise, I'm at the lower end of All Saints Street, in Hastings. How can I be here? But it is not quite the same as I remember it. There is no depth to it, like a painting on a canvas with a lack of perspective, with everything increasingly faded towards the edge of my vision.

There is movement. I see Hannah walking up the street towards me, calling out something. But I hear nothing.

I am here, Hannah, I try to say. But I have no voice and she runs right past me. Why did she not see me? I turn. She is calling to two people walking away, further up the street. They turn around. It is Dick and John.

I am with them now, but I have no sense of having moved.

Hannah runs up to us, stops suddenly; and bending forward with hands on hips, tries to catch her breath.

'Hannah, Dick, John, I'm here,' I mouth. But I make no sound and no one sees me nor hears my increasingly desperate silence.

They speak, but I cannot hear what they are saying. Dick moves a hand to his wounded shoulder. Hannah says something, excitedly.

Dick replies calmly. Hannah looks disappointed and speaks again. Dick replies calmly at greater length. Hannah arches forward, with eyes flashing, and spits out some silent words. Dick takes a deep breath, exhales slowly and replies only slightly less calmly than before. No one says anything for a moment: a silence more intense than the silence that has gone before. Hannah speaks with silent words, bursts into tears and runs off up the street towards her home.

I try to call out and to run after her, but I have no voice and cannot move.

Instead, my body twitches and I let out a breathless closed mouth moan to find myself barely awake in my cot. I roll over onto my back, take a couple of sharp gasps of much needed air and stare up at the deckhead. As my breathing returns to normal, I turn onto my side and manage to sleep again. For the first time in my life, I find myself plunging back into the same dream, or something like it.

It is dark. I do not know where I am, but I feel I am in familiar surroundings. Things begin to clear and I can see Hannah sitting on a stool, in her nightgown, by the hearth in the White Hart Inn. She has the smaller of the inn's two cats on her lap, stroking it, while the larger one rubs up against her legs purring. There is something beside Hannah. It is a bucket of water with something in it. It is a straw man, plunged headfirst into the water. I try to speak, but there is no sound. I move in front of Hannah, but she does not see me.

Hannah reaches behind her back and picks something up. It is a knife. And, with a sudden and swift movement, she slits the cat's throat. Blood spurts out like a crimson fountain, all over her nightdress, into the bucket and over the floor. Why on earth has she done that?

The larger cat retreats sharply, arches its back, hisses loudly and leaps at Hannah. Hannah throws it off, picks up the iron poker and brings it down sharply on its head.

Crying, bent over and moving about in a frenzy, like a soul possessed, Hannah picks up the dead cats and shoves them both in the smoke cabinet in the chimney. She slumps back on the stool, splattered with the cat's blood. She rocks from side to side with head in hands, as she wails bitterly but silently to my ears.

I hate to see her in such distress and move to comfort her.

My body twitches. I let out a breathless closed mouth moan and wake to find myself back in my cot, breathing heavily.

22

Tactics

The *Barque of Bulleyn* is running easily, leant over a couple of strakes by a fair south-westerly breeze, as we leave Newhaven behind us and make steady progress eastward along the Sussex coast.

I stand looking aft through the windows of the great cabin, thinking about the terrible dream I had last night before it melts away as most dreams eventually do. I do not believe that dreams are sent as portents of things to come, or of things that might be if we do not alter our ways. But, even if it were the case, I can make no sense of it. My thoughts are broken by a knock at the door. John enters. 'You asked to see me, Rob,' he says.

'Yes,' I reply, beckoning him to sit at the table. 'We've seen how the ship handles on our way from London, so I think it's about time we had our discussion on tactics.'

'It's straight forward enough, at least from a defensive point of view,' replies John. 'We keep well clear of ships of war that might pose a threat: those that can out gun us at range, and those who might have crews large enough to board us and take us a prize.'

'That sounds simple enough.'

'It's not quite as simple as it sounds. But we have a swift and manoeuvrable ship, and if we keep a weather-eye out we should be able to minimize the risks. As you know, the battle tactics of the Spanish and most other navies are still to get their hulks to ram ships and fire down on them with muskets from their castles before boarding. It would be extreme bad luck, or negligent on our part, for us to be caught by one of them.'

'I agree. Keeping away from the few potential threats should be our defensive aim. But how are we going to take ships at sea?'

'We'll patrol the main shipping routes looking for vulnerable, fully laden, merchant vessels: those riding low in the water, without ordnance or armed escorts,' states John, almost nonchalantly. 'There's no point in taking on ships running empty; or those that might beat us in a fair fight, when there are so many we can beat in a fair fight who we aren't going to fight fair with, anyway.'

'I don't really like these bullying tactics, John,' I say, realising the true nature of what we are about to do. 'I didn't give much thought to it when I jumped at the chance of this venture and persuaded Dick to agree to it. But I'm committed to it now, and it's probably the best way to minimize casualties.'

'Aye, it is.'

'So how do you propose we take these ships a prize, exactly?'

'It depends on a whole host of things: the target ship, the sea state, wind strength, direction of travel et cetera,' says John, slumping further back into his chair. 'In general terms, I think we ought to fly our Cinque Port ensign. A lot of the ships we come across won't know what it is, but it looks impressive and official enough. Then we'll close on them and hail them to heave to and be boarded. Hopefully, they'll do as we command. Then we board them and take possession of the ship and cargo.'

'But what if they don't heave to and make a run for it?'

'In that case, we put a shot across their bows. Hopefully, this will encourage them to comply.'

'What if it doesn't? It would defeat our objective to sink the ship and lose the chance of booty.'

'This is when we'll really have to earn our salt,' replies John, sitting forward. 'If we've picked our target correctly, we should have the better of her for speed and manoeuvrability. So we get into the position where we can take her wind, slow her down and force her to heave to. If we've done things correctly, we'll already have the weather-gauge. Hopefully, their captain will realize the game is up and will then submit. If not, we'll come closer and fire musket shot and arrows onto her deck and hope that encourages compliance. We might also consider using some of that quick lime the Board of Ordnance gave us, to blind the sailors if they look as if they might put up a fight when we board her.'

'I'd prefer not to use the lime, unless it is in defence of our own lives and liberty.'

'If you wish,' replies John, with a sigh. I sense he may be a little frustrated by my scruples.

'But what if the ship is sloop rigged and is better able to slip away toward the wind and continues to make a run for it?' I ask.

'That shouldn't happen, regardless of her heading, if we have the weather-gauge,' explains John. 'She'd have to anticipate what we are up to well before we've declared our intentions or be extremely nimble when we've closed on her. The only possibility is if she anticipates our intentions early enough and runs with the wind, then plays the wind and tides well enough to out manoeuvre us. In which case, fair dues to them. I suggest we shouldn't waste too much effort conducting a not so merry dance across the sea, unless we get in range and are prepared to dismast them.'

'I don't want to damage our prizes or risk killing anyone,' I say, quietly but adamantly.

'I agree, damaging our prize is self-defeating,' says John, 'but being averse to killing complicates things. Dead men tell no tales.'

'But, that's the way I want it, John. We offer people their lives in exchange for their co-operation.'

'And if we don't get their co-operation?'

'You can despoil them a little. But we should try to avoid killing, other than in self-defence, if at all possible. If we do that, we might get a reputation for fair dealing and encourage others to surrender to our will. If they think we'll kill them anyway, they might think there's nothing to lose by fighting – something we wish to avoid.'

'All right, we'll do it your way,' says John

'I'm glad that's settled. Now, how is Norris getting on with the gunnery?'

'The carpenter has made the gun carriages Norris designed. Unfortunately, we only have a few men with any experience of firing cannon. Norris and I have selected men to train to man the guns, and he's going to commence training immediately after the change of watch. Would you like to observe, Rob?'

'Yes, I'll join you on the gun deck before you conclude the drills to see how things are progressing.'

'In the meantime, I suggest you have a rest,' says John, with some concern. 'You are looking very tired, Rob; not quite yourself.'

'Thank you John, I slept poorly last night, troubled by a strange dream,' I reply. 'You Dick and Hannah were in it,' I add.

'What was it about?'

John sits there in silence, as I recount the first part of my dream; or as much of it as I can now recall.

'That's uncanny,' says John, with surprise in his voice. 'Dick and I did meet Hannah in All Saints Street under similar circumstances, two days ago, just before I returned to the ship.

'What happened?'

'Dick asked me not to tell you and cause you unnecessary concern before we sail,' replies John, hesitantly.

'Go on.'

'Well, I suppose this changes things and absolves me of my promise,' says John, with a heavy sigh. 'Dick explained to Hannah that you weren't coming to see her because you had met someone else, in London, more befitting a gentleman.'

'But that wasn't what I meant when I asked him to explain my absence to Hannah,' I say, with alarm.

'Be that as it may, but that's what he did. Hannah burst into tears and ran off home.'

'God, I wish he hadn't done that,' I snap, banging my fists on the table. I refrain from telling John the second part of the dream, as he will conjure up some sort of witchcraft story; something he had already accused Hannah and her mother of when we journeyed to Mayfield. I am sure the first part of my dream and what actually happened is just coincidence. It was predictable enough given that Hastings is a small place, and knowing Dick and his attitude towards Hannah. But the second part of the dream is too strange to be true. It must have been brought on by a combination of my subconscious guilt and John's accusations about Hannah.

I sit in my one comfortable wood and wicker chair and rest my eyes, intent on thinking no more of the disturbing dream.

23

The Foreland of Thanet

We arrive off Ramsgate, where we are greeted by the sight of a host of ships at anchor in Pegwell Bay.

'There're a lot more of them than I expected,' I say.

'Aye, there're quite a few, cap'n, but not nearly as many as there used to be in the old days,' remarks Cornish at the helm.

'We'll need to relay your plan for the convoy, Mr Hills.'

'Aye,' replies John, 'perhaps we should run through it again, in your cabin, and signal the captains to attend us aboard this afternoon.'

'Aye, agreed.'

'Bosun, let the fleet know the Flag Ship has arrived,' orders John, 'and that captains are requested to come aboard at the start of the forenoon watch.'

As the spring sun approaches its zenith, the captains of the merchant ships make their way to the *Barque of Bulleyn*. When they have assembled on the weather-deck, John takes a roll call from the list of ships he'd been given by Mr Parker. Three of them are missing and there are two additional ones that had been added as late substitutes.

Standing on the quarterdeck, I grip the rail in front of me with both hands and look down on the faces assembled below.

'Welcome aboard the *Barque of Bulleyn*, gentlemen,' I say. 'Thank you for coming. My name is Robert Isted of Hastings. I recognise a few faces amongst you, although there are quite a number who are new to me. We've a good many ships here to see safely to Sluis but I'll try to keep things as simple as possible. First of all, is there anyone amongst you who has an exceptional pilot who is experienced in the narrow seas and knows the Western Scheldt approaches to Sluis?'

'Aye, Rob,' answers one of the captains - a full bearded, middle-aged man. 'You know me, and my pilot - Jack Swallow. I'll wager Jack is as skilled a navigator as any. And he and I have plenty of experience in those waters.'

'Aye, I know you well, Will, and Jack and your ship the *Lutterell*. If you agree, I'd like you to take the van and Jack to be Pilot Major of the fleet. You'll need to identify yourself to the fleet by flying your Cinque Port ensign from your main mast. You'll also need to signal any course corrections, which I'd like every ship to acknowledge and repeat. Has everyone got that?'

'Aye,' comes the answer from the assembled captains.

'Oh, and Will, knowing Jack, you'd better keep him out of the taverns and whore-houses of Ramsgate for twenty-four hours before we sail,' I quip.

The assembled company laugh and some of the evident tension is eased.

'Now, are there any captains here with any ordnance?' I add.

'Aye,' comes the reply from three of the captains.

'How many pieces do you have?'

'I've two sakers aboard the *Dolphin*,' replies one.

'I've an old brass falcon and an iron saker, aboard the *Mermaid*, but neither have been fired in a good while,' says another.

'I've an old falcon and a minion aboard the *Rose*, but we haven't fired them for ages either, and we only have stone shot,' says the third.

'Hopefully, you won't have to use them. But you'll look the part, at least,' I add, in reassurance. 'I'd like you three, along with Captains Pykerden, Brodie and Conny, to establish a perimeter for the convoy. The three ships on the starboard side will fly the green and white striped Tudor livery flag, which I can provide. The other three, on the larboard side, will fly the *bandiera della sanitaria*. Perhaps these captains can all stay behind after the others have left so we can discuss the plan more fully.'

'Aye,' comes the collective reply in agreement.

'The *Barque of Bulleyn* will be in the rear, flying the Cross of St George atop her main mast to identify us as the flag ship,' I explain. 'The rest of the ships should take up loose formation within the established parameters. If anyone gets in trouble or spots danger they can make the appropriate signal. I know we are going to be in fairly tight company, but try not to take anybody's wind. Now are there any questions?'

There was a little murmuring amongst the captains, but no questions.

'I'll arrange for copies of the operation order to be drawn up in diagrammatic form and given to you all. I'll be maintaining watches while we're here and will allow only restricted shore leave, as Ramsgate isn't that big a place. I'll also have everyone aboard by the end of the last dogwatch, tomorrow. I'll leave it up to you what arrangement you make. However, we sail on the first tide on the following day. Perhaps our straggler will have arrived by then. Good day, gentlemen, and thank you for your attendance, attention and co-operation.'

As everyone disperses, I overhear a conversation between two of the captains. 'I don't like being told what to do by a young whippersnapper like Rob Isted. What experience has he got of this sort of thing,' says one.

'Well, he's a gentleman with a ship of war, who's just become a baron of the five ports. The master of his ship, John Hills, has been around the buoy a few times and it's not a bad plan,' comes the reply.

'Aye, I'll give you that. But it still don't stand well with me.'

After everyone else has left, the captains of the ships due to be in the van and to establish a perimeter attend John and I in the great cabin.

'I don't think there's much more I need to tell you, gentlemen,' I say, 'other than I received some intelligence from the Admiralty that some French pirates have been operating in the Channel, off the southern coast of Flanders. So I'd like Jack to plot a course that gives that part of the coast a wider berth than he might normally do; and enter the mouth of the Western Scheldt a bit further north, here,' I add, pointing to an X that marks the spot on the chart spread out on my table, 'a few miles southeast of the Westkapelle lighthouse.'

'It'll probably add a bit of extra time to our crossing with the normally prevailing winds. But it shouldn't be a problem,' replies Captain Will of the *Lutterell.*

'Good. It's also why I'd like the ships with ordnance to occupy the starboard position. That's where any danger is likely to come from.'

'What about the Watergeuzen?' asks Captain Will.

'The Admiralty doubts they'll wish to try to interfere with a neutral English wool fleet, even if the wool is destined for Spanish controlled Flanders. But in case times have changed and they want to disrupt our trade with the Spanish, we'd better keep an eye out for them and give them a wide berth. In any event, with the *Barque of Bulleyn* in the rear, we can provide cover to either flank.'

There were agreeing nods from around the table.

24

The Western Scheldt

As we can only move as fast as the slowest of the fleet, we only have the main and bonaventure masts rigged as we approach the point where we are supposed to be intercepted by the Watergeuzen. John and I nervously pace the decks keeping a lookout, but there is no sight of them. Then, suddenly, through the early morning mist, three Watergeuzen ships of war appear to larboard. The *Lutterell* spots them, recognises the potential danger and signals the fleet to change course toward a more acute southerly approach to the Western Scheldt.

'Well done, Will and the *Lutterell*,' I say quietly to myself.

The fleet responds to the signal, apart from the *Pelican*, *James* and *Anne Bonaventure* carrying the illicit ordnance. They are deliberately laggardly and lubberly in their sailing.

The fleet makes slow progress on this new heading as it is towards the extreme end of some of our square-rigged ships' ability to sail with the current wind direction. Of course, it would also be a problem for the Watergeuzen as well, if it were not the plan for them to continue to close on the deliberately tardy ordnance ships.

'Put us between them and our stragglers, Mr Hills,' I order, in a controlled manor, supressing my excitement.

'Aye, aye, cap'n,' replies John. 'You heard the cap'n, helmsmen. Make it so.'

'What do you think, Mr Hills?'

'We could keep them at distance, if not out run them. But, our stragglers can't. I reckon they'll overhaul us well within the hour. And we're no match for three of them if they're of a mind to engage us.'

'Your recommendation?'

'Keep going as we are. Then when there're a bit closer, signal them to keep their distance.'

'What if they don't comply?'

'Let's hope they do for now.'

The rest of the fleet puts a little distance between themselves and the *Barque of Bulleyn*, and the laggardly ordnance ships, as the Watergeuzen make steady progress in running us down.

'I think, we'd better sound the trumpet to call the men to action stations, as a precaution until we judge their intentions,' I say.

'I agree,' replies John. 'Sound the trumpet for action stations, Mr Johnston.'

Johnston grabs hold of the trumpet, hesitates for a moment, licks his lips and blows: '*ber, bup, bup, ber, bup, bup, ber, ber, ber; bup, bup, bup, bup, bup, bup, bup, ber, ber.*' He puts the trumpet down and gasps for breath.

'Well, I suppose that's close enough,' says John, physically wincing at the untuneful sound.

'I'll go below to check how the men are responding, and have a word with Norris while we've time before they close on us,' I say, as I leave the quarterdeck. 'You have the ship Mr Hills. But send for me if anything changes.'

I go below deck to discover that despite Johnston's woeful effort, it has had the desired effect on the crew. Partition bulkheads, furniture and utensils are being removed to be stowed in the hold to better protect them from damage and give the crew more fighting room. But more importantly, it will prevent injury by removing items that could be hit, thrown about, and splintered by any shot that might penetrate the ship.

Musket men and archers are moving this way and that, on their way to their stations on the quarterdeck and aloft.

Nick Long, the cook, douses the fire in the galley area to prevent it being spilled during action and accidentally start a fire, before he hurries along the gun deck to join the surgeon in the wardroom.

I look into the wardroom, where Long is now washing down the table on which the surgeon will operate. His skills as a cook in slaughtering animals and cutting carcasses into recognised joints is useful in assisting a surgeon in a ship of war, where amputations and tidying up severed limbs is commonly required.

The surgeon, Adam Sawyer, is laying out his instruments, along with a surgical book. I pick up the book: *The Fabric of the Human Body, by Andreas Vesalius.*

'Is there anything I can do for you, captain?' asks Sawyer.

'No. Don't mind me,' I reply. 'I'm just checking that everything is all right. You carry on and ignore me.'

'Can you break those eggs and separate the albumen, please, Master Long?' asks Sawyer.

'What?' asks Long.

'I'm sorry, will you separate the egg white?'

'Why? Do you want me to bake a cake?' replies Long, looking puzzled.

'No, I need it to mix with rose oil and turpentine to put on wounds to prevent necrosis.'

'Necrosis?'

'The flesh rotting and dying.'

'The last surgeon I assisted used hot oil.'

'Barbarous!' exclaims the surgeon. 'My preparation works much better. It was used by the ancient Romans and rediscovered a few years back by Ambroise Pare, at the siege of Bologna.'

'Well, I'll be…,' says Long, as he cracks and separates the egg white. 'Would you like me to get a small stove going, in case we need to cauterize any wounds?' he adds, handing Sawyer the egg whites.

'Yes, but only to heat water. I want to avoid cauterization if at all possible.'

'But amputees will bleed to death.'

'Providing we're not overrun and you can stem the flow of blood with a tourniquet until I can get to them, I'll perform a ligature as a part of the procedure.'

'A what?'

'I'll tie off the ends of any severed arteries. Cauterization with a hot iron is not precise enough and damages too much of the surrounding tissue. There are fewer complications and improved healing doing this and applying my preparation.'

I put the book down, and smile at the exchange between surgeon and assistant, as I depart to seek out Norris.

'The call to action stations is only precautionary, Mr Norris,' I say. 'I hope there's no need of your services, but I'm confident you and your men will acquit yourselves well after all your drills.'

'Thank you, cap'n,' replies Norris. 'We're ready willing and able, whenever you need to call on us. Aren't we lads?' he adds, turning to the gun crews.

'Aye!' they shout.

'I can see that lads,' I say. 'Stand ready and await orders.'

Back on the quarterdeck, John says to me, 'I think they're close enough for us to raise the signal, captain.'

'Make it so, Mr Hills.'

'Raise the signal, Johnston.'

There is no response to the signal from the Watergeuzen who keep closing.

'Signal our stragglers to change course to run with the wind and we'll cover them,' I order.

'They've changed course on our heading,' calls the lookout, a few moments later.

'Signal another change of course on a heading as close to the wind as the ships will bear, and we'll give them as merry a dance as we can in rejoining the main fleet,' I order. 'Take in some sail on the main mast, and hoist the sails on the mizzen-mast,' I add. 'We'll get closer to the wind with the lateen sails.'

'They've moved to a heading to intercept us,' calls the lookout.

'They're obviously after us and up to no good. What do you recommend, Mr Hills?' I ask.

'They're too much for us to handle,' answers John. 'We should re-join the bulk of the fleet. They have to be our main concern. We'll just have to leave the stragglers to their fate.'

'That's good and sensible advice. But I'm reluctant to give up on them without taking some action. We'll fire a warning shot close to the lead ship and see what happens.'

But before we have a chance to give the order, a flash is seen from the forward gunport of the lead Watergeuzen ship, followed in quick succession by the sound of a deep boom and a splash on our larboard side close enough for the resulting spray to reach the quarterdeck.

'To the gun deck, Mr Hills. Get Mr Norris to return a warning shot from the starboard side, towards the lead ship, as soon as I've got us into position,' I order.

'Aye, aye captain,' replies John, as he hurries below.

'Bring her hard about, helmsmen.'

Cornish, with the help of two other sailors, move the tiller as hard as possible. The *Barque of Bulleyn* heels hard over in response, with the sound of groans of complaint from her planking.

There is a flash and a loud boom from the first gun on the starboard side of the *Barque of Bulleyn*, followed by a splash short of the first ship. The lead Watergeuzen ship fires two shots from guns mounted in its bow that makes a huge splash on our larboard side, while it and the other two Watergeuzen continue to relentlessly run down our stragglers.

Bocas appears on the quarterdeck. 'Mr Hills's compliments, captain. He says the Watergeuzen must have a culverin aboard and could do us severe damage before we can hurt them.'

'My compliments to Mr Hills. Tell him to fire three shots on the upward roll even if we're a bit short of range. Then we'll make a turn to larboard to re-join the fleet.'

'Aye, aye, cap'n.'

Three shots boom out from our starboard side and we heel over further with the recoil of the guns. Two shots fall just short, as expected, but one tears through the main luff of the lead Watergeuzen ship.

'Hard to larboard, Cornish, we'll slip away as close to the wind as she'll bear. We'll make good enough progress with our lateen rigged masts. They'll not be able to close further on us. We'll just have to leave our stragglers to their fate.'

'Aye, aye, cap'n,' replies Johnston with noticeable relief, as another two cannon balls splash short and aft of the ship. Cornish and the other sailors move the tiller as quickly as they can, and we yaw off on our new course as the lateen sails take us close to the wind.

The *Barque of Bulleyn* makes good progress in re-joining the main fleet, while the three Watergeuzen close on the starboard sides of the ordnance ships forcing them to heave to.

John joins me on the quarterdeck and whispers to me, 'That's as good a piece of playacting as I've ever seen.'

'I know, but what happened with the shot that tore through their main luff,' I reply with a laugh of nervous relief.

'Unbeknown to me, Norris put an extra charge of fine corn powder, in a sort of pouch, down the barrel and it gave the shot some extra impetus.'

'I've never heard the like.'

'Neither have I. But I think he might be onto something, especially with using a packaged charge rather than ladling out loose powder. It could help prevent many an accident.'

'My compliments to Mr Norris and all the crew for their performance under fire,' I order. 'They deserve an extra ration of beer,' I add, smiling at John.

'I agree on this occasion,' replies John, laughing.

The wool fleet puts into Sluis before nightfall, while we remain at anchor in the Scheldt overnight.

25

Sluis

In the light early morning mist, the *Barque of Bulleyn* approaches its berth by the Bruges Gate set amidst the impressive sea defences and red brick city walls. Looking out from the quarterdeck, I notice several windmills behind the dykes that are used to pump water to drain the land that seems to be almost below sea level.

As the ship berths, a rotund man in fine apparel is waiting on the quayside. He comes aboard as soon as the brow is down. 'I'd like to speak with the captain,' he says.

'Who shall I say would like to speak with him,' enquires John, at the top of the brow.

'My name is Thomas Offley, Merchant of the Staple.'

'Take him to my cabin, John,' I call down from the quarterdeck. 'I'll be with you in a moment.'

'Captain, this is Mr Offley, Merchant of the Staple, to see you,' says John, as I join them in my cabin.

'I'm pleased to meet you,' I say. 'To what do I owe the pleasure?' I add, motioning for Mr Offley to sit at the table.

'It's a word of warning to the wise,' replies Mr Offley, as he fits himself snugly into a chair.

'You'd better stay for this as well, John,' I suggest, beckoning him to join us.

'The whole town is buzzing with talk of what happened at sea yesterday, from the stories of the sailors in the taverns,' reports Mr Offley.

'What talk, exactly?' I ask.

'The talk is of the capture of the three ships by the Watergeuzen. But it's mainly of your heroics in seeking to protect them and the rest of the fleet, against overwhelming firepower.'

'We were only doing our duty in fulfilment of our commission. I'm only sorry we couldn't prevent the taking of the three ships.'

'That may be so. But you can imagine my surprise, when I got all the manifests and discovered we'd received the total amount of wool we were expecting.'

'That's good, isn't it?'

'Yes. But I wonder who'll be taking the loss on the cargo of the other three ships, if indeed there is a loss?'

'I don't understand,' I say, wondering where this conversation is going. 'But if you aren't taking a loss, I wouldn't worry about it if I were you.'

'But I do worry about it.'

'Why?'

'I don't know what your game is, or even if you are party to a game at all,' adds Mr Offley, in an unpleasant manner. 'But there're a few things you should be clear about.'

'What?'

'First of all, the Merchants of the Staple are neutral with regards to matters of religion and politics, unless it interferes with our business and profits,' explains Mr Offley. 'Indeed, some say, the Staple's only religion and politics are business and profit. In any event, we won't let anything stand in the way of that. We had to move our homes and business operations from Calais, when the previous Queen's incompetence lost it to the French,' he adds in obvious annoyance. 'We moved to Bruges because it was, and still is, the best place for our business and profit. We're here as long as it suits us. But just as importantly, as long as it suits the Spanish governor whose concern for business is secondary to his interests in religion and politics.'

'I understand that. But what has any of that to do with us?' I say with a puzzled expression, although I now see where this conversation is headed.

'There are Spanish spies and government informers everywhere. It won't be long before word gets from the wool tellers to the authorities, that despite the loss of the three ships, we received all we were expecting. And it won't take long for the Spanish governor to wonder what the other ships were carrying and whether there was some form of subterfuge going on.'

'If there was, I know nothing of it,' I say, convincingly.

'Be that as it may, I don't care,' says the unpleasant Offley, who I suspect is the kind of man who might sell his own grandmother if there were some profit in it for him. 'And I don't care what happens to you, unless it impacts on the Staple's business, profit and security of tenure in Bruges. With that in mind, I suggest you're out of here before the authorities start putting two and two together and decide to seek to question you about the matter.'

'Hmm,' I murmur, thoughtfully. 'My intention has always been to be here overnight and to put to sea on tomorrow's early tide. And I have no intention of visiting the Spanish Netherlands again, within the foreseeable future.'

'I think that's a very wise decision,' says Mr Offley, as he rises, still wedged in the chair attached to his corpulent rear end.

John and I resist the temptation to laugh as the plump merchant turns in circles, like a dog chasing its tail, in an attempt to throw off the troublesome chair. Finally, John puts him out of his misery by giving the chair a sharp tug.

'Good day, gentlemen. I can see my own way out,' says Mr Offley, who turns and leaves without further ado.

Once Offley has gone, John and I burst out laughing at his undignified departure. 'I suppose we ought to be grateful to him for the warning,' I say, 'even if it was motivated by self-interest and delivered in an unpleasant manner.'

'Yes. I suppose we'd better take heed of it, although I'd hoped to get a couple of days alongside here and pick up some fine spun cloth for Mary,' replies John.

'I'm sure you can make time for that,' I suggest. 'Give shore leave to as many men as we can. But make sure they all return in good time for us to sail on tomorrow's early tide.'

'When're you going to tell the crew of our purpose and plans to sail for Lindisfarne?' asks John, reminding me that is a task I've yet to face.

'I'd thought of doing that before we sailed, as I'd like to establish a reputation for playing fair with the men,' I sigh at the thought of it. 'But in view of Offley's warning, and the possibility of Spanish spies being around, I think I'll do it once we're underway.'

26
Cadzand

John and I are already on the quarterdeck, as Johnston and the chief bosun's mate roust out the crew from their hammocks, and unceremoniously shunt down the brow several tired and dishevelled ladies of the town who had serviced many of the men aboard during the night.

'Weigh anchor, Mr Johnston, and get us underway as soon as possible,' orders John.

The *Barque of Bulleyn* eases away from the quay and into the channel, with a favourable light breeze, at the stand of the tide that makes it easier for us to manoeuvre in the confines of the harbour and the initial narrowness of the channel.

'What's our heading, cap'n?' asks Fisher.

'Just take us out of the Zwin along the Scheldt coast to Cadzand,' I reply. 'We'll drop anchor off shore for a short while. After that, I'll let you know our destination.'

'Aye, aye, cap'n. You heard the cap'n, Cornish,' says Fisher, relaying my orders. 'Now keep to the starboard side of the channel and when we're out of the Zwin, I'll give you our heading.'

As we make our way along the channel at little more than walking pace, some Spanish soldiers in a wagon, led by their captain on horseback, come alongside the ship on the towpath on our starboard side.

'*Venga al lado y preparese para ser abordado!*' hails the captain.

'Does anyone speak Spanish,' I ask.

'I speak a little,' says Fontane, the Frenchman.

'What did he say?'

'I think he wants us to come alongside and prepare to be boarded.'

'Ask him to say it again,' I order, playing for time.

'I don't like the sound of this,' says John. 'I suggest we get Norris to break out three of the hail-shot pieces and make them ready.'

'Make it so, Mr Hills,' I reply, mindful of Offley's warning.

'*Que dijo, capitan?*' shouts Fontane, as John leaves the quarterdeck to get Mr Norris and the ordnance.

'*Venga al lado y preparese para ser abordado!*' comes the reply.

'Does he want to board us?' I ask.

'He does,' reports Fontane. 'And he seems most insistent upon it, cap'n.'

'Tell him we don't understand. And ask him if he could say it again, in English.' Fontane looks at me, puzzled, but I simply smile and gesture with my hand for him to do as I say.

'*No entendemos. Puede repetirlo en ingles?*' calls out Fontane.

'*Yo no soy un idiota, capitan. Detenganse o vamos a disparar!*' replies the Spaniard.

'He says he's not an idiot and they'll fire on us, cap'n,' says Fontane, just as Norris and three soldiers appear on deck with the hail-shot pieces.

'He's an idiot if he thinks he can stop us with a few soldiers with handguns,' I reply. 'Carry on. And get the three hail shot pieces loaded and in position on the starboard side, Mr Norris, and be quick about it,' I order, quietly.

The Spaniards ride fast further along the side of the channel. They get out of their wagon, load their muskets and make ready to fire when we get abreast them, while Norris and his men hastily load the cast iron hail-shot pieces and fix them to the rail by means of the hook beneath the guns.

'Fire one of the hail shot pieces well over their heads, into the trees behind them, before we come abreast of them,' I order.

A hail-shot piece is fired, and the dices of iron rip into the trees behind the Spanish soldiers, felling some branches and stripping others of their leaves.

'Now hail their captain, Fontane, and tell him to lay down their weapons, or the next one will be aimed straight at them.'

'Dejen sus armas o el siguiente se dirigira a ustedes!' hails Fontane.

The Spanish soldiers duly oblige. I lift my hat to the captain and give a bow of my head as we pass him by, while the crew cheer and give the hapless Spaniards crude gestures: a mixture of the English two finger salute, the *le doigt d'honneur* and the *corte de mangas*[55].

We risk a little more sail than we would normally do in such confined waters and make steady progress out of the Zwin and along the Flemish coast until we are off Cadzand: a small fishing and agricultural village of no more than a couple of dozen houses.

'Heave to, haul down the sails and drop anchor, Johnston,' orders John. 'Then muster all hands on deck.'

I look down from the quarterdeck at the assembled crew. They are a motley bunch with many sporting cuts, bruises and signs of a surfeit of beer and a new local drink called jenever, from the excesses of the *run ashore* the previous evening. 'I don't

---

55 Le doigt d'honneur: the finger of honour – the vertically raised middle finger salute. Corte de mangas: cut sleeve – sometimes known as the Iberian slap, where one hand grips the bicep as the forearm is raised vertically.

know what our enemies will think of them, but by God they frighten me,' I say quietly to John.

'Avast there,' shouts John. The assembled crew quieten, turn and look up to the quarterdeck. 'Your captain - Cap'n Rob Isted.'

I move forward. 'Good day, men,' I say, gripping the rail with my left hand. 'I know many of you have been speculating about the ultimate purpose of a ship rigged out and crewed as we are. Well, I'll end that speculation now. Here in my right hand, I have two documents with two great seals of state,' I add, holding aloft two parchments bearing impressively large wax seals. 'These are letters of marque: one bearing the great seal of England, and the other bearing the seal of the Prince of Orange. With the authority and protection these contain, we're going privateering. Each man will get a share of the prize money according to his rank or rate. And there should be plenty enough of that to go around. But if there's anyone not willing to commit to this venture, they can collect their things and be safely put ashore at Cadzand with my good wishes. Now are you with me lads.'

There is a moment's silence before Fisher the pilot shouts, 'Aye, we're with you cap'n. Lets hear it for Cap'n Rob.'

'Aye,' shout the assembled crew, followed by shouts of 'Cap'n Rob, Cap'n Rob, Cap'n Rob.'

'Thank you men,' I reply, extending my arms out in acknowledgement. 'Get us underway, Mr Hills. Mr Fisher, plot a course for the Holy Island of Lindisfarne.'

'Avast there,' shouts John. The crew quieten. 'Weigh anchor and get us underway, Johnston; and lets be quick about it.'

27

The North Sea

As we weigh anchor and set sail, I speak quietly with the pilot. 'Thank you for your support, Mr Fisher,' I say, gratefully.

'It was my pleasure, Captain,' he replies.

'I'm grateful, nevertheless. It got a positive response from the men.'

'There was never any doubt in that, cap'n. They just needed a nudge,' says Fisher, with a smile. 'Most of us had guessed your purpose in London. Some may not have signed on otherwise. And with your and Mr Hills handling of the ship with the wreckers at Seaford, the escort of the wool fleet, the engagement with the Watergeuzen, and now in dealing with the Spanish soldiers, everyone realises we've a good ship in good hands.'

'That's very gratifying.'

'Of course, the letters of marque you showed us are a real bonus. None of us wants to end up on the Admiralty gibbet.'

'Amen to that.'

As the *Barque of Bulleyn* makes steady progress northward towards the Holy Island of Lindisfarne, John and I, with the assistance of Johnston, Fisher and Norris, put the men and ship through drills to ensure we are ready for almost every eventuality that might arise in taking ships at sea.

In the early morning, less than a day out from Lindisfarne, John and I survey the surrounding sea from the quarterdeck.

'I think we're as ready as we're ever likely to be, and not a ship in sight,' I say.

'We should come across something soon on this heading,' replies John.

'I confess I'm apprehensive about it. But the sooner we cut our teeth on something the better.'

'There's no need to worry,' says John, reassuringly. 'We've a good ship and crew. Everyone knows what to do. We've run through all the drills and I'm impressed with the results.'

'It's not that what I'm apprehensive about. I've never done anything like this before and I don't want to foul up in front of the crew.'

'You'll be all right. There has to be a first time for everything. We'll select something completely harmless for us to board first. Anyway, as captain, your place is in the ship,' explains John. 'All you have to do is bring us alongside to a position where we can board them. Hopefully, this will be with their acquiescence or, if not, forcibly. I'll take the boarding party and conduct the dirty end of the business,' he adds, as if he is relishing the prospect.

Our conversation is interrupted by a shout from the lookout in the crow's-nest, 'Sail ahoy on the larboard bow.'

'What are your orders, captain?' asks John.

I hesitate before replying more loudly than necessary, 'Close on her so we can better make out what she is.'

'You heard the captain, Mr Fisher, make it so,' orders John.

'Aye, aye, sir,' replies Fisher, smartly. 'Two points to larboard Cornish to steer a course to close on yonder ship,' he orders.

A little while later the lookout calls down, 'She looks like a small but well laden Dutch flyboat.'

'It doesn't sound like much, but sufficient for us to cut our teeth on,' advises John. 'What're your orders, captain?'

I swallow hard, and say with more confidence than I feel, 'Plot an intercept course. We'll hail her to stop and be boarded. Strike our colours and call the men to action.'

'You heard the captain, Mr Fisher, make it so.'

'A point to starboard, Cornish,' orders Fisher.

The *Barque of Bulleyn* responds swiftly to the helm and with a favourable wind makes straight for an intercept point on the flyboat's heading.

'Sound the trumpet for action stations,' orders John.

Fontane takes the trumpet and blows a tuneful call, now that Johnston has found someone who can actually play the instrument.

There is a flurry of activity with archers and musket men taking up positions on the forecastle, quarterdeck and in the rigging, and with Norris and his gun crews assembling on the gun deck. Then the red and blue ensign of the Cinque Ports, displaying three golden lions conjoined with the sterns of three ships above one another, is unfurled atop the main mast.

'Bring us in closer to take the wind from her sails and force her to heave to,' I order. 'Then come alongside her on the starboard side. Now where's our Dutch speaker?'

'It's Fontane. He's here, cap'n,' replies Johnston.

'When I've brought us close alongside, I want you to hail her skipper to keep a steady course, lower her sails and prepare to be boarded. Have you got that Fontane?' I say.

'Aye, cap'n.'

'Good luck with the boarding, Mr Hills,' I add, as John takes his leave to join the boarding party.

The Dutch flyboat is closed on its larboard side and forced to heave to into the wind.

'Koers blijven volgen, lager dat zeils en komen de aan boord,' hails Fontane.

The skipper of the flyboat duly obliges.

I ease the ship alongside and John and a boarding party of ten, including Fontane, swing aboard the flyboat.

I move to the ship's side and look down on the flyboat's lower quarterdeck, in earshot of where John and Fontane join its captain.

'Fontane, ask the captain where he's from, where they're headed and what's on his manifest,' orders John.

'Waar kom je vandaan en waar ga je heeen. En wat is uw manifest, Kapitein,' asks Fontane.

'There's no need of that, I speak English,' replies the captain. 'But I must protest, we've done nothing wrong to be stopped by a Cinque Port ship.'

'Ah, you know of us,' remarks John.

'Yes, I'm well acquainted with the Cinque Ports. I attend the Herring Fair at Yarmouth most years and have had dealings with the bailiff at the fair.'

'I still require your heading and manifest.'

'I'm just returning from the herring fishing grounds in the North Sea, laden with fish for the market in Antwerp.'

'I'm afraid it's your bad luck that we've a letter of marque from the Prince of Orange to seize ships bound for Spanish held territory that might aid his enemies.'

'But I'm no lover of the Dons. The fish will feed the civil population and help support our families.'

'I can't help that. But as a fellow fisherman, I'll give you quarter in exchange for your co-operation,' offers John. 'If not, we'll simply confiscate your ship and cargo.'

The Dutch captain looks around him at the fierce and heavily armed boarding party, before sighing and saying, 'Very well. I suppose I've little choice.'

'A wise decision. Now if you give me your parol to follow my orders and not try to escape, I won't confine you and your men,' offers John.

'But I thought you were going to give us quarter and let us on our way,' says the captain sharply.

'I will, but we have neither sufficient nor suitable space for your cargo,' explains John. 'So you'll sail with us to a place where we can dispose of it and then we'll let you go. You can even return via the fishing grounds and recoup your losses if you wish, without further hindrance from us.'

'But you might as well take all our cargo, with the time it'll take us to do that and return to Antwerp.'

'I was going to do that anyway. The quarter I'm offering is your life and ship.'

'This is intolerable,' exclaims the Dutch captain, with genuine anguish.

'As intolerable as the alternative?' asks John, looking menacingly at his unsheathed sword. 'You can take it or leave it. It makes little difference to me. Now what is it to be?'

'*De drivel hale je, Minheer,*' exclaims the Dutchman, bitterly. 'You have me at a complete disadvantage. You have my parol on it.'

'A wise choice,' says John, sheathing his sword. 'I'm leaving Brown here, as prize master, with some armed men to ensure you keep your word. You're to follow Brown's instructions explicitly. But if you cross me, there will be hell to pay for it. Do you understand?'

'Yes, I understand. You have my word on it.'

'All right, Harry, keep in as close company as you can, but failing that we'll foregather at Lindisfarne,' says John to Harry Brown, one of our men from Hastings.

'Aye, aye, John,' replies Harry.

'Good luck,' adds John, before he and six of the boarding party return to the *Barque of Bulleyn* to cheers from the remainder of the crew.

John proceeds to the quarterdeck to join me, while the two ships separate and make ready to proceed in convoy on course for Lindisfarne.

'Well done, Mr Hills,' I say with some relief.

'We all played our part, cap'n,' he replies, with little indication of any pleasure. 'Unfortunately, it wasn't much of a prize. The ship is only carrying fish. Still, we can seek to sell it on somewhere. In agreement for the captain's parol to obey our orders, I've agreed to let them go with their ship once we've done that.'

'I heard it all from the quarterdeck. You did exactly as I'd have wished.'

'But we'll have to do better than this, otherwise we'll be operating below subsistence rate.'

We make steady progress during the remainder of the morning with a favourable wind, sea state and visibility.

'Ahoy. Two ships on the starboard bow, in close company on a northerly heading,' calls the lookout, from the crow's-nest.

'Can you make out what they are,' shouts John.

'They look like a couple of hoys, sloop rigged and well laden.'

'Your orders, captain?' asks John.

'Plot a course to intercept them,' I order. 'Your recommendations, Mr Hills? Can we take both, or should we content ourselves with one?'

'I think we could try for both,' he replies, as if relishing the challenge. 'We're faster than they are and we've the weather-gauge. I suggest we close on them. Take the wind of the hindmost and signal it to heave to. Then we can close on the other and force them to do the same. Put a boarding party on the second ship and then return to the first and put another party aboard her.'

'I agree. If we stop to board the first one when we force it to heave to, the other will almost certainly get away,' I say. 'You lead the boarding party into the first ship to be boarded and I'll lead the one into the second.'

'You don't need to do that, Rob,' whispers John. 'Fisher can lead the second boarding party.'

'I know. But I feel I ought to do this, both for myself and to show the men I'm not one of those gentlemen privateers who takes the lion's share of the booty without taking a proper share of the risks.'

'I don't think they'll think that, and it doesn't matter if they do. Nevertheless, I can see the benefit of it, if you're sure.'

We make good progress over the next half an hour in closing on the two hoys, which maintain a steady course and speed.

'Ahoy. They're both Dutchmen,' shouts the lookout.

'Strike our colours, Johnston. Sound for action stations and get Fontane ready to hail them,' I order.

'Aye, aye, cap'n,' comes the quick response.

'Cornish, I want you to approach the hindmost ship so we take her wind. Then I want to pass her on the starboard side close enough for us to hail her to heave to, while maintaining a position where we'll have the wind to haul off and do the same to the other ship. Can you do that?'

'Aye, aye, cap'n,' replies Cornish, seemingly relishing the challenge.

Cornish steers the ship into exactly the right position to take the wind from the hindmost hoy's sails.

'Well done, Cornish,' I say.

As we pass the hoy on its starboard side, Fontane hails, *'Koers blijven volgen, lager dat zeils en komen de aan boord.'* Their captain obeys. We haul off to close on the second ship, which runs with the wind.

As we veer off in pursuit, its erstwhile companion makes a run for it, sailing close hauled, six points to the wind. 'The first ship is making off,' reports John. 'We'll have to let her go.'

'Not if Cornish is able to pass the second ship close enough for you to board her while we're still on the move,' I reply. 'Then we can haul off and re-intercept the first one.'

'I can get us in real close,' replies Cornish, 'if the boarding party are prepared to take her on the move.'

'You just make sure you get us in real close and personal, and we'll swing across on ropes and take her,' says John, with determination.

'I'll do that, don't you worry.'

'That's settled then,' I say. 'Good luck, Mr Hills, I think you'd better join the boarding party now and tell them the change of plan.'

'Aye, aye. Good luck to you as well, captain,' replies John, as he hurries off to join his boarding party.

Cornish brings the ship in close enough for the crews to reach out across the bulwarks and shake hands, if we were on cordial terms. But we are not.

John and the boarding party swing aboard the hoy while the ships are moving, under cover of the musket men on the forecastle and quarterdeck of the *Barque of Bulleyn*. This gives those swinging into the hoy's rigging sufficient time to cut the mainsail to quickly bring the hoy dead in the water. As we veer away, I can see the hoy's crew are not giving in easily, but attack the boarding party on the deck with cudgels.

'The same procedure as before, cap'n?' asks Cornish.

'No, not this time,' I reply. 'I doubt she'll meekly heave to now and will no doubt be prepared for a small boarding party swinging across. I want you to bring our bow across her, ahead of her mast. Can you do that?

'Aye,' replies Cornish. 'It's a difficult manoeuvre, but we can do it.'

'And Johnston, just as we turn into her, I want the sails moved to contrary positions to cancel each other out to bring her to a halt quickly,' I order. 'We'll then get some men in her rigging to bring down her mainsail. Our musket men, in the forecastle, can cover her crew and be prepared to rake her deck if there looks like being any resistance. If all goes well, the boarding party can simply climb down and take her.'

'I'll join the boarding party,' states Fisher.

'No. I'll lead the boarding party on this occasion,' I say. 'You'll have the ship in my absence.'

'As you wish, cap'n.'

After half an hour of playing cat and mouse across the sea, I manage to seize the opportunity to end the game. We take the wind from the hoy's sails and ease alongside her on her starboard side.

'Hard to larboard, Cornish,' I order.

Cornish immediately obeys, with the assistance of two other sailors at the tiller. And with Johnston's sailors exercising their orders explicitly, the *Barque of Bulleyn's* bowsprit is gently brought across the hoy just ahead of its main mast.

'Now get some men in her rigging and cut her mainsail. And take in our sails at the double,' I add, as I make my way to the larboard side of the quarterdeck, where the musket men and bowmen have taken aim on the captain and crew below us.

In contrast to the chase, it is all over in a matter of moments. The Dutchmen on the hoy lay down their weapons faced with the sight of the musket men taking aim at them. So it is an easy matter for me and the boarding party to lower ourselves onto the hoy.

'Fontane, ask this man whether I've the pleasure of addressing the captain,' I order.

'*Ben jij de kap…*'

But before Fontane can finish, the Dutch captain interrupts, 'I am the captain,' he says in perfect English.

'What is it with you Dutchmen, you all speak better English than the crew,' I remark. 'Do I have your surrender, captain?'

'You do. I see I've little choice.'

'Thank you,' I say, before turning and shouting to Johnston aboard the *Barque of Bulleyn*, 'The ship's secured. Now get our bow off her and tie her up alongside, before we do any further damage.'

A sound of clashing blades is heard forward, followed by a cry of pain. 'What's going on?' I shout. The sound of a scuffle continues before there is silence and Beattie appears.

'Nick Lowing's been injured. The first officer sliced off his nose with a sword, before we could bludgeon him into submission,' reports Beattie.

'Get him aboard our ship and get Mr Sawyer to see to him,' I order, before returning my attention to the captain. 'Now, where were we, captain? Oh yes, I know. Where are you from and where are you heading?'

'We're a ship of Utrecht, heading for Bergen,' replies the captain.

'That's good, from Spanish held territory. What's your cargo?'

'Five tons of sugar from Santa Caterina, two hundredweight of galls and sundry items for painters and apothecaries.'

'That should fetch a pretty penny. Now, captain, will you give me your parol to follow my orders in sailing the ship to Lindisfarne, in exchange for not confining you for the remainder of our voyage?'

'You have my ship, crew and cargo, but I'll be damned if we'll lift a finger to help you,' he replies with understandable bitterness.

'I understand. But I regret I'll have to cage you and your crew until we reach port and dispose of your cargo.'

'Then what?'

'I'll release you and your ship to return to Utrecht, or go onto Bergen or wherever you will.' The Dutchman looks taken aback and then relieved, but he makes no response. 'Take the captain to join his crew, Fontane, and find somewhere to cage them for the time being.'

The Dutch captain walks off with Fontane. He stops, then turns to me and says, 'My compliments captain, to you and your crew, on your seamanship. I thought I might be able to slip away when you went after my compatriot's ship. If I'd known you were so daring and capable of such manoeuvres I wouldn't have bothered. And, I'm heartily sorry for the unnecessary injury caused to your crewman.'

'Thank you, that's most kind,' I reply, surprised at such a courteous compliment and apology under such circumstances. 'Would you like to reconsider my offer, captain?'

'No, I wouldn't,' he says, with a dismissive laugh, as he continues to walk away, shaking his head.

I leave Tom Cox, as the prize master, in command of six sailors and two soldiers aboard the hoy to re-rig the sails and make her ready to get underway.

I return to the *Barque of Bulleyn*, to resounding cheers from the crew. It feels good to have completed a successful boarding and received the approval of the crew.

Fontane and I proceed straight to the wardroom to see how Lowing is fairing.

'How's the patient, Mr Sawyer,' I ask.

Sawyer removes a swathe of material staunching the blood flowing from what's left of Lowing's nose. 'As you can see, it's a good clean cut. Now where's your nose.'

The usual nasal sounding Lowing tries to speak, but the lack of a nose and the bleeding wound makes him sound incomprehensible.

'We looked for it but couldn't find it,' states Fontane. 'I suspect it went over the side.'

'That's a pity. It might have just been a simple case of sewing it back on,' replies Sawyer, studying the wound intently. 'Never mind, when we get to Lindisfarne, I'll fix it. For now, I'll simply clean it and bandage it up.' He sucks up some red wine in a syringe and uses it to irrigate the wound, to ensure it is clean and free of any extraneous particles. He then applies some of the preparation of egg white, rose oil and turpentine to the wound that he and Nick Long had made prior to the engagement with the Watergeuzen. Finally, he places a clean wad of gauze on the wound and secures it in place with a bandage. 'That will hold for now. I'll see you again when we get to Lindisfarne and I'll sort it out then.'

'How are you going to fix it?' I ask, thinking there is nothing that can be done.

'There're three options: we can let it heal as it is; we can make a silver cover for Lowing to wear; or I can make him a new nose.'

'Make a new nose,' I exclaim in astonishment, as I've never heard the like.

'Yes. If Lowing chooses the latter option, it'll be painful; it'll incapacitate him for sometime; I can't promise it'll look as good as the one he lost, although it wasn't the prettiest to start with; and the operation isn't always successful. But, I've done it before, at Berwick.'

'You decide what you want Lowing,' I say. 'You seem to be in good hands with Mr Sawyer.'

'Now you go away and think about it, Lowing,' states Sawyer, tidying away his instruments. 'And have a shot of medicinal brandy to dull the pain. But don't drink too much. Getting hung-over will only add to your troubles.'

I return to the quarterdeck. A little while later, the other hoy comes alongside and John joins me.

'That went well, Mr Hills, thanks to all your drills,' I say, delighted by our success.

'Yes, but we didn't get to practice that last manoeuvre of yours,' replies John. 'That was very well executed indeed.'

'I appreciate that, John. How did things go on your hoy and what cargo is she carrying?'

'We had some resistance, but nothing we couldn't handle. Her holds are full of grain bound for a Hansa merchant in Bergen. We've repaired the main luff we cut in taking her, and I've left Tomlyn in charge as the prize master.'

'We should get a pretty penny for that and the sugar, galls and apothecary stuff on mine. A little bit more than subsistence level now.'

'Aye,' agrees John. 'The crew are pleased with their work, as they should be, and now they'll see some reward for it.'

'Johnston, will you kindly give my and Mr Hills' compliments to the crew on a job well done,' I say. 'And make arrangements for them to have an extra ration of beer once we reach Lindisfarne.' John and I both laugh at my almost habitual ordering the issue of extra rations of beer. But the men have certainly deserved it for their day's work.

'Aye, aye, sir,' replies Johnston. 'And may I say, captain, that was as fine a bit of seamanship as I've seen in all my years at sea.'

28
Holy Island

'Ahoy there! Land on the larboard bow,' shouts the lookout from the crow's-nest.

'That'll be Bambrough Castle on the headland, cap'n, with the Farne Islands and Holy Island just beyond north and east of there,' says Fisher.

'Well done, pilot,' I reply. 'That's good, John,' I add, quietly, 'we'll be at anchor by nightfall. Then tomorrow we can pay a courtesy call on the Captain of the Garrison and conduct our business with the Queen's Storehouse. Then if Henry Knollys and Fernando Fielding are there, arrange to meet them and see if we wish to throw in with them or not.'

'That's up to you, Rob,' answers John, in equally hushed tones. 'But unless they have a better plan, as we are at this latitude, I suggest we sail east to intercept some of the Baltic trade to or from the Hansa League[56]. Then perhaps we can seek to dispose of the prizes in Edinburgh, if they'll be well disposed towards us there. But if not, then further south.'

'While it's my decision, John, I value your input and I'd like you to be part of the discussions with Knollys and Fielding. I also like your idea about the Baltic trade and Edinburgh.'

'I'm sorry, cap'n, but I couldn't help overhearing your conversation with Mr Hills, especially about Edinburgh,' interrupts Fisher.

---

56 The Hansa League was a commercial and defensive confederation of merchant guilds and their market towns that dominated trade along the coast of Northern Europe during the 16th century.

'Hmm,' I grunt, a little annoyed with Fisher, John and myself. 'I'd be obliged if you'd keep it to yourself, Mr Fisher.'

'You can rely on me, cap'n. I wouldn't have mentioned it, but I might be able to help.'

'How?'

'I come from Leith and know Edinburgh well,' replies Fisher. 'I think we'd be able to do business there, providing we leave alone Scottish ships and ships trading with Scotland. I know people in authority in the port and could check with them if you put me ashore there before we take any prizes into the port.'

'Hmm. What do you think, Mr Hills?' I ask.

'It'll be as well to check it out,' replies John, thoughtfully. 'It might even be best to do it now, rather than later, as we may have to be here awhile to meet with Knollys.'

'I agree. All right, Mr Fisher, we may have to be at Holy Island for a while. Can you arrange to get to Leith and back in a week's time?'

'Aye, I should be able to take passage to Leith from Holy Island, or via Berwick-upon-Tweed, but it won't give me much time in Leith,' replies Fisher, whom I suspect is saying that in the hope of extending his time in his home port.

'That's agreed then.'

As the *Barque of Bulleyn* approaches Lindisfarne harbour in the fading daylight, I look out on the silhouette of the newly built fortified garrison high up on Beblowe Crag with the remnants of the old wood and turf fortifications adjacent to it. On the other side of the bay is the beacon that has just been lit. Just beyond that is St Cuthbert's Island, barely visible through a descending light sea mist, where the venerated St Cuthbert had first retreated to live the life of a hermit.

As we drop anchor in the harbour, I count four armed flyboats and a hulk amongst a host of fishing boats.

'I suspect the flyboats are rigged out for the same trade as us,' remarks John.

'Yes, I wonder if one's Captain Fielding's?' I muse.

'We can enquire ashore in the morning.'

'We'll do just that,' I say, keen to get things underway. 'Will you make arrangements for the boatman to get the longboat ready after breakfast, Mr Hills?'

'Aye, aye.'

'We'll go ashore with Brocas, the quartermaster, and Fisher; make a courtesy call on the Captain of the Garrison; see if we can get Fisher passage off the Island; get news of Knollys and Fielding; and then visit the Controller of the Queen's Storehouse to discuss disposal of our captured cargo.'

John, Fisher, Brocas and I land on the eastern side of the bay; the opposite side from the reddish-brown stone ruins of the 12th century Priory that has been abandoned since the dissolution of the monasteries. Since then a great deal of its masonry has been used to build the garrison fort and other buildings in the small village of Lindisfarne.

We make our way along the shore and up the slope to the top of Beblowe Crag, which gives the garrison fort a complete view of the island and the surrounding sea for miles.

At the gate of the garrison fort we are greeted by a halberd-bearing sentry, wearing a simple morion helmet and a breastplate over a white and green jacket. 'Who goes there?' he demands.

'Captain Robert Isted, here to pay a call on Sir William Read, Captain of the Garrison,' I answer.

'Is he expecting you?'

'Mr Henry Knollys has informed him we'd be coming, but we don't have a specific appointment.'

'Wait here gentlemen. I'll see if he's free to see you.'

We wait in the guardroom to the right of the main entrance. A few minutes later I am escorted through a long gallery to a small room. There, a tall angular gentleman of military dress and bearing is standing looking out of a window that commands a view of the harbour and its entrance. 'Captain Isted to see you Sir William,' announces the escort.

'Come in captain,' says Sir William. 'I received a letter from Henry Knollys to say you'd be calling. I'm afraid I can't spare you much time, as I'm off to the garrison at Berwick shortly. However, if there's anything I can assist you with while you're at Holy Island, don't hesitate to ask and I and my men will do whatever we can.'

'That's very kind,' I reply. 'We're hoping to dispose of some cargo in the Queen's Storehouse, find passage off the Island for one of my men to go onto Leith, and to meet up with Henry Knollys and Captain Fielding.'

'If you call on Mr Yeman, the Controller of the Queen's Storehouse, which is in what used to be the old Priory Church, he's used to providing that service for gentlemen such as yourselves. I'll also be happy to transport your man to Berwick, with me. He should be able to take passage in a coastal ship to Leith from there.'

'Thank you. Are Henry Knollys and Captain Fielding here, or do you know when they might arrive?'

'I'm expecting them, but I'm not exactly sure when. I might find out more about that when I'm in Berwick. I suspect Knollys will be combining his visit here with a visit to his uncle, Baron Hunsdon, who as Lord of the Eastern Marches is my commanding officer.'

'Thank you. We'll remain here until we have news.'

'You're welcome. However, I'm afraid the island has few attractions for those who have been at sea for a while,' says

Captain Read. 'So I'd be grateful if you would ensure your men maintain good order and discipline, especially in their dealings with the locals. This is all I ask in exchange for providing you with a safe haven.'

'I understand, perfectly. I'll do all I can to ensure we cause no trouble.'

'Now, if you'd excuse me, I've a few things to do before I depart in half an hour,' says Captain Read, extending his hand.

'I fully understand,' I reply, shaking his hand. 'I have a lot to do as well. I'll leave my man Fisher at the guardroom, to wait for you,' I add, as I leave the room.

John, Brocas and I return to the longboat, row the short distance across the bay and make our way to the old Priory Church.

'Do I have the pleasure of addressing Mr Yeman?' I ask, as we enter the office of the Controller of the Queen's Storehouse.

'You do. Who do I have the pleasure of receiving?' replies the tall but portly man struggling to his feet.

'I'm Robert Isted, Captain of the *Barque of Bulleyn*. This is John Hills, master of the ship; and John Brocas, my quartermaster.'

'You must be the gentlemen who arrived in the ship of war yesterday evening, in company with a couple of hoys and a flyboat.'

'Yes, we are.'

'It's a pleasure to meet you gentlemen. What can I do for you?'

'We've taken the three ships under letters of marque. I'd like to dispose of the cargo and hope you'll be able to help in that.'

'I'll do what I can. What do you have?' says the Controller, rubbing his hands in delight.

Brocas hands me the manifests and I pass them to the Controller.

187

'Hmm. The sugar, galls, paints and apothecary stuff should fetch a good price,' he murmurs, with a nod of satisfaction. 'I can take them and the grain off your hands, but I can't help you out with the fish.'

'That's a good start anyway. How much will you pay me for them,' I say, getting down to the nub of the matter.

'I can't give you much in the way of coin; I don't hold that much, currently. But I can give you some and a promissory note for a good proportion of what I expect to make for it at market.'

'How much will that be?'

'Twenty pounds in coin and forty pounds in a promissory note.'

'But we could get much more for it on the open market.'

'You're welcome to try,' says the Controller, sitting back at his desk. 'But with the greatest respect, captain, your kind aren't welcome everywhere. Even where you are, the price drops. Besides, there are expenses in transporting and selling the goods,' he adds, leaning back, opening his hands in a wide shrug. 'Her Majesty takes the risk of selling them on, and I have to show her a profit on what I deal with on her behalf.'

'Of course, I understand,' I say, understanding full well that he has the advantage of us. 'It's just that I'd hoped for more, especially more coin for provisioning and showing the men for their efforts,' I add in an effort to squeeze a little more from the scoundrel.

'As it is your first time here, captain, I'll give you thirty pounds in coin and a promissory note for the same.'

I look at the Controller straight in his eyes and realise I'll get no more from him, before saying, 'Agreed. But where can I exchange the promissory note.'

'I'm afraid there's nowhere around these parts,' explains the Controller. 'But if you return here sometime after I've sold the goods, I might be able to redeem it for a small consideration,' he adds, with a twinkle in his eye at the chance of making a little personal profit. 'But if you want full value for it, you'll have to redeem it with the Exchequer in London.'

I control my irritation and merely ask, 'When do you want the goods and when can we get the money?'

'We're handling some goods from some others of your trade today. If you start tomorrow morning, I'll have men ready to receive it.'

'Agreed. Now before we go, do you have any suggestion of what we can do with the fish?'

'A polite one I hope,' mutters John.

'Your best bet is to take it to Francis Clarke, on Inner Farne. He leases part of the former monastery, from the Dean and Chapter of Durham Cathedral,' replies the Controller. 'Clarke runs a chandler's for the fishing fleets that use the islands from time to time. But more importantly for you, he has a fishery with a large smokehouse, facilities for salting, and a fish-flake for air-drying. You might try to sell the fish to him, or make a trade for some provisions.'

'We'll do that,' I say, 'as soon as we've unloaded the other cargo.'

'But I wouldn't count on him giving you much for it; well below the usual wholesale trade,' adds the Controller.

'Thank you for your advice,' I reply, realising this is going to be the way of things from now on. 'I'll call again for our money, once we've landed everything.'

'It's my pleasure, gentlemen. Good day,' says the Controller with a self-satisfied smile.

'Good day, sir,' I reply, as we leaves the office.

'I realise we're in a somewhat dubious trade, but these so called respectable people are the real crooks,' exclaims John.

189

'I know what you mean, John, but what could I do?' I say, in frustration. 'These people hold the whip hand and they know it. I suppose Dick might've struck a better deal. That's more his strong point than mine.'

'I'm not blaming you, or making unfair comparisons with your brother,' exclaims John.

'I know you aren't. I am,' I add, quickening my step past the storehouse men carrying sacks of flour. 'Let's go back aboard, arrange to get the cargo ashore, and then set sail for the Farne Island and dispose of the fish.'

'What shall we do with the hoys?' asks John.

'We'll take them with us and release them whilst we're in the Farne Islands. I don't want to do that here in case they cause trouble, and I'd rather they weren't aware of our movements once we let them go.'

'I think that's wise.'

'I'd also like to provide them with sufficient victuals for their voyage home,' I add, 'rather than leave them with nothing so they have to make port in England, beg for provisions and make complaint about us to the authorities.'

'I don't think that's necessary,' says John, 'but it's your decision. I only hope we can get all we need from Clarke in exchange for the fish.'

John, Brocus and I board the *Barque of Bulleyn* to find most of the crew standing in a circle on the weather-deck. In the midst of them, Lowing is seated on a high backed chair to which his arms, legs and head are strapped, making it impossible for him to move. Sawyer stands next to him, with his surgical instruments laid out on an adjacent table and Nick Long standing nearby in attendance.

'What's going on here, Mr Sawyer?' I ask.

'Lowing has opted for a new nose, captain,' replies Sawyer.

'Well, I'll be… I'm sure we'd all like to see that, but why are you doing it out here.'

'It's a nice day, we're steady at anchor and it's a little too dark below deck for such a delicate operation, even with lamps.'

'I'll send the men away and let you get on with it in peace.'

'No. That's not a problem for me, providing they remain quiet. The men might find it instructive and comforting to see what can be done with modern surgical procedures.'

'If you're sure about it; carry on.'

Sawyer undoes the strap securing Lowing's left arm to the chair. He then picks up a wooden and leather contraption.

'This was made to measure by the carpenter to my instructions,' announces Sawyer, as he places Lowing's arm into the contraption. He then raises it so that Lowing's hand is held flat on top of his head. Sawyer secures it in place with straps from the moulding at the elbow that are buckled at the back of Lowing's head. He then takes another longer strap attached to the moulding on the inside of the elbow, runs it under Lowing's right arm, across his back, up under his left arm and secures it to a buckle on the moulding on the outside of the elbow.

Sawyer stands back, checks his work and tightens the straps a little further. 'Now take a good draught of this brandy,' he says, as he places a straw in a goblet to Lowing's lips. Lowing sucks hard on the straw and empties the goblet with a hollow slurp. 'Now bite hard on this and try not to move,' adds Sawyer, placing a leather bite in Lowing's mouth.

Sawyer removes the dressing from Lowing's nose and washes the wound with a syringe of wine. He then picks up a silver nose shaped moulding. 'This was made to measure, by Norris, from small silver coins given by Lowing and some of his shipmates,' he announces. He then places it against the remnants of the bone and cartilage of Lowing's nose. Lowing winces at the touch. He removes it, bends it a little with the aid of some small pliers and tries it again for fit. Lowing winces again. Sawyer makes two further iterations, before he is satisfied that it is a good fit, before setting it aside.

Sawyer picks up a small curved knife with a fine sharp blade and speaks softly to Lowing, 'I hope the brandy has started to take effect, because I'm afraid this is going to sting quite a bit.' He then cuts three sides of a rectangular flap of skin from the upper part of Lowing's arm. Lowing bites hard on the leather, grimaces his face and lets out a muffled cry. Sawyer pulls back the flap of skin to examine it and then replaces it. 'I'm sorry, Lowing, but this is going to hurt even more. I'm going to have to resurface the area around your nose where it has already started to heal a little.' He then scrapes and cuts the knife along the wound until it reopens and starts to bleed. Lowing bites hard on the leather, then expels it from his mouth to let out a scream before passing out. 'That's probably for the best,' states Sawyer.

Sawyer irrigates the wound with a further syringe of wine and holds a clean dressing to the wound. 'Hold this wad in place, Long,' he orders, and Long duly obliges. Sawyer then tightens the straps to move Lowing's upper arm much closer to his face. He then lifts the flap of skin and sews the upper end of it to the wound at the top of what is left of Lowing's nose. He then puts the silver nose moulding in place and moulds the flap of skin around it and sews all but the bottom bit in place. He then makes another adjustment of the straps. 'That's to avoid any strain being put on the skin now attached to both Lowing's nose and his upper arm,' he says. He then irrigates the wounds with another syringe of wine, and applies the preparation of egg white, rose oil and turpentine.

'That's all I can do for the moment,' states Sawyer 'I'll leave Lowing secured to the chair until he comes around, to make sure he isn't going to struggle against the confinement of his arm while he regains his senses.'

'What happens then,' I ask.

'Lowing will have to wear the contraption for a while, to ensure a good blood supply to the graft from his arm,' replies Sawyer, loudly, so that the gathering can hear him. 'Then when it becomes better established, I'll sever the flap from his arm and reconstruct the bottom of his nose.'

The assembled company applaud and cheer loudly. Saywer takes an appreciative bow.

'Where did you learn to do that, Mr Sawyer,' asks one of the men.

'It's a technique pioneered by Gaspare Tagliacozzi. I studied with him for a time nearly ten years ago, at the University of Bologna. It's proved useful for cases such as Lowing's, although the technique was developed to treat *saddle nose.*'

'Saddle nose?'

'Yes. Where the bridge of the nose collapses and rots away as a symptom of syphilis,' says Sawyer. 'Looking around here, I can see a few potential patients in the offing.'

The men laugh. But looking about me, I can see Sawyer may well be right.

'Now back about your business men,' orders Johnston, and the men disperse to attend to their various duties.

29

The Farne Islands

It takes a day and a half to shuttle the cargo of the captured hoys ashore in the longboats, where it is loaded onto handcarts and taken to the Queen's Storehouse.

On the following afternoon we set sail with our prizes for the nearby Farne Islands, in a fresh south-westerly breeze and a moderate sea state.

No sooner than we are out of the bay, the breeze and sea strengthens surprisingly quickly. I decide to press on, as our destination is no more than ten miles away. Unfortunately, the wind continues to strengthen, blowing us towards a more easterly course.

As we approach the Farne Islands in fast fading light, it is blowing a gale.

'I think we'd better take what little shelter there is to be had in the lee of the Wamses and Big Harcar Islands,' suggests John. 'Then tomorrow, if the storm has blown over, we can make a safe approach to Inner Farne.'

'I agree,' I reply. 'Make it so.'

'Signal the other ships to follow our lead, Johnston,' orders John. 'We're going to seek shelter in the lee of yonder islands. And double check that everything's fully battened down.'

With a wave height of twelve feet or more, we sail towards the hoped-for shelter from the storm.

'There's no need for both of us to stay above deck and get drenched in this weather, Rob,' says John, 'Why don't you retire to your cabin and get some rest?'

'All right, John. But call me if there are any problems or when you need relief,' I say, as I depart the quarterdeck for the dry and relative comfort of my cabin.

I'm summoned to the quarterdeck less than half an hour after I had left it.

'What's the matter, John?' I ask.

'I don't know what Harry Brown and the captain of the flyboat are doing,' replies John. 'They're going too far and too close to the sandbanks. Are they blind?' he adds, with alarm.

John, Johnston and I watch on helplessly, as the flyboat runs aground on the sandbanks. The waves crash into her and she turns on her side. There is a loud crack, perceptible even above the sound of the raging storm, as her masts are torn from their seating and she breaks her back.

'She's lost,' cries John.

'Can you see anything of the men?' I shout, in order to be heard above the storm.

'I can't tell at this distance, in this light, and we daren't attempt to get any closer.'

'What can we do?'

'I'm afraid there's nothing much we can do for the moment,' states John, with the wind and rain lashing into our backs. 'I suggest we wait for dawn, then assess the situation and hope there are men alive that we can do something for.'

The long night passes, made seemingly longer by the perilous storm and concern for the fate of those aboard the flyboat. I awake suddenly in terror, shivering and covered in sweat, from a nightmare: a vision of my drowning in water that turns red with blood. Could this be a premonition of things to come, I wonder? I wipe the sweat from my body and try to dismiss this thought as nonsense and something brought on by sleeping while the ship is tossed around by the storm. I get dressed and venture out onto the windswept deck to relieve John early.

Dawn breaks and those of us aboard the *Barque of Bulleyn* can see the flyboat has completely broken up on the sandbank with the force of the waves. We can also just make out some bodies on the rocks beyond - the Blue Caps. 'I think some of them are moving,' shouts the lookout, from the bow.

'Your recommendation, Mr Hills?' I ask.

'There isn't anything we can do for them. We can't get the ship any closer because of the sandbanks, and the sea is too rough to put a boat in the water,' replies John.

'But they've been clinging on all night and can't last much longer.'

'I know,' states John, acknowledging my concern. 'But the best we can do is wait until things subside, retrieve whatever bodies haven't been washed off the rocks and give them a decent burial at sea, otherwise we'll only be adding to the dead.'

'I won't accept that, John,' I say, determined we should do something positive. 'Get a boat in the water on the leeward side of the ship,' I order. 'I'll call for a volunteer to go with me.'

'You'll get no one to go with you in these seas and that'll erode your authority,' cautions John.

'The effect on my authority is of comparatively little importance.'

'Don't do it, Rob. It isn't worth it.'

'I must.'

'Well, if you're going, I'm coming with you.'

'I appreciate that, John. But one of us has to stay here in command. And on this occasion, it's you.'

'All right, have it your own way,' says John, in face of my determination. 'But I suggest you ask Andrew Reid to accompany you, rather than call for a volunteer. He's about the strongest and best boatman we have; and his brother-in-law, John Sinclair, is one of the men I left on the flyboat.'

'Thank you, I'll do that,' I say, wondering why John had not suggested Reid in the first place, unless he withheld the information to prevent me going.

'Johnston, get the longboat ready on the leeward side, and ask Andrew Reid to join the captain and me on the weather-deck,' orders John.

'This is Andrew Reid, cap'n,' says Johnston, introducing a sturdily built, red haired sailor.

'I'm sorry I've not got to know you yet and that we have to meet under such circumstances,' I say. 'But I'm taking the longboat out to rescue the men shipwrecked on yonder rocks. I understand you're the best boatman amongst the crew and I'd like you to volunteer to come with me.'

'Aye, count me in, cap'n,' replies Reid. 'My brother-in-law was aboard the ship. He'll have got to those rocks and will be clinging on for dear life, if I know him.'

'Thank you, Reid,' I say, with grateful relief. 'I suggest we row parallel with the islands and sandbanks, to make best use of what little shelter there in their lee. Then we'll turn south and row hard against the waves, across the submerged sandbanks until we reach the rocks.'

'Aye, aye cap'n. But we won't be able to put the boat in on the rocks without coming to grief ourselves.'

'If you can hold her off the rocks, Reid, I'll go ashore and help the survivors into the water and the boat. Do you think you can do that?'

'If anyone can, I can.'

'That's the spirit. Now lets go before anyone else gets washed off those rocks.'

'Good luck, captain, and you Reid,' says John.

I set aside the fears of my nightmare as Reid and I climb over the side of the ship into the boat on the raging sea.

We row on as planned, in defiance of the raging wind, swollen sea, drenching spray and the deafening noise. When we reach a point level with the rocks we turn toward them, directly into the wind and waves. 'Pull hard now, Reid,' I shout. There is not a sound from my shipmate. But we pull hard together on the oars, straining every sinew of our bodies in the physical effort of slowly propelling the boat against the elements.

'We daren't get in any closer,' I shout above the deafening noise of wind and waves. 'Hold her here as best you can,' I add, as I ship my oars. I plunge into the raging waters and swim hard toward the rocks, dragging a long rope attached to the boat. For every two strokes length forward, I seem to go at least one stroke length backwards. Finally, I ground my feet, stagger ashore coughing up water and tie the rope around a small crag. Looking around, I see some dozen prostrate bodies lying on the tiny exposed rocks. There are more than I'd expected. I go to the closest one - a Dutch sailor. He is dead. So is the next one, and the one after. 'Am I too late?' Then a body moves. It is the Dutch skipper of the flyboat. Then another moves - Reid's brother-in-law, John Sinclair. Altogether, there are five Dutchmen, along with all four of my own crew that are still alive in various states of health.

'Can any of you make it out to the boat with the help of the rope,' I shout, above the storm.

'I think we all can, if the stronger ones help the others,' replies Sinclair, who is as robust as his brother-in-law in the boat.

'Aye, with perhaps the exception of young Hans over there,' says the Dutch skipper, pointing to a young Dutch sailor clinging to one of the dead bodies.

'I'll see to him,' I reply, as I bend down to try to get the young man to his feet.

'*Ga weg, ga weg. Ik ben net mijn broer vertlaten,*' he screams.

'Leave him,' shouts the Dutch skipper. 'He won't leave his dead brother and I doubt he'll survive much longer himself.'

'I'll get him aboard,' I say. 'Tell him we'll come back for his brother.'

'*Hij is dood. We komen terug on hem later te komen,*' shouts the skipper. The young man's only response is to cry out in anguish and cling ever tighter to the corpse.

'Come now,' I say, in as soft and comforting tones as I can manage against the raging storm, as I kneel by the young sailor. Even though he doesn't understand the words that are spoken it has a calming effect and I manage to raise him to his feet, as he relaxes his grip on his dead brother's body.

'I'll help you with him, cap'n,' offers Sinclair.

The survivors make their precarious way in ones and twos out to the boat with the assistance of the rope, with Sinclair and I bringing up the rear with the weak and distraught young sailor. All the while the boat is tossed around on the waves with Reid struggling to keep her off the rocks.

We all clamber aboard the crowded boat, barely avoiding it capsizing, with the young Dutch sailor left with his skipper in the stern. I let loose the rope and Reid and I pull away from the rocks, and run with the wind and waves towards slightly calmer waters on the lee of the other side of the sandbanks.

The crowded boat is tossed about on the heavy seas. It starts shipping water and is in danger of sinking.

'There are too many of us in the boat,' shouts the Dutch skipper. 'It'll capsize and we'll all drown.' I ignore him to save my breath, as Reid and I continue to struggle to keep the boat on as even a keel as possible. Then as we row over the crest of a wave and fall some twelve feet into the trough, amongst heavy spray, I notice the young man is gone. We row on a little easier now we are a little lighter, less cramped, shipping less water, and more buoyant. We reach the point where we had turned south on our way to the rocks, then turn westward and strike for home towards the safety of the *Barque of Bulleyn*.

Alongside the more sheltered side of the ship, the crew help the shipwrecked sailors off the bobbing boat. Reid and I come aboard last, to resounding cheers from the crew. All the survivors are wrapped in blankets, given brandy to drink and taken below deck.

John attends me in my cabin.

'I'm greatly relieved you made it, Rob,' says John. 'God knows what I'd have told Mary and Dick had you perished.'

'You were right to give me the advice you did, John,' I reply, slumping back in my chair. 'But I felt responsible for those men and had to try.'

'And you succeeded against the odds. But now the storm is beginning to subside a little, what are your orders? We've lost the fly boat and the reason for coming here.'

'I don't know,' I reply, with my head in hands and elbows on the table. 'Perhaps we should put into Inner Farne anyway, take on some provisions and send the two Dutch hoys on their way with the survivors from the flyboat. Is there anything they need?'

'Probably only beer for the few days it will take them to return home. We could do with some as well, with all the extra rations you keep awarding the men for jobs well done,' adds John, with a laugh.

I smile. 'Make it so, John. Oh, and while I think of it, I'd like to recover any bodies that remain on the rocks and give them a decent burial at sea. I'd also like to speak with Reid and Sinclair when we've all had a chance to recover a little, to personally thank them for their courage and good work.'

'Aye, aye, Rob. And might I say, for someone who just said he didn't know what to do, you've just made a number of good decisions.'

John enters my cabin, late in the afternoon, and reports. 'We've retrieved four bodies, Rob – three from the rocks and that of a young Dutch sailor from the sea. There're more that are lost, some of which the sea will give up to the land over the next few days. But we can do little about them.'

'Thank you, John. Will you make the necessary arrangements for the burials, as soon as possible,' I reply.

'Aye, aye, Rob. I've brought Reid and Sinclair to see you, as you requested.'

'Show them in, please, John.'

'Now sit down lads and have a glass of brandy with me,' I say, as I pick up a ships decanter and three small goblets. 'I want to thank you both for all your efforts during the rescue.'

'I was grateful for the opportunity,' replies Reid. 'If it weren't for you, I'd never have had the chance to rescue my brother-in-law. I don't know how I'd have broken the news to my sister.'

'I should be thanking you as well, cap'n, for coming to get us in such treacherous conditions,' adds Sinclair.

'But if it wasn't for your assistance, Sinclair, I certainly wouldn't have got that young sailor off the rocks and into the boat. It's only a pity he was washed overboard on our way back,' I reply, sadly.

'But he weren't washed overboard.'

'What do you mean?'

'His skipper helped him over the side as we came off the crest of a huge wave, just after he'd complained there were too many of us in the boat.'

'I suppose the poor lad must have died from the ordeal.'

'He was certainly in a bad way, but I'm sure he was alive at the time. I'd swear to it.'

I am shocked and angry at the thought of it, but I try to hide it from Reid and Sinclair. 'Thank you for that information, Sinclair. I'll question the captain of the flyboat about that later. Now have another brandy and tell me something about yourselves.'

John enters the cabin nearing the end of my conversation with the brothers-in-law. 'The bodies are almost ready for burial,' he says. 'Would you like to attend and say a few words, captain?'

'Assemble the ship's company and I'll be out shortly,' I reply, not relishing the task. 'It's best we get this done as soon as possible.'

I emerge from my cabin, onto the weather-deck, to see the last body - that of the young Dutch sailor we had lost from the longboat - being sown into a hammock, along with a cannon ball to ensure it sinks. The customary final stitch is put through the corpse's nose to make sure he's dead before burial; as if there were any doubt in it.

With it done, John asks, 'Would you like to say a few words over them captain?'

'Hmm. Of course,' I reply, not quite sure what to say. Then after composing myself, I say, 'I commend the bodies of these poor sailors to the deep and their souls to the mercy of Almighty God. Now let's bow our heads and take a few moments to remember our shipmates.' We hold a minute's silence. 'Thank you, men. Now, cast them into the deep.'

The bodies are lifted one by one and unceremoniously cast over the side of the ship.

'Please arrange for the men to have an extra half ration of beer when we reach Inner Farne, Mr Hills,' I order.

'Aye, aye, captain,' replies John, without further comment.

'I'd also like to see you in my cabin, Mr Hills, with the captain of the flyboat, as soon as possible.'

John enters the great cabin with the flyboat's captain. 'I've Captain Lademaker with me, as you requested,' he says.

'It's been reported to me, captain, that you cast overboard the young lad you wanted me to leave behind on the rocks,' I say, accusingly, staring the captain straight in his eyes. 'What do you have to say for yourself?' I demand, making no attempt to disguise my anger.

'He was dead, or soon would have been. The boat was too crowded and unstable. We might have all perished if I hadn't done it,' answers Captain Lademaker, without any sign of remorse or apology.

'Well, I hope you can live with it on your conscience.'

'I'd rather that than be drowned,' he snarls, defiantly. 'And while we're talking of conscience, I hope you can live with yours. If it weren't for your actions we wouldn't have been in that position in the first place. Instead, young Hans and his brother would've been home by now in the bosom of their family.'

'Get him out of here, John, and off my ship as soon as possible,' I order, angrily, not wanting to engage any further with the Dutch skipper.

'Aye, aye, captain,' replies John, as he rough handles Captain Lademaker from the cabin.

John returns to my cabin. 'I've had Captain Lademaker and the remainder of his crew transferred to one of the Dutch hoys,' he reports. 'I've ordered that he's confined until we release the ships.'

'Thank you, John,' I say, gratefully. 'Sit down and help yourself to a brandy. As much as I didn't like it, Lademaker had a point,' I add, in a more reflective mood.

'I know. While I wasn't there, if I'd been in his place and thought we might all otherwise perish, I might well have slipped the lad over the side if he was the least likely to survive.'

'While I don't like it, I can accept that, John,' I say, with a heavy heart. 'But it's the other things he said that bothers me. It all seemed a jolly adventure when I eagerly persuaded Dick that we should do all this. But is it right? And what about the unintended consequences of our actions?'

John sits there in silence for a moment and then takes a sip of his brandy. 'You know me, Rob,' he says, 'I do the best I can for my family and me. This is the best opportunity I've had for that and I'm grateful for it.' He takes another sip of his brandy and continues. 'The politics don't play much of a part in it for me. But we've letters of marque from two Sovereigns to seize ships in their service to help confound the Dons, the spread of their religion and the inquisition; not to mention our getting cannon to the Watergeuzen in their struggle for freedom. Most Englishmen would see that as a good thing. You're also helping Hastings meet its obligations to the Crown, to protect its charter privileges. So why not carry on doing what we do the best we can. And if things don't work out exactly as we wish, that's just too bad.'

'Thank you, John, for your sage advice,' I say, with a reluctant smile. 'I know you're right. I just needed to hear it said. I promise I'll try not to get melancholy over it anymore.'

The next morning, in calm seas, we sail the short distance to Inner Farne. As we approach the island, I can see seals basking on the rocks and a whole host of different birds nesting in the cliffs and on the shore: guillemots, puffins, kittiwakes, common shags, Sandwich terns, eider ducks, amongst other species.

We drop anchor in St Cuthbert's Gut, below the Pele Tower. Brocas purchases thirty-five tons of beer from Clarke the chandler and puts sufficient of it aboard the two Dutch hoys to last them on their voyage home. The hoys depart on the following tide, while we remain at anchor engaged in make and mend.

The next morning a small carvel sails into the Gut and drops anchor at our stern. Its longboat is put into the water and is rowed the short distance to our ship. Its passengers climb the ships ladder and come aboard.

I am summoned from my cabin to greet our visitors and am surprised to see Fisher with Captain Read.

'Good morning, Captain Isted,' says Captain Read. 'I was coming here to do the weekly relief of troops stationed in the Pele Tower; and I thought I'd also return your man, Fisher, to you. You might also like to know that Captain Fielding arrived just after you sailed. And Henry Knollys arrived on horse across the causeway, at low tide yesterday afternoon.'

'Thank you for that news and for bringing Fisher with you,' I reply. 'I'll be leaving for Lindisfarne tomorrow, after some further make and mend as a result of damage caused by the sudden storm. In the meantime, can I offer you some refreshment in my cabin?'

'That's very kind, but I've to attend to duties ashore and return to the garrison this afternoon.'

Captain Read departs, leaving John, Fisher and I to talk.

'How did it go in Leith, Fisher?' I ask.

'I didn't have a lot of time there. But I met with David Crawford, a gentleman of the Port,' reports Fisher. 'He told me you'd be welcome in Scotland if you were the Queen of England's servant and had a good and relevant cause.'

'Thank you for that report, Mr Fisher,' I say. 'I suppose we more or less fit that description. It's good to know we have the option of visiting Scottish ports. We'll make a decision on that and where we go hunting after our meeting with Knollys and Fielding.'

30

The Partnership

In contrast to our outward journey, it is a calm and sunny day as we sail into the harbour at Lindisfarne.

'Captain, there's another ship of war in the harbour of a similar size and number of guns to ours, with a hulk at anchor nearby,' reports John.

'I see it, Mr Hills,' I reply. 'It must be Captain Fielding's ship. Drop anchor half a cable's length from her on her starboard side. We can make enquiries later.'

'You heard the captain, Mr Johnston. Make it so.'

I am in my cabin resting, when John enters followed by a young sailor. 'Captain, you've a messenger from yon ship of war.'

'Captain Isted, Mr Knollys and Captain Fielding send their compliments. They'd be pleased if you and your first officer would join them aboard the *Elephant*, for supper and some entertainment, at five bell on the last dog watch,' says the young sailor, politely.

'My compliments to Mr Knollys and Captain Fielding,' I reply. 'Thank them kindly for their invitation. I, and Mr Hills, will be pleased to accept. Now, if you would like some refreshment before you row back to your ship, I'm sure our cook, Master Long, can find something for you in the galley.'

'Thank you kindly, sir.'

'Get someone to show him where it is please, Mr Hills, and then come back.'

'I'm not sure there's much for us to discuss, John. It's just a matter of listening to what they say and then making up our mind whether or not to throw in with them,' I suggest.

'With two ships like ours operating in concert, we could go after some much bigger prizes. Even Spanish and Portuguese treasure ships won't be beyond us. That's where the real money is,' states John who seems excited by the prospect, probably with thoughts of his share and of getting closer to his ambition of buying into the Cinque Port franchise. 'Of course, it's your decision, entirely,' he adds, more soberly.

'But I value your opinion, John. It all depends on the terms, but all things being equal I'd like to go for it. Then, perhaps, we can do a little more than bullying defenceless merchantmen.'

'As you know, taking helpless merchantmen is fine with me. But I'm not averse to taking risks, if the prize is worth it. Minimising risk and maximising profit is my motto. I want to make sure we're around to enjoy the benefits.'

'I agree. Perhaps that should be our maxim from now on. You know, John, you're quite the philosopher,' I add, with a laugh.

'Your cousin, Thomas, once accused me of that. One of these days I'll have to find out what it means.'

We both laugh, as I pour each of us a brandy. 'Now, let's drink a toast to our new maxim.'

'Maximise profit and minimise risk,' we say, before I down my brandy with a renewed sense of purpose and optimism.

'Now if you don't mind, I'd like to rest for awhile, before we meet Knollys and Fielding,' I say.

'You've been looking a little tired lately. Is there anything wrong?' enquires John.

'No. I'm just not sleeping too well, with the same recurring nightmare.'

'Not the dream you told me about on our way to the Foreland of Thanet?'

'No!' I think for a moment, then add, 'I remember telling you about a dream, but much of the detail of that is lost to me now. This one's of me drowning in a red coloured sea, which started the night of the storm and has recurred every night since.'

'All I can suggest is you don't put yourself in danger of drowning, in case it's a omen.'

'A fat chance I have of doing that, given our occupation,' I say.

We both laugh.

At the appointed hour, John and I scale the ladder of the *Elephant* to be greeted on deck by Henry Knollys and a large well-built man with a full red beard.

'Welcome aboard, gentlemen,' says Harry, 'This is Fernando Fielding, the captain of my ship, the *Elephant*.'

'Thank you Harry,' I reply. 'I'm pleased to make your acquaintance, Captain Fielding. I've heard a lot about you. I'd like to introduce the master of my ship, my brother-in-law, John Hills.'

'I've started to hear good reports about you two, and your ship,' states Fielding shaking my hand with a vice-like grip. 'Now if you'd like to make your way to the great cabin, we'll have a drink and talk of mutual interests before we eat and make merry.'

'There're also some pressing matters to discuss, in addition to my proposal of a partnership,' adds Harry.

On entering the great cabin, I am struck by how well it is furnished and adorned; compared to my cabin, with its begged, borrowed, and now stolen furniture from the Dutch hoys. But by far the greatest adornment is a strikingly beautiful woman, dressed in finely tailored male clothing, with an ornate dagger hanging from a tightly drawn leather belt highlighting her trim waist. Her breeches are similarly tight and reveal shapely calves and ankles below the fastenings at the knee.

'Gentlemen, I'd like you to meet my wife, Lucia,' says Fielding.

'I'm pleased to meet you, Mrs Fielding,' I say, with a bow of my head.

'Lucia Jaramillo,' replies the lady, extending her hand toward me. I'm not quite sure whether I should kiss it or shake it, not knowing what the etiquette is for a lady wearing men's clothing. But I decide upon the kiss.

'Lucia prefers to use her maiden name,' explains Fielding. *'Podrias disculparnos, Lucia? Tenemos asuntos importantes que atender,'* he adds, turning to his wife, who stretches up to kiss him before bowing in the male style and sashaying elegantly from the cabin. 'She doesn't speak much English and wouldn't understand what we're saying, but I find she can still be quite a distraction when discussing business.'

'She's very intriguing,' I remark. 'How did you come to meet?'

'It's quite an interesting story,' says Fielding, with a smile. 'Lucia is from an old family, from Extremadura in southeast Spain. Being somewhat headstrong and free spirited her family thought the best thing for her was to become a nun. So they sent her to La Coruna, to her mother's family - the Andrades. From there, she was to be taken to the Santo Domingo convent in the nearby Santiago de Compostela. But as luck would have it, I took the ship she was travelling in. I was going to hold her for ransom. But we got talking, took to each other and now she's as good a privateer as any.'

'That's very interesting. We've never captured such a prize,' I remark. 'I also notice you speak excellent Spanish, Fernando.'

'My mother was Spanish, my father was English and I was brought up bilingual. I'm as happy with one as the other. It comes in handy sometimes in our chosen trade.'

'Well, that's enough of that for now, Fernando,' interjects Harry. 'I've some urgent news to impart to Rob before we get down to the matter of our partnership.'

We all sit around the captain's table, as Fielding pours us all a goblet of wine. 'Things have changed a little since we last saw each other in London,' adds Harry. 'Walsingham's spies discovered the Spanish preparing an armada in Cadiz, with the intention of sailing to Ireland to stir up trouble; after we've only just put an end to the Desmond Rebellion[57]. If the *Geraldines* take up arms again, the Queen won't have any qualms about confiscating the Earl's lands for good and forcing him into exile.'

'What's that to do with us?' I ask.

'The Queen has ordered the Fleet to be made ready. Winter and Hawkins have been appointed vice admirals, and twenty-seven of Her Majesty's ships are being prepared for service on the Medway. Additionally, all ships of war in private hands, including those of the Cinque Ports, are being called to arms. They're to report, by mid July, to any of the dockyards on the Thames, or at Chatham or Portsmouth and await orders. I've spoken with the other captains here: Winteris, Storey, Higgins, Anderson and Calles, with mixed results; and now with you.

'The Queen can count on us to do our duty.'

'Good! I'm sailing with Fernando for London tomorrow, where we'll sell on the captured hulk and its cargo before reporting for service. We thought you might like to sail back in company with us.'

---

57 The first Desmond Rebellion took place between 1569 and 1573. Its supporters were known as the Geraldines, after the Earl of Desmond's family name – FitzGerald.

'There's nothing I'd like better,' I exclaim, with a sigh. 'But we need to earn some money first. Our commission for escorting the wool fleet was spent on storing the ship before we sailed, and our commission from the Wealden ironmasters went back to them for providing us with cannon. What we've made to date has barely covered our costs. I certainly can't afford to pay the crew for any service to the Crown we're obliged to provide under the Cinque Port's charter obligation, as things stand.'

'That's very disappointing,' exclaims Harry, with a frown.

'I'm not seeking to renege on my obligation to the Crown,' I quickly add, in case that's what Harry is thinking. 'It's just that we'll have to earn a bit more and may not arrive until much closer to the deadline.'

'I'm not doubting your honour, Rob. But I must impress on you the seriousness of the situation.'

'I understand that, and we will be there. You have my word on it.'

'Anyway, it's possible our ships won't be kept in service too long,' adds Harry. 'Walsingham has very cleverly let the Don's spies know we're expecting them and are making preparations to meet their threat. We know this has been successful as he intercepted a letter, from Antonio Guerras, to Pedro Menendez de Aviles[58]. We hope our preparations might make them think twice about their proposed venture. Spain's a great power and has much greater resources than we do. But its war in the Low Countries, and its adventures in the New World, have stretched them a little too thinly. So you can see how important

---

58 Calendar of State Papers Foreign, Elizabeth, Volume 10, refers to an intercepted letter, written by Antonio Guerras, giving an account of the naval preparations that were being made in England under Vice-Admirals Winter and Hawkins to oppose Spain's armada on the coast of Ireland.

your mission was to get those cannon to the Dutch rebels. The longer we keep that war going the better for us.'

'I'd like us to be able to help further in that cause in our normal operations, as well as be ready to bolster the English fleet when necessary,' I say.

'That's good. You're thinking along the same lines as Fernando and I, which brings me nicely to our next point: our proposed partnership.'

'I've discussed it with my brother, Dick. He likes the idea, in principle, and has left it up to my discretion.'

'That's excellent news.'

'It does, however, very much depend on what's involved and the terms.'

'Of course,' states Harry. 'Our thoughts are we'd lay up over the winter, after we've dealt with the Spanish threat and release most of the crew. We can then do whatever refit is necessary, provision and train for our campaign in the spring.'

'Which will be what, exactly?'

'Intercepting Spanish treasure and supply ships between Spain and the New World.'

'Excellent! They are exactly the thoughts that John and I had.'

'Lucia will also be delighted,' adds Fielding. 'Her father's elderly cousin, Don Juan Garcia Jaramillo, was a conquistador who went in search of El Dorado, in New Granada. He never found it, but stole lots of gold from the Muisca and Zenu peoples, and opened up mines in some of their tribal areas. It'll be doubly pleasurable if we can relieve them of some of those ill-gotten gains.'

'What about the share of the prize money?' I ask.

'As far as the prize money is concerned, our ships are comparable and I suspect they require roughly the same complement,' states Harry. 'So I'm content to split the prize money according to ownership and the rank and rate of both our crews, as if we're of one ship. So I'd get half an owner's share of the combined take, and you and your brother would divide the other half between you.'

'And what about command?'

'That should go to Fernando, of course, as he's by far the greater experience.'

'Hmm,' I muse.

'Rob has more than proved his worth,' interrupts John. 'He's also a baron of the Cinque Ports and a gentlemen. It wouldn't be fitting for him to play second fiddle to the likes of Fernando.'

Fernando stands sharply, stares hard at John with fire in his eyes and growls behind his full red beard. John stands equally sharply, returns his stare and moves his hand to the hilt of his sword in response.

'Now, now, gentlemen,' says Harry. 'I'm sure John meant no offence by it.'

'Quite!' I say, placing a restraining hand on John's sword arm. 'In any event, I'm not going to stand on rank or privilege. However, I've an option to purchase another ship from the Admiralty, which would be of benefit to our venture. In which case, I'll be bringing more to the table, and that would change the balance somewhat.'

'I agree, another ship would be very useful,' states Harry, thoughtfully. 'But, as things stand, you have no money to buy it. Whereas I do.'

'That's a fair point, although the Hastings franchise might be prepared to put up the money.'

We all slump back in our chairs and sit in thoughtful contemplation for a moment, until Harry breaks the silence. 'I propose we buy the third ship. I'll pay for it all, but Rob and his brother will have an option on a half share of it, if they choose to raise the money. If they do, Rob can choose its captain, perhaps John here, providing Fernando has command as the admiral.'

'That seems eminently fair to me, providing I can persuade John to sign on again after this voyage,' I say, looking at John.

'I'll do it,' states John, without any apparent thought to our previous agreement or the promise he made to Mary.

'That's agreed then,' says Harry, with relief, amongst accompanying smiles from John, Fernando and me.

'I do, however, have one proviso,' I add.

'What might that be?'

'I want us all to be able to agree the strategy and some battle tactics in advance, to ensure we all know what we're doing and no one is taking an unfair share of the risk. Once we're at sea, communications between ships is limited and we need to have some confidence in what each other will do to cover various contingencies.'

'That's no problem with me,' states Harry. 'I'd like to be in on the strategic planning, but I'm more than happy to leave the tactics up to you and Fernando to agree. Are you happy with that Fernando?'

'Aye, it's an acceptable plan. I'm sure Captain Isted, designate Captain Hills, and I can work together amicably enough,' states a conciliatory Fernando, seemingly content with his admiral's share if not the limitations on his command.

'Are we all agreed then?' asks Harry.

'Aye,' we respond collectively.

'When do we start this partnership?' I ask.

'Why not now?' replies Fielding.

'We could. But we have to go to work before we can join the English fleet, while you'll be taking your prize to London without much chance of adding to it.'

'I can see Rob's point,' interrupts Harry, sensing another potential disagreement. 'But I can see the advantage of our

215

starting now, even though we may have to operate separately in the first instance.'

'I'm happy with that, but I'm not sure how we can do that fairly.'

Harry thinks for a moment, then says, 'I'll take the risk. I want to make sure that Rob joins the fleet on standby to meet the Spanish threat, and he needs funds to ensure he can meet his commitment to the Crown and his crew.'

'So what do you propose,' asks Fernando, with a concerned look.

'I suggest we divide up the proceeds of whatever Rob gets with what we receive for the hulk we've already captured.'

'What!' exclaims Fernando with alarm, no doubt thinking he is being asked to take a share of the risk.

'I haven't finished yet, Fernando,' states Harry. 'I'll make sure you and your crew don't lose out, from my owner's share of the hulk and my personal wealth if necessary. However, I don't expect to have to do that. I've every confidence that Rob will earn his full share and perhaps even provide us with more than we would have otherwise received. For his part, Rob gets a guaranteed amount that will go someway to meet his pressing financial needs. And the Queen will be sure of getting a more satisfied and better motivated additional ship for the fleet.'

'If you put it like that, I agree,' says Fernando.

'I do as well,' I say. 'We'll do our best to make sure that you're not out of pocket, Harry.'

'On that account, I suggest we each exchange two members of crew to testify to what each other takes and receives,' suggests Fielding.

'Agreed. We can make arrangements to do that in the morning,' I add.

'Excellent!' exclaims Harry, seemingly pleased with the deal he has struck. 'I'd like to offer a toast,' he adds, as he pours everyone a large brandy. 'A bloody war or a sickly season.'

'That's an odd sort of a toast, Harry,' I say.

'What you need to realise, Rob, is the opportunity that a war with Spain represents,' says Harry, earnestly. 'Those who're good enough, strong enough and lucky enough to do well and survive it will fill the places of those who aren't. You aren't very different from Winter and Hawkins at their age. Indeed, you've a head start on them, being a baron of the Cinque Ports and a partner of the Queen's cousin. You and Fernando could be the coming men.'

'A bloody war or a sickly season,' we all say, before draining our goblets.

'Now that's done, let's get on with some serious drinking and merrymaking,' suggests Fielding, as he rises from the table and leaves the cabin. He returns a few moments later followed by his steward carrying bottles of wine and brandy, a Spanish lady carrying a tambourine, and three sailors carrying musical instruments: a vihuela, a lira da braccio, and a drum.

The musicians start playing and the Spanish lady starts singing a strange melody, which sounds like musical wailing to my ears. The cabin door flings open with Fielding's wife, wearing a Spanish dress, striking a dramatic pose in the frame of the open doorway. She then moves sensually into the body of the cabin with her back and neck arched, thrusting her bosom forward, all the time turning with exaggerated movements of her raised arms and hands. Then suddenly, in time with the music, she makes clicking noises with some wooden implements attached to her fingers. And with her heels moving quickly below her skirts, she makes loud, rapid and rhythmic tapping sounds on the wooden deck. As John and I watch on, mesmerised,

Fernando starts clapping in a strange broken rhythm with periodic stronger claps: '*clap, clap, CLAP, clap, clap, CLAP …*'. After a short while, Lucia moves towards her husband with outstretched hands. Fernando takes them and rises swiftly to his feet and joins the dance, moving his large frame deceptively nimbly. Then after some seemingly frantic heel tapping and body contortions, he collapses back into his chair pulling Lucia onto his lap to laughter and applause from Harry, John and I.

'I told you she was a wild one,' says Fernando, giving his wife a kiss and a cuddle.

'That was quite something,' I say. 'I've not seen anything quite like it before.'

'It's a dance of the Gitanos of southern Spain. Lucia loves it. It's one of the things her high born parents frowned upon.'

The cabin door opens and in walks Anne. 'Anne!' I exclaim, in surprise, as I rise to my feet.

'You seem surprised to see me,' says Anne.

'That's my fault,' interjects Harry. 'Anne insisted on accompanying me on my journey north. I don't know why,' he adds, with a sly wink to me. 'She's been staying with my uncle, Henry Carey - Baron Hunsdon, Governor of Berwick-upon-Tweed and Lord Warden of the Eastern Marches. I sent Anne a message as soon as you dropped anchor yesterday, but I wasn't sure she'd be able to come.'

'You were just being mischievous Harry. You knew full well that I'd come,' says Anne, in a scolding tone.

'I'm very pleased you did,' I add, recovering my composure and giving Anne a gentle kiss on her cheek.

'That's better,' sighs Anne. 'Perhaps you can show me later how pleased you really are to see me,' she adds in a whisper.

'I'd be delighted, if we get the opportunity.'

'I'm sure that can be arranged.'

'Now let's have some more music and dancing,' says Fielding, lifting Lucia from his lap and gesturing to the musicians. 'Lucia and I'll teach Rob and Anne some of the steps.' He takes Anne by the hands and Lucia drags me more reluctantly to join the dance. Fielding and Lucia then proceed to guide us slowly through the basics.

'I think I'd better take my leave, gentlemen,' says John. 'If we're going to take some prizes and join the Fleet by the appointed date, we'll have to make ready to sail as soon as possible and I'll need a clear head for that in the morning.'

As John exits the great cabin, Anne and I begin to move more freely with the rhythm of the music – '*clap, clap, CLAP, clap, clap, CLAP …*'

31

The Mouth of the Skagerrak

I ease my weary body from the ship's ladder, over the bulwark, to the relative safety and stability of the deck.

'Good morning, captain. I trust you had an enjoyable night of merrymaking,' says John, with a smile.

'Very good, John,' I reply, feeling as if someone was banging a quoin into my head with a commander, from inside out. 'I think I'll spend a little time alone in my cabin today.'

'But what are your orders, captain?'

'Oh! I suppose you'd better come with me to discuss the matter.'

I slump in my chair at the table in the great cabin and John sits opposite me.

'Correct me if I'm wrong, John, but I think we concluded a partnership with Harry and Fernando,' I say, trying to remember all we agreed. 'I also recall something about our swapping two men from each of our crews, before going off to take some more prizes. Then return to London to share out the takings and join the fleet to defend the realm against a possible Spanish armada.'

'That more or less sums it up,' says John, trying not to smile at my discomfort.

'Will you make the necessary arrangements for the exchange of crew, before the *Elephant* puts to sea today.'

'I've already arranged that with the master of the *Elephant*,' reports the efficient John. 'I sent over Tomlyn and Harry Brown. But I think they got the better of the deal.'

'What do you mean?'

'As you know, Tomlyn and Brown are excellent and trustworthy men from our homeport of Hastings. But in return they sent us Loutton, a gentleman from Yorkshire, who for some strange reason has been working as a carpenter of sorts on Fernando's ship. The other one, whose name I can't recall, looks as if he's seen better days; all of which were very many years ago. I doubt either of them will be of much use to us.'

'We're hardly short of good men and the main purpose is for them to testify what prizes we take,' I say. 'We can come to a better long-term arrangement when we meet up in London.'

'I suppose so. I've put the gentleman in with me, in the wardroom.'

'That's fine. Is there anything else?' I add, hoping to bring the proceedings to an end and take to my cot.

'There's the question of where we're going hunting.'

'You mentioned the trade going in and out of the Baltic, the other day. Nothing better has come to my mind since.'

'The Baltic trade it is then,' agrees John, before adding more reticently, 'There is also the question of what we take.'

'What do you mean?' I ask, thinking the answer obvious.

'Up to now, we've done what men of Hastings have traditionally done: taken the goods of ships they stop and let the ships and crews go. But Fielding and the other privateers here generally take the ships as well. That's where much of the money is to be made.'

'I know. I've had similar thoughts, and I'm content to do the same.'

'That's a relief.'

'But I'm still insistent we leave the crews alive.'

'Where do you propose we do that, as we'll be taking their ships?'

'I reckon we need to take two merchant ships to make sure we earn our salt and ensure Harry doesn't lose financially in underwriting us,' I say. 'Once we've done that, we'll stop or capture a third and put all the captured crews on that, or the lowest value of the three.'

'It's likely to a bit more complicated and more difficult than it sounds,' says John, who I know likes to keep things simple. 'I'd also like to remind you that if we're ever caught by an unfriendly power, we'll be executed for piracy, whether or not we've spared everybody's lives.'

'I know that, John. When we go after Spanish treasure ships with Fernando, I'll be content to relax that policy, without engaging in any unnecessary slaughter. But for now, with the shipping of other nations, that's the way I want it.'

'Aye, aye, Rob; fully understood,' replies John, who knows I won't be budged on this point. 'We've still got some make and mend to do after the storm. So I think the earliest we can make ready to sail is sometime tomorrow.'

'That's ideal for me. Before we sail, I'd like to inform the crew of our plans.'

'Aye, aye, Rob,' says John, as he leaves the great cabin while I ease myself from the chair and sink heavily into my welcoming cot.

The crew are assembled on the weather-deck as I climb the ladder onto the quarter deck to address them. They look more familiar and less intimidating than when I'd first addressed them at Cadzand.

'Avast, there,' shouts John. Everyone stops what they are doing, turn toward the quarterdeck and give me their attention.

'We're going hunting for some fat ships, of some fat Hansa merchants, coming out of the Baltic,' I announce.

'Hurrah!' The crew cheer loudly.

'Then we'll dispose of the ships and cargo, before making for London to make merry and spend some of our gains.'

'HURRAH!' The crew cheer even louder.

'Then we'll be joining the Queen's fleet under Vice-Admirals Winter and Hawkins, in fulfilment of our obligation as a ship of the Cinque Ports, to prepare for a Spanish armada making ready to come out of Cadiz.'

There are loud cheers from some, while others remain silent and appear less keen at this news.

'That's all. Get us underway, Mr Hills,' I order.

'Three days at sea and not a sign of anything worth our while,' I say to John, as we survey the expanse of empty sea around us.

'The wind and waves have forced us to take a more northerly course than I'd have liked,' replies John. 'I reckon we're a day or so away from the northern end of the mouth of the Skagerrak. We should find plenty of game there.'

'Sail ahoy on the starboard bow, heading north,' cries the lookout from the crow's-nest.

'Let's have a closer look at her, Mr Hills,' I order.

'Aye, aye, captain,' replies John, 'Two points to starboard, Cox.'

'She's a Norwegian, riding high in the water,' the lookout calls, as we close to less than two cables.

'She's probably not worth our while, but we might as well stay on this heading and make sure,' suggests John.

As we approach the Norwegian ship, no more than a shackles length on her larboard side, John reports, 'She's a timber ship running empty, captain, probably on her way home after delivering timber to the Low Countries.'

'Let her be and resume our course, Mr Hills,' I order, as I leave the quarterdeck, longing to get things over and done with and then head south to join the English fleet for a more honourable, if less profitable, task.

'It's the best part of two days since we spotted that empty timber ship, and not a sign of another sail since then,' I say, pacing the quarterdeck.

'Sails ahoy,' shouts the lookout in the crow's-nest. 'There're a great many sails dead ahead on the horizon, on a southerly heading.'

'At last. Let's get amongst them, full sail.'

'You heard the captain, Johnston. Get the whole nine yards up,' orders John. 'We're going hunting.'

As we close on the ships the lookout calls down, 'Ahoy. They're a whole fleet of merchantmen - mainly Dutch.'

'Are there any ships of war escorting them,' shouts John, in response.

'Not that I can tell.'

'Let's hope that's the case,' I say.

'I doubt they'll be escorted,' states John. 'It's probably just the herd of deer strategy: travelling in numbers, knowing they'll lose one or two of the weakest if they run into wolves like us, but that the rest will go unmolested. Any armed merchantmen that may be amongst them will be lightly armed and won't bother us. They'll just be glad we've left them alone.'

'Let's get amongst them and cut out a couple of slow fat ones,' I order.

'There are so many of them, I suggest we cut one out and let Fisher lead the boarding party this time,' suggests John. 'Then we can haul off and take another more leisurely than we did last time. I'll board that with the other party. Then you can haul off and cover us both, in case any of the others are foolhardy enough to come to their aid.'

'I agree. You and Fisher had better make ready. Sound for action stations.'

'You're with me Mr Fisher,' orders John, as he and Fisher leave the quarterdeck to join their boarding parties.

We approach a merchant ship astern on its starboard side, take the wind from its sails and force it to heave to. Fisher and the boarding party swing aboard, as we bring the *Barque of Bulleyn* alongside to observe and stand ready until I am sure the ship is taken and secure.

'Round up the captain and crew and confine them in the hold,' orders Fisher.

'I must protest,' shout two gentleman from the quarterdeck, in unison.

'And who might you be to protest?' demands Fisher.

'I'm Lucas Zeleson, the captain of the *Fair Born Son*, and this is Cornelius Johanson, the owner of the cargo,' replies one of the men.

'You mean the ex-captain and ex-owner. Throw them in the hold with the others,' orders Fisher, before calling to me on the *Barque of Bulleyn*. 'The ship's secured, cap'n.'

'Well done, Mr Fisher,' I call back. 'Check their credentials and foregather with us, when you're ready. Now, get us underway, Johnston,' I order. 'I want to pick out another fat one, for Mr Hills.'

We close on a second merchant ship in a similar manner to the first, with exactly the same result. However, the ship's captain and crew resist John and his boarding party.

John makes straight for the quarterdeck and attacks the captain with ferocious slashes of his sword. The captain defends himself but against such an onslaught he can offer no reply other than stubborn defence, until he stumbles to the ground. John puts the point of his sword to the captain's throat. 'Do I have your surrender?' I hear him snarl.

'You do,' says the exhausted captain.

John hauls him roughly to his feet and pushes him towards the rail overlooking the weather-deck where their men are fighting. 'Now tell your men to put down their arms and surrender,' orders John, 'or, I'll slit you from ear to ear,' he adds, menacingly, holding his dagger to the captain's throat.

'Leg je wapens neer. Ik heb het schip overgegeven,' shouts the terrified captain.

John pushes the captain down the ladder onto the weather-deck. 'Lock the captain and crew in the hold. And be quick about it,' orders John. 'The ship's secure cap'n,' he adds, calling to me overlooking him from the quarterdeck.

'Well done, Mr Hills. Check their credentials. I'm going to stop another ship, as we planned. Foregather on me when you're ready.'

'Mr Johnston, we'll intercept that slow moving Norwegian ship laden with timber that we passed to larboard awhile back,' I say.

'But we can't take her cargo and she's so slow, it will take us ages to get her to port. There are better prizes to be had.'

'We're not going to take her or her cargo. We're just going to put the crew of the Dutch ships we've taken aboard her, and be on our way with the prizes we've already got,' I explain.

'I'm sorry, captain, I didn't mean to question your orders,'

'That's all right, Johnston. I should have informed you of my plans. Now, four points to larboard, Cox. We'll catch her easily enough and ease ourselves alongside, within hailing distance of her. Now Mr Johnston, do we have a Norse speaker?'

'Aye, I think Andrew Reid has a few words, from trading between his homeport of Aberdeen and Bergen. I'll fetch him.'

We close on the Norwegian ship within a shackle's length on her starboard side.

'Now, Reid, I want you to hail her captain, and tell him to heave to and we'll do them no harm. Can you do that?' I ask.

'Aye, captain,' answers Reid, who immediately turns and hails the Norwegian ship, *'Lempe til captain, du har ingenting a frykte fra.'*

The Norwegian captain complies without comment, and we gently come alongside.

'Reid, tell the captain, we'll be putting the crew of the two ships we've taken aboard his ship and then letting him go on his way,' I order.

Reid leans over the side and calls down to the Norwegian captain standing on his quarterdeck below, *'Captain, vi vil vaere a sette mannskapet pa to skip ombord og deretter la deg pa vei.'*

'Jeg har ikke mat eller vann,' replies the Norwegian captain.

'He says he doesn't have enough victuals for them cap'n,' reports Reid.

'We're low on provisions ourselves. But we'll give him a little beer and they'll just have to make do with that until they make landfall.'

We put the crews of the captured Dutch ships aboard the Norwegian timber ship, along with a small quantity of beer, and let them go without further molestation.

'Well done, John. What did we get?' I ask, as John reports to the quarterdeck.

'It's a good haul,' replies John. 'One is laden with thirty-two lasts of rye, forty-one lasts of salt and six large bundles of linen. The other has twenty lasts of rye, nine and a half lasts of beer, six kilderkins of spruce beer, a hundred dry cowhides, and twelve stacks of planking.'

'That and the ships will more than cover our needs. By the way, where were the ships from?' I ask, wishing confirmation they are covered by our letters of marque.

'Returning from Danzig, to the same place as the others we took before,' replies John.

'Ah, more men of Utrecht.'

'Your orders, captain,' asks John, somewhat abruptly.

'I'd like to plot a course straight back to London. But with the current wind, sea state and the slowness of our heavy laden prizes, I wonder whether we might be better running in a more west sou'westerly direction, towards Leith.'

'Aye, I agree. We could dispose of our prizes there, and then make better time tacking south on our own.'

32

The Storm

'We made the correct decision, John,' I say. 'Even with the hoys in company, we've made much better time than on our outward leg. I estimate, we're no more than a day out from Leith.'

'Aye. But the wind has changed to a less than helpful south-westerly. I don't like the look of those dark clouds gathering fast upon us, in that direction,' replies John.

Within half an hour the wind starts singing and whistling strangely in the rigging, the sea swells and roars, and the sky turns black to extinguish any light from the setting sun and any stars that might otherwise have lit the heavens.

'We'd better take in more of the sails,' advises Johnston. 'I doubt she'll bear much more than half a fore-course in these winds, if you choose to run before the storm.'

'I think it might be better to heave to into the wind, while we still can, as I suspect it's likely to strengthen further,' advises John.

'I agree, John. Make it so, Mr Johnston,' I order.

'Get more men on the tiller,' yells John, as the storm gathers pace. Four men and then six hold the tiller and are barely enough to keep her steady in the storm as the rain and sea spray wash across the decks.

'Cap'n, cap'n,' shouts Andrew Reid, as he appears on the quarterdeck. 'She's spewed the oakum we repaired the leaks we got in the storm off the Farne Islands, and I fear we've sprung more caulking elsewhere. We've three feet of water above the ballast.'

'Man the pumps and get every spare man working with buckets,' I order. 'Ask the carpenter, cooper and shipwright to meet me on the gun deck. You have the ship, Mr Hills,' I add, as I leave the quarterdeck to investigate.

I set the carpenter, cooper and shipwright, with candles in hand, creeping along every rib, viewing the sides, searching every corner, and listening everywhere to hear for running water. Many weeping leaks are found and caulked with oakum.

'There must be more leaks, cap'n,' says Reid. 'We've caulked all we've found, we've had both pumps and all the spare men working with buckets for more than two hours and we're now nearly four feet above the ballast.'

'We must be damaged below the waterline, in the bilges,' I say. 'Get plenty of oakum, two caulking hammers and irons, a few wooden bungs and wedges, two coils of rope and a couple of strong men; then meet me at the hatch to the bilges.'

On my way, I notice one of the young boys cowering, shivering, amidships on the orlop deck, but I have no time to stop to give him any words of comfort.

Looking through the hatch into the bilges, I see there is very little room above the floodwater. And with the rolling of the ship, the free surface water washes from one side to the other up to the deck-head.

'We can't take any light down there; it will just be extinguished,' I say, as Reid joins me at the hatch leading to the bilges. 'We'll just have to feel our way along in the dark, and hope we can find and repair any leaks before we drown. I say we, but I'm not giving you an order, Reid. I'm asking you to volunteer again.'

'I'm with you, cap'n. If we don't get it done, we could all drown.'

'Good man!'

Reid and I remove our boots and strip to the waist, tie one end of each of the ropes around ourselves and sling a canvas bag of caulking materials over our shoulders. 'Now you two men hold onto our ropes and feed it out gradually to keep some tension on it,' I say, to Goliath and the ex-slave Isekeri: the two strongest men aboard. 'If either of us tugs hard on it three times in quick succession, I want you to haul us in as quickly as possible. Reid, you work down the starboard side. I'll take the larboard and we'll try to repair any damage we find.'

'Aye, aye, cap'n,' replies the willing Reid.

I step through the hatch and plunge into the shivering cold water up to my chest. A few moments later, Reid follows suit. The ship rolls and the free surface water washes me off my feet, plunging me below water and against the larboard side of the ship. I regain my feet quickly. The ship rolls again and I've headroom once more. I take two quick gasps of air before I am submerged again. I want to turn back but force myself onwards, as the fear of being seen to be afraid and failing is stronger than the fear of the physical danger I face.

I work my way slowly along the entire length of the ship, with my head below water every time the ship rolls to larboard. A few yards from the bow and about three feet above the ballast, I feel an irregular shaped hole a little bigger than the size of a man's fist. I struggle to take an appropriately sized wooden bung from the canvas sack and hammer it home into the hole, with my body braced against one of the ship's ribs. I'm periodically under water for a few seconds at a time that seem like an eternity. Finally, when the wooden bung is as secure as I can make it, I fill the remaining space with oakum and small wedges, which I hammer home as tightly as I can with the caulking hammer and iron. With that done, I make my way aft as quickly as my exhausted body will take me. As I approach the hatch, the ship rolls and the water washes over me. I stumble in my haste, hit my head on the bulkhead, turn turtle and sink. I look up to see light from the hatch shimmering through the water tinted red with blood from my wound. I remember to tug on the rope: one tug and then another.

I know not whether I tugged upon the rope a third time, as the next thing I know, I am being pulled through the hatch, barely conscious, coughing up water. 'Thank you, men,' I gasp, as I regain my senses. Was that my dream playing out? Has it been fulfilled? Has a curse been lifted? Stop thinking like that, I say to myself as I start to recover.

I recover a little more and notice a similarly drenched, bedraggled and tired Reid. 'What did you find, Reid?' I ask.

'Not much I could do much about, cap'n. I suspect we've spewed a fair bit of oakum, but it's impossible to see where in all the water and amongst the darkness,' gasps Reid in reply.

'I suspect you're right. I found a hole that I've made watertight, but I'm not sure it can account for all this much water. We'll just have to hope it's enough to hold her with the pumps until we make landfall and can get her bailed out and repaired properly.'

I make my way back to the quarterdeck, holding my linen shirt to my head to staunch the blood flowing from my wound. When I arrive there, I find several men mesmerised by a little round light trembling along halfway up the main mast. It shoots from shroud to shroud, rests momentarily, sparking in a little blaze and darting off again.

'It's St Elmo's fire,' says John. 'I've seen it often enough in storms. I've never known it to be a harbinger of either good or ill. But it's got the sailors paralysed with fear.'

'Come on, men, get back to work,' I shout. 'It's a sign from St Elmo, to say that it's only by our own efforts that we'll be saved this night.' With that, the men slowly regain their senses and return to their duties.

'Well done, Rob,' says John. 'I couldn't reason with them. What's the situation below?'

'It's not good. We've done all we can. I only pray that's enough and we'll be able to hold her with the pumps. Nevertheless, we need to make port at the first opportunity to undertake proper repairs.'

'I've no idea where we are,' replies John. 'There's not a light in the sky we can take a reading from. Where the storm has blown us is anybody's guess. But we must be a fair bit north of our mark and being blown further from it. Now you'd better go below and get Sawyer to stich up your wound.'

The night passes slowly. But as dawn breaks, we find ourselves in sight of the coast. To my astonishment, our two prizes are still in sight and looking in good order.

'I only hope they didn't have to jettison any of the cargo to weather the storm,' says John.

'That's the least of our worries. Do you have any idea where we are Mr Fisher?' I ask.

'Aye, cap'n. If I'm not mistaken, we're off the Angus coast, just south of Montrose. I know this area well,' replies Fisher.

'Do you think we can risk putting up some sail and make our way safely into Montrose?'

'We could try the bonaventure with a half a fore-course,' states John.

'Make it so, Mr Hills. We may have struck lucky.'

33

Montrose - Safe Haven?

We limp into Montrose harbour with our two prize ships. In the relative calm of the harbour the prize ships find space to come alongside, one astern the other. With limited space I berth the *Barque of Bulleyn* outboard one of the prizes: the *Fair Born Son*.

'Thank God we've made it safely here, John,' I say, with obvious and heartfelt relief. 'It's the second time I could've drowned in a storm, lately. And this time in the bilges of my own ship.'

'I'm not sure what part God may have had in it,' replies John. 'But, we can be proud that the ship and men held strong in adversity. And I'm pleased you've confounded your dream.'

'But, we've no time to sit on our laurels. We've much to do to determine the damage, get it repaired and be on our way to meet our deadlines.'

'Quite right, captain. I'll get Mr Johnston to make her secure. Then, perhaps, you and I, and the shipwright and carpenter, can give the ship a good inspection.'

'Make it so, Mr Hills, and send Brocas ashore to inform the harbour master we're here and what our status is, and see what port dues we might owe.'

At berth, in the shelter of the harbour, we succeed in pumping out the bilges and the damage becomes obvious. As well as the hole that I had temporarily made good, the ship has spewed a good deal of oakum caulking and is weeping water in a number of places below the waterline. We fix all we can find, but there is still seepage through the ballast. We move the ballast and find some more sprung seams. We undertake a makeshift repair to hold it overnight with the intention of making it good the next day, after the men have had a well deserved rest following a well earned extra half ration of beer.

I sleep well during the night without a recurrence of my nightmare, which I hope has been well and truly put to rest. When I awake, the storm has abated a little, but insufficiently for us to risk putting to sea in our current state of repair.

'I'm not sure how long we're going to be stuck here in this weather, Rob,' says John.

'I was wondering that myself,' I reply. 'As we're getting hard pressed for time, I think I'll go ashore to see if I can sell our prize ships and cargo here. It probably won't fetch the price we might have got from merchants in Edinburgh or London. But as long as we make enough to cover our coming expenses, and the reduced price is worth forgoing the inconvenience of taking them elsewhere, I'll strike a deal.'

'That's a good idea. In the meantime, I'll ensure we're as shipshape as possible. Then if the weather abates sufficiently, we might be able to sail on the first tide tomorrow.'

'I'll go ashore with Brocas, and Fisher as he knows the area, to see what sort of a deal we can make,' I say. 'You'd better keep all the craftsmen at work. We can make it up to them later. But let a third of the rest of the ship's company go ashore on each watch. Oh, and you'd better include Reid in the first batch ashore and anyone else you consider performed especially well during the storm. Oh, and you'd better also include the two boys who must have been frightened stiff during the first real storm they've had to ride out at sea,' I add, remembering one of the poor little devils I saw cowering on the orlop deck during the height of the storm.

As I make my way ashore with the off duty men and the two boys, I notice a Scottish ship entering the harbour seeking refuge from the storm.

'Cap'n, cap'n,' shouts Reid, as he bursts through the door of the tavern where I, Brocas and Fisher are waiting to meet the merchants about our prizes; and where Johnston, Sawyer, Norris, Fontane and Loutton are sat drinking. 'Men from the ships we took are in town and the provost has sent the baillies and their men to seize our ships.'

'Quickly men, back to the ship,' I order, standing sharply.

The men jump straight to their feet and follow me out of the door, displacing some of the furniture in our haste. Along the way we meet Sinclair who had been with his brother-in-law Reid when they had learned the news, and who had subsequently found Cox, Long, Cornish, Benkis and the two boys. Together, we all rush back towards our ship.

As we round the corner onto the quayside, we stop in our tracks at the sight of three score or more armed men boarding the *Fair Born Son*, while outboard of her, those aboard the *Barque of Bulleyn* cut their cables and run, leaving us stranded.

'Look, it's more of the pirates,' calls out a naval looking gentleman, pointing an accusative finger at us.

'Stop, where you are,' orders one of the baillies.

'Quick men, fall back,' I order, and we run headlong back the way we came.

'Apprehend those men,' shouts the baillie, as he, followed by half the armed men, set off in hot pursuit.

'We can't outrun them, captain, with all the running we did to get to the quay,' says a breathless Johnston, as the militia gain on us.

'Those of you with breath left, make a run for it. The rest of you, take refuge in the tavern with me,' I order, not wishing to desert any of my men, needing time to think and an opportunity to speak with our pursuers before the inevitability of being taken.

We stop outside of the tavern, with the exception of Fisher, Reid and Sinclair who run on and dart around the next corner. The soldiers close on the remainder of us before we can all enter the tavern. A skirmish ensues with Norris and I keeping our attackers at bay while everyone barely makes it through the door. We hastily barricade the door behind us and gasp for breath, thankful for any respite from the chase.

The soldiers barge against the door, but to no avail.

'What shall we do now, captain?' gasps Johnston.

I sit silently for a moment, trying to catch my breath and give myself time to think. 'I'm not totally sure,' I say. 'I'll try to talk to the baillie, see what he has to say and take it from there. But if anyone else comes up with a plan, I'll be pleased to consider it.' I make my way upstairs, open a window and call down, 'Why are you pursuing us, sir.'

'Who am I addressing,' asks the baillie.

'My name is Robert Isted, captain of the *Barque of Bulleyn*. Who is asking?'

'Captain Isted, I'm Robert Lichtoun, one of the baillies of Montrose. Some Dutch merchants, who claim to own the two ships you arrived with, accuse you of piracy. I've been commanded, by the provost, to seize the ships and apprehend you and your men to answer the charge.'

'But we are innocent.'

'Then you have nothing to fear.'

'Your actions up to now,' I reply, 'suggest the contrary.'

'That is only because your ship cut and run, and you and your men fled before we could make known our intentions. Those are not the actions generally associated with innocent men.'

'Faced with sixty or seventy armed men, for an unknown cause, and fearing what might happen next, our actions seem entirely reasonable to me.'

'You have a point. But I'm afraid it's one that I'm unable to debate with you now. You are to surrender yourself and your men, immediately.'

'And if I don't?'

'I'll be forced to break into the tavern and take you by force.'

'Hmm,' I muse, looking at the heavily armed band of men below, delaying my answer to play for a little more time to think.

'Now be reasonable, Captain Isted,' says Mr Lichtoun. 'Don't make things any worse than they already are. There's been little damage done so far. If I have to break in and take you by force, which I will succeed in doing, there will be damage to property and possibly serious injury or loss of life. If that happens, the full force of the law will hold you accountable for it, whether or not you are innocent of the charges already laid against you. If you surrender now, you will receive fair treatment and it may count in your favour in the provost's judgement.'

'You make a convincing argument, Mr Lichtoun, and I don't wish to see any unnecessary loss of life,' I reply, realising this is our only reasonable course of action. 'We'll lay down our arms and be out shortly.'

I go downstairs to address my men. 'I suspect you heard most of that, men. I'm afraid we've little alternative but to lay down our arms and surrender. The baillie seems a fair man. I only hope his master, the provost, is the same.'

34

The Provost

My captured men and I, including Reid and Sinclair who had been apprehended by the other baillie and his men, spend an uncomfortable night in three small cells in the jail, in the Steeple. I assume Mr Fisher made good his escape and is still on the run.

'I'm sure we can sort this out in the morning, when we see the provost,' I say, trying to reassure the men. 'We have a letter of marque to take Dutch ships loyal to Spain.'

'Are you sure that's what they are?' asks Johnston.

'Mr Hills told me they were of Utrecht, which is a part of the Netherlands in Spanish hands. Do you have cause to doubt that?'

'No,' replies Johnston, cautiously. 'But, I did overhear him and Mr Fisher talking about you being too particular in following the terms of our letter of marque and the difficulty of distinguishing which Dutchmen were loyal to Spain or not. I didn't hear everything else, but Mr Hills concluded by saying, "Ask no questions and be told no lies".'

'I can assure you, Mr Hills would not have lied to me,' I say, sternly. But it makes me think whether John had told me they were from Utrecht, or whether I had just assumed that from what he said. While he may not have lied, he may not have told me the whole truth. In any event, we have little choice but to base our defence on taking them in accordance with our letter of marque.

We are led in chains to the courthouse, at mid morning, where we are sat on benches at the front and left of the courtroom. Behind us stand two armed sentries. At the back of the court stand two further armed sentries, at either side of the door. To our right, across the aisle, sit our accusers who look at us furtively, avoiding making any eye contact.

The Provost of Montrose, dressed in his red velvet robes and wearing his gold chain of office, enters the courtroom by a side door, followed by two armed guards.

'Be upstanding. The Provost of the Royal Burgh of Montrose, The Much Honoured John Erskine, Laird of Dun,' announces the Clerk of the Court. Everyone stands. The provost sits on a large chair behind an oak desk on a high rostrum, with his guards standing to attention at a respectful distance to the rear. We all retake our seats.

'Captain Isted, you and your men are charged with piracy on the high seas,' says the provost. 'How do you plead?'

'Not guilty, Your Honour,' I reply in a strong voice, as I rise to my feet.

'What is the case of the accusers?' Our three accusers stand up. 'No, one at a time, please. You first,' adds the provost, pointing to the one nearest to him.

'Thank you, Your Honour. My name is Lucas Zeleson, captain of the *Fair Born Son*. We were forcibly stopped and boarded on the high seas, by pirates in a ship I now know to be the *Barque of Bulleyn*. We were rough handled and confined in our hold before being forcibly put aboard a Norwegian timber ship: the *Ingrid of Olden*, under the command of Captain Tormod Hansen, bound for Ostend. The Norwegian ship forgathered with a Scottish ship, commanded by Captain George Pantoun that was bound for Leith. And as we heard some of the pirates speak in a Scottish tongue, he granted us passage so that we could make complaint to the authorities in

Edinburgh. However, a storm blew up and we were forced to seek safe haven in the harbour of Montrose. To our astonishment and good fortune, we discovered our ships were tied up on the quayside in the possession of our assailants.'

So that is how they came to be here, I think to myself, shaking my head in disbelief.

'Do you recognise any of your assailants in this court,' asks the provost.

'I recognise the captain, who I saw standing on his quarterdeck,' replies Captain Zeleson, pointing an accusing finger at me.

'Thank you, Captain Zeleson. You may be seated. Is there anything you would like to add,' says the provost, pointing to the next of our accusers.

'Thank you, Your Honour,' says the Dutchman getting to his feet. 'My name is Cornelius Johanson, the owner of the cargo aboard the *Fair Born Son*. It was as Captain Zeleson testified.'

'Thank you, Mr Johanson,' says the provost. 'If you have nothing further to add, you may be seated. Do you have anything you'd like to say,' he adds, looking at the third of our accusers.

'Thank you,' says the man. 'My name is Herman Johanson, Your Honour. I am the owner of the other ship, the *Duifje*, or the *Little Dove* as you would call her, and the owner of part of her cargo. I and my ship were treated exactly the same as Captain Zeleson said in his testimony.'

'Thank you, gentlemen. That's very clear and concise. Do you still maintain your innocence Captain Isted?'

'I do, Your Honour,' I say, as I stand up.

'Do you mean it wasn't you that took the ships and cargo of your accusers by force?'

'No, Your Honour, we certainly did that.'

'Then how can you plead not guilty?'

'We took them lawfully under a letter of marque, issued by the Prince of Orange, to take ships loyal to the papist Governor of the Spanish Netherlands. These men and their ships are of Utrecht, under the governance of Spain.'

'But…' cries Cornelius Johanson before being interrupted by the provost.

'Be quiet,' orders the provost, addressing the accusers. 'You will get your opportunity to answer this later. But for now, I'm questioning Captain Isted. Now, captain, can you show me this letter of marque?'

'I'm afraid not, Your Honour,' I reply. 'It is aboard my ship at sea.'

'How very inconvenient. But if you had this letter of marque and are innocent, why did your ship put to sea and leave you stranded ashore? That doesn't seem the action of innocent men.'

'If sixty or seventy armed men came to seize you for some unknown reason, what would you do, Your Honour?'

'Hmm, perhaps. But that's not really the issue here, Captain Isted. I'm trying to establish proof of your innocence or guilt. Even if I discount the circumstantial evidence of the flight of your ship and you and your men, I've heard nothing to do either, so far. Do you have anything else you wish to add?'

'Thank you, Your Honour. Although it may not be totally relevant to my taking these Dutch ships, you may wish to be aware that I also have a letter of marque issued by the Queen of England; and I am working in partnership with Captain Fernando Fielding, of a ship owned by the Queen's cousin.'

'Thank you, Captain Isted, but I assume you can't produce proof of that either.'

'Sadly, that is also true, Your Honour.'

'You may be seated,' says the provost, with a courteous nod of his head towards me. 'You have heard what Captain Isted has said in his defence, regarding his right to take your ships,' he adds, addressing the accusers. 'What have you to say to that?' All three of the accusers get to their feet. 'No, one at a time please, gentlemen. You will all get your chance. You first,' adds the provost, pointing at Cornelius Johanson, who was first to his feet.

'Your Honour,' says Cornelius Johanson, while the other two sit down. 'I doubt that Captain Isted has ever had such a letter of marque. But even if he had, he had no right to take our ships. I'm from Dordrecht, which is loyal to the Prince of Orange. My ship, the *Falcon*, perished at Danzig and I hired Captain Zeleson and his ship, the *Fair Born Son*, to transport my goods to Dordrecht.'

'Can you corroborate that, Captain Zeleson?'

'I can, Your Honour,' says Captain Zeleson, as he gets to his feet. 'It's as Mr Johanson said. I and my ship are of Emden, which is also loyal to the Prince of Orange and where I was due to return with the remainder of my cargo from Danzig, after visiting Dordrecht.'

'Thank you, gentlemen. Have you anything to add to that,' adds the provost, looking at Herman Johanson.

'I'm from Tweisk, near Maneblik, in the north of Holland, which is loyal to the Prince of Orange,' says Herman Johanson. 'I was taking my and my partner's cargo from Danzig to Encusen, which is also loyal to the Prince.'

'Thank you, gentlemen. That seems clear enough and you corroborate each other's stories. You may be seated. Now, Captain Isted, in the face of that testimony, do you wish to change your plea, or add to your testimony, or say anything else in your defence.'

'Thank you, Your Honour,' I reply. 'Well, they would say that, wouldn't they? They have had plenty of time to collude and get their story straight between them. But can they prove it? And as far as my testimony is concerned, I'm confident the twelve men sitting with me in the dock will also corroborate what I have said.' All of my men nod fervently in my support.

'That's a fair point, well made,' says the provost. 'Can you prove what you have said, gentlemen,' he adds, looking at the three accusers.

The three accusers look at one another uncomfortably, before Cornelius Johanson replies, 'What do you mean, Your Honour?'

'It's simple enough. Do you have any papers or documentation to prove your testimony: bills of sale, or bills of lading, showing your port of destination, or the ships logs, or anything else that might corroborate your statements?'

'I'm afraid not, Your Honour,' replies Cornelius Johanson.

'Why not?'

'The pirates must have destroyed them,' states Captain Zeleson, quickly.

'Hmm. How very inconvenient, or convenient, whichever way you look at it.' The provost frowns and thinks long and hard before announcing, 'The case is not proven on the evidence presented so far. But neither can it be properly refuted. There are also national and international political issues, which this court does not have the competence to properly take into account. I have, therefore, decided to refer the matter to the Privy Council. I'll write a letter to the Regent and send it along with the accused and their accusers to Edinburgh. Lord Robert of Orkney's ship of war, the *Andrew*, came into Montrose this morning, to repair some minor storm damage, en route to Leith. I'll ask her captain to take the letter, and transport the accused and their accusers to Edinburgh when he sails. Do you have anything to say?'

'But what about our ships and cargo?' asks Cornelius Johanson, anxiously.

'They'll have to remain here until the Privy Council reaches a verdict, when it will no doubt release them to whoever they determine has the right.'

'But, Your Honour, some of our cargo may perish in the meantime and we have customers waiting for it in the Netherlands.'

'That is not my concern. You can raise the matter with the Privy Council in Edinburgh.'

An obviously disgruntled Cornelius Johanson takes his seat with the two other equally unhappy Dutchmen.

'Do you have anything more you want to say on the subject, Captain Isted?'

'Thank you, Your Honour,' I reply. 'As no case has been proven against us, I humbly request that you release us from these chains in return for our parol not to escape. Or will you be sending our accusers in chains, to Edinburgh, as we accuse them of bearing false witness against us.'

The provost laughs. 'A nice try, Captain Isted.' He laughs again, before slumping back in his chair more thoughtfully. Then after a little deliberation he adds, 'No, I'm afraid not. It's true I can prove nothing against you, and I'd like to take you at your word, given your conduct in this court and during your arrest as reported to me by Mr Lichtoun. However, I'm not obliged to proceed on the presumption of your innocence to that degree. Experience in this court has shown me that even those with letters of marque do not always confine their activities within their terms. Also, your ship cutting and running, and you and your men fleeing from the baillie in the town, makes me believe the chances of you and your men trying to abscond are too great; especially given the seriousness of the alleged offence and the consequences of being found guilty.'

'And what about those we accuse of bearing false witness against us,' I ask.

The provost thinks again, while our accusers look on nervously, before he says. 'As for your accusers, I'll make no comment on their conduct. However, Scotland is not at war with Spain. And as far as I'm concerned, they have done nothing wrong in living in or taking cargo to Spanish-held territory, even if you can prove your right to take them on the high seas. Although I'm an advocate of the religious reforms in Scotland, I have a record of religious tolerance. Whether they are papists, or not, is of little relevance to this case regarding your claimed legal right to take their property, as far as this court is concerned. I, therefore, consider the chances of their absconding, without their ships and cargo, is extremely small. So you and your men go in chains, while your accusers go on their own recognizance. However, their failure to appear in Edinburgh will result in the forfeiture of their property, and no doubt that would help prove the veracity of your claim.'

'Thank you, Your Honour, for your kind words, consideration and explanation; even though your answer is disappointing,' I reply, while our accusers sit there looking relieved and in silence, despite the conditions imposed on them by the provost.

'All rise,' shouts the Clerk of the Court, and the provost exits as he came in.

35

To Edinburgh

My men, the two boys and I, are brought out of the Steeple jail into the watery sunlight and cool early morning air, and are bundled into an open cart. The cart trundles slowly through the streets towards the harbour. At berth near our captured prizes, is the *Andrew*: an armed merchantman, owned by Lord Robert of Orkney, the Scottish King's elder bastard brother who has a reputation as a privateer.

As we near the ship, a hostile crowd greets us. A few women and small children shout, 'Dirty pirates', and pelt us with fish heads and rotten vegetables. Then a small wiry man tries to clamber into the cart. He grabs hold of me roughly, snarls, gives me a wink and clasps my hand, leaving a small piece of paper behind. He is dragged off and cast aside by a member of the militia.

'That looked remarkably like Beattie,' whispers Johnston. 'I don't know what he's doing here. He wasn't one of the off duty men ashore when we were taken.'

'Mr Hills must have put him ashore to learn of our fate,' I whisper in reply. I look surreptitiously at the small piece of paper. 'Mr Hills says, "Hold fast. I'm coming".'

'He'll be too late. He can't know we're being transported to Edinburgh.'

'Maybe not, but I wouldn't be too sure about that. Anyway, we've not been forgotten, lads. And if there's a way of releasing us, Mr Hills will find it.'

We are bundled out of the cart, led up the brow of the ship, to more shouts of 'dirty pirates', taken below deck and confined in a small brig.

Within an hour of sailing, there is a commotion on deck. Sailors are shouting and scurrying around, with more sail being hoisted quickly; accompanied by a sense of a course correction, a quickening of our speed with the ship running leant over by a couple of strakes or more.

'What do you make of that, cap'n?' asks Reid.

'I don't know, Reid, but they seem more concerned with speed than a smooth passage, all of a sudden,' I reply, daring not to say what I am hoping.

As we are brought some food - some thin gruel, bread and water - I ask the sailor, 'What was that earlier commotion above decks?'

'We spotted a ship rigged out for war, which turned on a heading to intercept us. And the captain, fearing it might be your confederates, decided to try to put some distance between us.'

'And is it my ship?' I ask, eager to know if a rescue may be in the offing.

'I know not.'

'But what's happening?'

'Nothing much, now. The other ship kept pace with us for a time, but we kept our distance, and then after a while we suddenly outstripped her for speed,' says the sailor, proudly. 'So if they were your mates, they'll not be rescuing you while you're aboard this ship.'

'Do you think it was Mr Hills and the *Bulleyn*, cap'n,' asks Johnston.

'Maybe, bearing in mind Mr Hills's note. It is certainly something Mr Hills would try,' I reply. 'Under normal circumstances, I would expect the *Bulleyn* to be more than a match for this tub for speed and much else. But without a chance to effect proper repairs to the storm damage, it may not have been able to stay the pace.'

The men look forlorn, as if our last chance of freedom was gone.

'Don't be too downhearted, men,' I say as cheerfully as I can muster, despite my own feelings. 'We've not been forgotten. Mr Hills will no doubt seek another chance. We'll also get our day in court when the Privy Council hears our case, as our accusers can't refute our claims.'

My men, the two boys and I, are brought out onto the deck of the *Andrew* as it berths just inside the Water of Leith. After being confined in the darkness of the brig, even the weak sunlight is painful to my eyes. We are led down the brow in chains and are bundled into the back of a cart pulled by two horses.

'That's where we'll be taking you,' says our guard, pointing at Edinburgh Castle, some three miles in the distance, standing high on the top of Castle Rock.

The cart trundles off.

'That's the newly rebuilt St Ninian's Church,' says our guard. 'The old church was destroyed some thirty years ago by you Sassenachs.' He spits in a display of contempt.

We proceed along the Edinburgh road, at the end of which our attention is drawn to the Palace of Holyroodhouse, and the parish church of Cannongate that is all that remains of the once Holyrood Abbey.

Then at Girth Cross our guard draws our attention to a guillotine. 'That's the Maiden, recently acquired by the Regent, the Earl of Morton. You never know, you might get a more personal introduction to it later,' he suggests, laughing.

Then further up the hill, we pass through the Netherbrow Port in the Flodden Wall and into the High Street. We trundle on over the cobbles, passing by St Giles Kirk and the Toll Booth.

'Now that's where John Knox, the religious reformer lived, until he died recently,' says our guard, with surprising pride and sadness in his voice.

Then onward we go into the part of the High Street known as the Land Market, where we see that cloth and other textiles are sold. Beyond the Land Market, we pass through a derelict area of the city that had been cleared of houses.

'The houses were knocked down to create a killing ground for the slaughter of those attacking the castle during the *Lang Siege*,' reports our guard. 'A bloody shame,' he snarls.

As we get closer to the castle, we can see that it has suffered severe damage from artillery fire.

'The devastation was caused by Sassenach cannon fire, from Castle Hill, under the command of that devil, Sir William Drury,' reports our guard, with a snarl. 'A bloody shame.' He spits again.

'But this brought an end to the *Lang Siege*, in favour of your master, the Scottish Regent,' I remark.

'Aye. It's an ill wind that blows no one any good.' The guard spits. 'Bloody Sassenachs,' he snarls.

We enter the castle through the gatehouse, surrounded by rubble.

'That's what's left of David's Tower and Constable's Tower,' says our guard. 'Bloody Sassenachs.' He spits. 'Bloody shame.'

Onward we go, to the top of the hill, past what we are informed is St Margaret's Chapel that appears to be the only building in the castle to have completely escaped damage.

Perhaps there is a God that looks after his own. If so, I wish I had paid more attention to religious observance.

The cart stops outside the door of the dungeons. My men, the two boys and I, are dragged out of the cart. We are pushed in single file down the narrow, dark, winding stone stairs. At the bottom, we enter a large chamber with a number of torches attached to the walls that provide the only light. In the centre of the room there is a half-naked man stretched out on a rack, with his ankles and wrists fastened to rollers at each end of the rectangular wooden frame. To one side of the rack, a brazier burns with hot irons protruding from the top. On the other side, we are greeted with the horrific spectacle of a naked and unconscious man suspended from the ceiling on a pulley. Copious amounts of blood and faeces are running down his legs from his anus. Below him we see the cause of his injury: the blood-and-faeces-covered Judas Cradle - a pyramid shaped wooden seat.

'Greetings, Ruari,' says our guard, as he enters the chamber behind us. 'I've a few more sinners for your tender care,' he adds, laughing.

'Greetings, Hamish. I wasn't expecting anyone,' replies Ruari.

'What have they done to deserve my hospitality?'

'They've been sent here from Montrose, to be examined by the Privy Council, on a charge of piracy.'

'I expect I'll have the clerk up from Holyrood Palace with a list of questions for them, in the next day or so. Then we can get down to business,' says Ruari, rubbing his hands with glee. 'Anyway, they're just in time for a demonstration of the sort of entertainment we have to offer them in this establishment. This is, eh,' Ruari hesitates. 'Oh, I forget his name. It matters little. He's some sort of jeweller caught minting coins in the exiled Queen's name.' He then takes a red-hot iron from the adjacent brazier and places it against the sole of the jeweller's right foot. There is a marked sizzle. The jeweller lets out a terrifying scream and passes out. The smell of burnt flesh fills the air. One of the boys throws up over Andrew Reid's breeches, while the other one falls in a dead faint. 'Bring him round,' says Ruari, to his assistant.

'Which one?' asks the assistant.

'Both of them.'

The assistant throws a bucket of water over the jeweller on the rack and the boy who had fainted. They are both shocked back to consciousness. 'One final demonstration,' adds Ruari, with a devilish laugh, as he pulls on a lever attached to a ratchet fixed to the top roller of the rack. The roller rotates and the ratchet clicks into place holding the man in a new, longer, stretched position. The man screams but remains conscious. My men and I wince at his pain.

'Would you like to see that again? Of course you wouldn't,' says Ruari, cackling with delight, as he pulls on the lever once more. The roller turns, the ratchet clicks and there is a loud popping sound. The man screams again and passes out. 'Now that popping sound you heard were his shoulders dislocating. I can tell by the sound. There's a subtle difference between that and the sounds of cartilage, ligaments and bones snapping. But it takes an educated ear to distinguish them.'

The boys start crying and Loutton tries to bolt for it back up the stairs. But as he is chained to the rest of us, he makes little progress and falls shaking and sobbing.

'I think that's a sufficient demonstration. No doubt you're now all looking forward to being entertained here within the next day or so,' says a chuckling Ruari. 'Lock them up, Hamish. You'd better put the gentleman in the important person's quarters,' he adds, pointing to me.

Hamish leads us away. He unchains me from the others and puts me on my own in a small dark cell with the floor strewn with straw covered in blood, excrement and piss. 'Phew!' I exclaim, screwing my face up at the stench.

'I know, you're wondering what the non-important person cells are like,' says Hamish. 'They're just the same as this, but without the straw,' he adds with a laugh.

36
Ambassador Killigrew

'Aaaaaarrrrggghhhh, aaaaaaarrrrrgggghhh.' The agonising screams of a man in acute pain and torment come echoing through the dank darkness.

That's Peter Fisher on the rack, I say to myself as I lie alone in chains on a pile of straw reeking of my own stale blood and piss. Since being here, I've come to distinguish the cries of most of my men undergoing the various forms of '*examination*' on offer in the castle dungeon. The iron maiden, the Judas Cradle, the boot and hot irons engender subtly different squeals than those of the rack. And Fisher is proving to be quite the squealer, since he was captured a few days later than the rest of us, in St Monan, having made his way there via Brechin, Torry and St Andrews. He was making his own way to Edinburgh, where he is now being tortured. But I suspect the irony is lost on him.

I know Fisher cracked yesterday and admitted to more than he should, in the hope of bringing an end to his torment. I do not blame him for that. That was just the way it was. I had almost succumbed myself. But I had sustained myself with the knowledge that they had no proof, and without a confession they had little on us. I still hold onto the thought that while there is life there is hope, even though hope had faded markedly for Fisher and probably for the rest of us by association. Unfortunately, for Fisher, his confession only provided him with a short respite. He was now under 'examination' again, to extract information about further matters unrelated to those that had led us here. I do not know, and do not care, whether

Fisher knows anything about these other matters. I suspect the Scottish authorities do not much care either. But they have a squealer and they are going to make further use of him for their own purposes.

The screaming stops. I assume Fisher is ready to add to his confession. Whether truth or lies, it matters little to me, or even Fisher for that matter. But some other poor bastards, the authorities have it in for, are likely to be fingered for similar treatment. And so it will go on.

I hate this *examiner* with every fibre of my broken body. Nevertheless, I recognise the skill of his craft, inflicting the maximum amount of pain while keeping each subject alive and conscious. But I suppose that is to be expected from a master of his craft, who has had the opportunity to perfect it in the capital of a kingdom in strife, under its fourth Regent in less than six years since their Queen went into exile and imprisonment in England.

I try to escape into thoughts of happier days filled with promise and adventure that are a far cry from the sorry state I now find myself in. I think of Anne, but this only reminds me of the misadventure that led me here. I take a moment's comfort in thoughts of Hannah and my carefree life in Hastings. I would forgo all the rank, privilege and adventure I have had and might have had, if only I could escape and return to the simple life in Hastings with a woman who loved me. But then I wonder how long that would last before a shinier object comes along that I want to possess, like some sort of human magpie I may have become.

The lock turns with a clunk. The cell door opens and the large frame of the jailer fills the space. 'Here's some water,' says the jailer, as he places a bowl of water on the floor in front of me. 'Wash yourself and smarten yourself up.'

'Am I to be released?' I ask, hopefully.

'Ha, ha, that's a good one.'

'What then?'

'You've a gentleman here to see you.'

'Who is it?'

'I don't know, but you won't find out if you don't get a move on.'

I hurriedly clean myself up as best I can and am half led and half carried out of my cell, past the cells holding my men, to calls of, 'Good luck, cap'n. God bless you.' Onward I go through the *examination chamber* containing the instruments of my torture. I avert my eyes to avoid confronting the painful memory and then climb the stone steps out into the glaring sunlight. I shut my eyes tightly against the painful light, while turning my head skyward to feel the sun's warmth on my face. But this small pleasure is interrupted, by my being pushed through a door into a room, where a man of about forty-five years of age stands dressed in black, apart from his white ruff.

'I'm Ambassador Killigrew[59],' says the man. 'How are you, Captain Isted?' he asks. I raise my hands in chains, shrug my shoulders and give him a crooked smile. 'I'm sorry, that was a stupid and indelicate question,' he adds.

'Never mind,' I say. 'Are you here to get me released?'

'Unfortunately, not. Walsingham has only instructed me, on Her Majesty's behalf, to report on the matter and to see you are being treated as well as can be expected while you are in custody.'

'But a word from Her Majesty, or Walsingham, or even Henry Knollys, supporting the fact that I was operating under letters of marque, should be enough to acquit us.'

---

59 Sir Henry Killigrew was dispatched to Edinburgh as England's emissary to Scotland, in 1574, on a secret mission, to deal with what is referred to in diplomatic correspondence as 'the Great Matter'.

'Maybe so, but I've been instructed not to interfere and let Scottish justice take its own course.'

'But why have I been abandoned and treated so, especially after the service I've recently provided in the Netherlands.'

'I'm afraid that very service may have, in part, been your undoing. I understand the Spanish authorities wanted to question you about the wool tallies and what might have been aboard the ships the Watergeuzen captured, and that they sought to detain you from leaving Sluis. But you fired on their soldiers and made your escape.'

'I didn't fire on them. I just gave them a warning shot not to fire on us.'

'Be that as it may,' says Killigrew, dismissively, 'the fact is, that is what the Spaniards said in complaint to Her Majesty. In reply, she said she knew nothing of the incident, or what you may or may not have been up to, other than you were a private ship engaged to do nothing more than escort the wool fleet. If we interceded now, on your behalf, that might put Her Majesty's account into question. That could compromise our position ahead of the negotiations we are due to have with the Spaniards at Bristol,[60] or even put end to our precarious peace with them.'

'Damn it! But you said that might only be a part of it,' I say, wanting to know the full reasons for their betrayal of me.

'I'm afraid, I've said too much already and I'm not at liberty to say more.'

'But if my men and I are going to die for it, I think I deserve to know,' I demand. 'I'm hardly likely, or in a position, to tell anyone. And if I did, who'd believe me.'

The ambassador paces the floor in thought, stroking his beard while he walks.

---

60 England and Spain concluded the Treaty of Bristol, a few weeks later, in August 1574.

'All right, Captain Isted, if you give me your solemn word you will repeat nothing of what I tell you.'

'You have my word.'

'First of all, the Scots have repeatedly complained about English pirates disrupting their trade in Scottish waters and being allowed to use the facilities of the garrisons at Holy Island and Berwick-upon-Tweed. We've promised much and delivered nothing to curtail it. This has adversely impacted on Anglo-Scottish relations. And seeking to interfere on your behalf won't help that and might be the difference between success and failure of my mission – the *Great Matter* - for which I've recently been dispatched from London to Edinburgh.'

'And what is this *Great Matter* you speak of?'

'I've said too much already.'

'But you can't leave it like that. And you have my solemn promise.'

'All right, Captain Isted, you deserve to know why your life is left in peril,' says the Ambassador, with a heavy sigh. 'I'm here to negotiate the return of Mary Queen of Scots, to face the justice of her own subjects. Then, hopefully, they will dispose of her for her complicity in the murder of her husband, Lord Darnley, The King Consort of Scotland, after he had murdered the Italian, Rizzio.'

'I know about Lord Darnley, but who is Rizzio?' I ask, as I am not over familiar with past affairs in Scotland.

'Rizzio was an Italian courtier who was rumoured to have been the lover of both the sodomite Darnley and Queen Mary, and of being the real father of their son King James.'

'But surely, that would give Her Majesty leverage in all sorts of things, including securing my release.'

'It would, if only that were the case, as it once was, when Queen Mary first sought exile in England. Unfortunately, the Scots have cooled on the idea. The Regent, knowing that blood is thicker than water and fearful of the future when the King comes of age, now sees advantages in leaving her a prisoner in England rather than disposing of her himself; or of keeping the charismatic Mary in prison from where she would seek to cause trouble or exercise influence over the King. Whereas, Her Majesty now wants rid of her cousin after the Ridolfo Plot, and other rumoured plots against her in favour of Mary.'

'Why doesn't Her Majesty have her executed? She has just cause.'

'She has and some of her Privy Council and other advisers have urged her to do this. But Her Majesty, being a pious woman, believes that killing "God's anointed" is a mortal sin and might set an unfortunate precedent.'

'I'm not sure that God will make that much of a distinction between doing the deed and being complicit in bringing it about,' I say, as the distinction is lost on me. 'Or what he'll think about me being abandoned as a consequence.'

'We're all in God's hands. Perhaps he'll deliver you yet. Unfortunately, I am constrained by my instructions from doing more than protest about the conditions in which you are held. Now good day, Captain Isted, I now have to attend to my purpose: the *Great Matter*. But remember your solemn promise. If you renege on this, or seek to implicate the Crown in your actions, I cannot answer for any action that may be taken against your kin and associates in England.'

37

The Scottish Privy Council

The lock of my cell door turns again with another clunk and the door creaks open.

'You're to come with me,' demands the jailer.

'Where to, now?' I ask, hoping that Killigrew had received instructions to secure my release following our meeting of yesterday.

'You're to appear before the Privy Council.'

'At least I'll get a hearing,' I reply, a little downcast, as it looks like there will be no intervention from England.

I retrace my steps back through the dungeon past the cells holding my men.

'I'm to plead our case before the Scottish Privy Council, men,' I shout as I'm pushed along. 'Perhaps I can yet persuade them of the justice of our claim.'

'Good luck, cap'n. God bless you,' shout the men in response.

At the top of the steps outside the dungeon, I'm bundled into the back of a cart. The cart proceeds past St Margaret's Chapel, past builders busy with the continuing repairs and improvements to the defences, and then on past the *Lang Stairs* and out through the gatehouse.

I look around now my eyes have grown more accustomed to the light. Unfortunately, the first thing I see clearly is the still burning embers of an execution pyre; and a charred body, burned at the stake.

'That's a witch burnt at the stake by the Witches Well, earlier this morning,' says my guard, disdainfully, who then spits towards the embers. 'We were robbed of our sport by some misguided, pitying soul, or fellow necromancer, who managed to get a bag of serpentine powder tied around her neck. Bloody meddler. Mind you, it was a pretty flash which near took her head off and put the fear of God into the crowd,' he adds with a laugh.

We drive on past St Giles Kirk on the right, where I offer up a silent prayer for my salvation; and for the poor woman, no doubt burned as a witch by misguided, superstitious, religious zealots, manipulated by the authorities for political purposes.

At the bottom of the hill, we pass through the gatehouse of the Palace of Holyroodhouse where the cart stops at the entrance to the Great Hall. I'm bundled out of the cart, through the door, and seated on a bench in the atrium. Slumped over and in pain, I look around and notice my three accusers; clean, and smartly suited and booted in contrast to myself. The three Dutchmen look back at me with disdain, before turning away and continuing their conversation in whispers.

We are escorted into the Great Hall and are left standing in front of a long oak table, behind which there are three large chairs with a smaller one at one end. A door opens to our left and a herald enters. 'Be upstanding for their Lordships: John Lyon, Lord of Glamis; George Sinclair, Earl of Caithness; and Robert, Lord Boyd,' says the herald, strangely. Strangely, because my accusers and I are the only ones there and we are already standing and have no seats.

The three lords enter, followed by a clerk, two soldiers and two stewards. The lords and clerk take their seats at the table. The soldiers stand at attention behind them and the stewards stand either side of the door.

'First on the agenda is the case of the English pirates commanded by Captain Isted,' states the clerk.

'You mean the alleged pirates,' states the Earl of Caithness.

'Have it your way. The alleged pirates,' says Lord Glamis. 'Make a note of that, clerk. And while we're at it, get the gentleman a chair.'

The two stewards pick up three chairs between them from the side of the room. 'No, no, not for the tradesmen, they can stand in our presence,' says the Lord of Glamis, condescendingly. 'Didn't you hear me, I said the gentleman – Captain Isted – who looks as if he's about to fall down.' The three Dutchmen look taken aback and offended.

'Thank you, My Lord,' I say, gratefully, slumping onto the chair. Then the oddest thought flashes through my mind: thank God they didn't use the Judas Cradle on me.

'There's no need to thank me, Captain Isted. It is likely to be the only kindness shown to you by this council.'

'Nevertheless, I'm grateful for small mercies,' I say, although it sounds like they have already decided upon my guilt.

'We've read the testimony given to the Provost of Montrose,' states Lord Glamis, glancing at a document before him. 'To sum it up: Captain Isted, does not dispute the fact that he took the ships in question by force, but contends that he had the right to do so, under a letter of marque lawfully issued by the Prince of Orange to seize the ships and goods of those of the parts of the Netherlands governed by Spain. But you cannot prove this, as the letter is on your ship, which made its escape to sea when the baillies of Montrose came to seize it. Is that correct, Captain Isted?'

'It is, My Lord.'

'And the accusers claim they are from the territory loyal to the Prince of Orange and that you had no right to take their ships and goods. But they have no proof of this either. Is that correct.'

'Regrettably, it is My Lord,' say my accusers, in unison.

'What about the results of the *examination* since the alleged pirates have been in Edinburgh?' asks Lord Glamis, looking towards the clerk.

'There are some inconsistencies in the evidence given under *examination*, Your Lordships,' replies the clerk. 'But it more or less tallies with their previous account; although one of their number has admitted to piracy.'

'Our *examiner* can usually get most people to swear black is white. He's either slipping, or the others are made of sterner stuff,' says Lord Boyd.

'Or they're innocent,' adds the Earl of Caithness.

'Who admitted to piracy?' asks Lord Glamis.

'Peter Fisher, the pilot, a fellow Scot, admitted to previous acts of piracy, but not on the occasion in question,' replies the clerk.

'Have we had any representation from the English Ambassador?'

The clerk shrugs and says, 'Not that I've been informed of, My Lords.'

'The Regent told me that he'd informed Killigrew of the matter when he saw him recently, and that he'd only complained about the conditions Captain Isted was held in,' says Lord Boyd.

'I don't think we can construe a lot from that,' states Lord Glamis. 'I doubt those held in the Tower of London would have faired any better, or worse. So we have to decide who we believe, if anybody, and what to do about it. Any thoughts, gentlemen,' he adds, turning to the lords on either side of him.'

'I'm not sure I believe any of them,' says Lord Boyd, making no attempt to conceal what he says from us. 'But the Regent told me he wants to send a clear message to all the English pirates that are the scourge of our coast.'

'Deterrence is an important part of sentencing, but it's no reason to condemn innocent men,' interjects the Earl of Caithness.

'But there is evidence.'

'What?'

'The ship cut and run to avoid being detained by the baillies, and Captain Isted and his men ashore tried to make their escape as well,' adds Lord Boyd. 'They are not the actions of innocent men.'

'Aye, but faced with armed men and fearing the sequel, we'd probably do the same,' replies the Earl of Caithness.

'Maybe. But there is also our previous experience of those with letters of marque exceeding their scope, which is what the accusers say. In any event, privateers are much the same as pirates to me.'

'I'm not sure I believe the accusers either, and I would hate to see papists profit from such a deception,' states Lord Glamis. 'What do you think, George, given all this,' he adds, looking to the Earl of Caithness.

'Although the evidence against Captain Isted and his men is circumstantial, I suppose it's enough to give the Regent what he wants, especially as the English have been informed and they've made no representation,' replies the earl. 'But we could delay the execution of sentence for a while in case representation is made. In any event, we don't need to believe the accusers sufficiently to return their property to them, at least not immediately.'

'What do you mean?'

'We could sell the ships and goods and retain the money, until they provide proof of what they say,' suggests the earl. 'If they do so, we can give them the money, but have the use of it in the meantime. And if they don't we can keep it.'

'I like it,' says Lord Boyd. 'It provides the greatest benefit to us. The Regent will be well pleased with such a result. But I see no need to delay the execution of sentence.'

The three Lords then huddle together in further conversation and I can hear nothing more. I sit there angry and frustrated, but unsurprised by what was said given my meeting with Ambassador Killigrew. But I am too exhausted to rail against anything I am powerless to prevent; and mindful of Killigrew's threat against my kin and associates in England, I say nothing. I am not sure whether my accusers could have heard or understood what was said in a tongue that is not their own, and in a dialect that might be more alien to them. I assume not, as they seem happy enough. In any event, I've come to the conclusion that the English and Scottish governments will turn out to be the biggest crooks in this case.

'Captain Isted,' says the Lord of Glamis, looking at me. I attempt to stand. 'You may remain seated.'

'Thank you, My Lord,' I reply, slumping back on the chair.

'After considering all the evidence given by you and your men under *examination* and the testimony of your accusers, I find you and your men guilty of piracy.'

I sigh, having expected this verdict. I only hope that some good can come of it for the greater good of England.

The Lord of Glamis continues, 'You will be taken to whence you came. From there you and your men will be taken to the place of execution, on Leith Sands, on the eighteenth of July. There you will be chained below the high water mark and your bodies left for three days as a caution to others.[61] What is left of

---

61 Drowning was a common form of execution, particularly in coastal towns. It was abolished in England in 1623 and in Scotland in 1685.

your remains will be removed and buried in an unmarked grave in the Kirk of Our Lady, in South Leith. May God have mercy on your souls.' There is a short pause, before he adds, 'Captain Isted, is there anything you would like to say?'

I sit there in shock for a moment. I am to be taken to Leith to be drowned. Was there something in my dreams? Did Hannah actually curse me after all?

As soon as I have composed myself, I say, 'I beseech Your Lordships to be merciful to the two boys taken with my men and me. They are both half starved and one is sick with a fever.'

Lord Glamis turns to the others and asks, 'Shall we grant this request?'

'I think it's a concession we can make. It may touch Queen Elizabeth's female heart and ease any contention this might otherwise cause,' says the Earl of Caithness.

'I doubt there's a female heart beating in that breast. But I'm inclined to do it anyway,' replies the Lord of Glamis. 'Your request is granted, Captain Isted. I will arrange for the boys to be sent to Ambassador Killigrew, with instructions that it is our desire that he returns them safely to their kin in England.'

'I'm grateful, My Lord,' I reply, with some small measure of relief.

'As for you three,' says the Lord of Glamis, addressing the three Dutchmen who were looking pleased with the judgement and my misfortune. 'While we're content that Captain Isted and his men are guilty of piracy and deserve their fate, you have no proof of your testimony and there is something about you that makes us doubt your veracity.' The smiles disappear from the Dutchmen's faces. 'Your ships and cargo will be sold by the baillies in Montrose, and the proceeds delivered to Mr John Heriot, Burges of Edinburgh, while you have the chance to provide proof of your case.[62]'

---

62 Scottish Privy Council Meeting, dated 25 June 1574, NAC PC1/7 refers.

'But, My Lord, if Captain Isted is guilty of piracy, you have no just cause to retain our property,' pleads Cornelius Johanson.

'It is for this council to determine whether there is just cause,' states Lord Glamis, sternly. 'I'll warn you only once. If you wish to challenge our judgement, I'll be happy for you to undergo the same sort of *examination* as Captain Isted and his men have had in the dungeon of Edinburgh Castle. Then we'll see how well your story holds up,' he adds, loudly, in a threatening manner.

'I spoke hastily, My Lord. Please forgive me,' stutters a frightened Cornelius Johanson. 'We accept the wisdom of your judgement and will make haste to the Netherlands and return with our proof.'

'Be off with you then. If you aren't back here within ninety days, the money is forfeit.'

The three Dutchmen leave the room in haste, in case the Lord of Glamis changes his mind and makes good his threat to put them to torture.

I am lifted from my chair. I bow my head to the Privy Council, turn and am led unsteadily away in my chains. 'I've said it before, and I'll say it again: it's the so-called respectable people that are often the biggest crooks,' I whisper under my breath, with a faint smile flickering across my pain-etched face.

38

Leith Sands

The lock of the cell clinks, the door creaks open and a dark figure fills the frame. 'I'm a minister of the Kirk,' says the dark figure. 'The authorities thought you might like to see me before your execution tomorrow.'

'What!' I exclaim. 'But it's not due until the eighteenth.'

'The Regent's had it advanced, to coincide with the horserace.'

'A horserace?'

'Yes. The one King James IV introduced. It's not been run for many a year, but the Regent decided to reinstate it now things are more settled after the *Lang Siege*,' says the minister, disapprovingly. 'It's against the Kirk's advice. It only encourages gambling and licentious behaviour. The Regent's far too much of an Episcopalian for the Kirk's liking.'

'In the overall scheme of things, it matters little when the execution takes place,' I say, having already resigned myself to it. But is the horserace really the reason for the unseemly haste, I wonder. Or is it just an excuse, in the Anglo-Scottish and Anglo-Spanish political interests, to dispatch us as soon as possible?

'I suppose you want me to confess my sins?' I add.

'You can, if you want. But I can't intercede for you with God. The Kirk doesn't believe in that.'

'Neither do I. So what's the point?'

'The Kirk believes in public confession and people having the opportunity to mend their ways. I suppose there isn't much opportunity for that in your case. But you might like to confess anyway, before you meet your Maker.'

'I've been thinking about what brought me to this sorry state. It was quite some coincidence, and extreme bad luck, that the men whose ships I captured took passage in a Scottish ship blown by the same storm into the same port as my ship.'

'Or the intervention of an omnipotent God who has a purpose for everything.'

'Perhaps. But if he has a purpose in this case, I know not what it is and can't immediately see what good there may be in it.'

'There may be no good in it for you. But maybe it will provide a salutary lesson for others.'

'I'll give some thought to that. Maybe I'll say something publicly tomorrow. And if my story is ever told, perhaps some good may come of it for some other poor soul.'

After the minister has gone, I spend a restless night filled with unwanted thoughts of what brought me to this sorry end. Then as I finally fall into a light sleep, the cell door creaks open. 'Are you ready to meet your Maker?' says the jailer, with a laugh.

'No, is anybody?' I say, under my breath.

The jailer rough handles me to my feet and pushes me along through the torture chamber, up the stairs and out into the bright summer sunlight. My men are already sitting in the cart, ready to transport us to our place of execution on Leith Sands, with the exception of Fisher whose execution has been delayed pending further questioning.

All of us are in a sorry state, physically weakened by the rack and the effects of dysentery caused by the insanitary conditions in which we have been detained. A number of the men also have eruptions on their skin and sit their sweating and shivering:

symptoms typical in cases of *jail fever*. We sit there in silence as the cart trundles over the cobbles towards the castle gatehouse.

Cox breaks the silence. 'Drowning's a bloody awful way to be executed. They don't do that where I'm from.'

'Where's that, and what do they do there?' asks Sawyer.

'Worcester. We'd be hanged there.'

'And that's a good way?'

We all make a painful and involuntary laugh.

'Drowning is the usual form of execution in Lowestoft, and for many of us who live on the coast,' says Benkis.

'Why's that?' asks Cox.

'Well, we ain't short of water, and it saves the trouble and cost of building a scaffold.'

We all laugh again, less painfully and more freely.

'Yes, in Hastings, and all but one of the Cinque Ports, they simply tie up the condemned and unceremoniously cast them into the sea,' I report.

'What do they do in the other Cinque Port, captain?' asks Cox.

'At Sandwich, we'd be buried alive on the beach.'

'It's a bit of luck we're not in Sandwich, then.'

We all laugh again, with incongruously raised spirits. I have seen gallows humour before but I've never understood it, until now.

'I don't want to break this mood, men, but I'd like to say a few words to you before we get amongst the crowd in the town,' I say, getting everyone's attention. 'First of all, I'm sorry I've brought you all to this end.'

'It's not your fault, captain,' says Sawyer. 'It was just bad luck. No one could've foreseen them Dutchmen coming across a Scottish ship and taking passage in it, and then being blown into the same harbour as us by the same storm. What were the chances of that?'

'Maybe, but they were my decisions that brought us here. It seems the whole world can turn on things of seemingly little significance. Anyway, I want to say, if I'm going to die, and I don't want to, I couldn't wish to die in better company.'

'I don't want you to die either, captain. But if you're going to die, I wish it were in someone else's company,' says Johnston.

We all laugh again, which strangely eases the horror of our plight.

'That's the spirit men. But you know what I mean.'

'We do, and I take some comfort from that too,' says Sawyer.

'Aye,' say all the others.

'Thank you, men,' I say, feeling a sense of relief knowing the men do not hold a grudge against me. 'I also want to say that we can expect the crowds to be swelled and more boisterous because of the festivities. They'll no doubt be hostile towards us, pelting us with things and poking fun at our expense. We can either rise to the bait and fight back, or try to maintain our good humour and bear it with courage and dignity as best we can. Whatever we do, I'd like us to do the same together.'

'I'd like to fight back, captain,' says Norris, ever the soldier. 'I don't believe we should meekly go into the darkness without a fight.'

'I'd agree, if we had a chance of escape,' says Reid, weakly. 'But I see no chance of that. Like many of us, the rack's stretched my muscles so much I've little power in them. My brother-in-law, John, and Cornish, have had their shoulders dislocated while some others are weak with the fever.'

'I agree entirely, Reid,' I reply. 'I wouldn't give up without a fight if there were a point to it. I suggest we show these people that while they may have been able to break our bodies, they can't break our spirit. And if by some chance Mr Hills and the *Barque of Bulleyn* come sailing over the horizon to our rescue, we may have some strength left to get out of this mess.'

We all laugh at the thought of such an unlikely but welcome prospect. Everyone agrees, including Loutton, displaying considerably more fortitude than he had demonstrated in the face of torture when he had tried to lie his way out of trouble by pretending to be a passenger and not a member of the crew. I had never got to the bottom of why a gentleman, such as Loutton, was working as a carpenter, let alone one aboard a privateer. Perhaps this, and his earlier behaviour, was all an act for his own advantage.

The cart trundles on over the cobbles into the Land Market and the High Street beyond, where we endure a barrage of abuse, rotten vegetables, dung and stones as we pass through the crowds. One woman from an upper window of a house shouts, 'Gar'dy'loo,' and then empties her slop bucket over us to the delight of the crowd below. With our spirits and skins dampened, we trundle on out through the Flodden Wall, into Cannongate, and onto the road to Leith. The crowds are now more spread out and more intent on making their way to the horserace on Leith Sands, than to spend too much time on prematurely baiting some of the day's sport. No doubt, they will get their chance later.

We reach the shore where the crowds are thickest, to shouts of, 'Dirty English pirates.'

'They can call me a dirty pirate if they like, but I'll be damned if I'll stand idly by while they call me English,' says Reid. 'Dirty Scottish pirate, if you please,' he shouts at the crowd, as he stumbles in an attempt to get to his feet.

The crowd surges around the cart and some people try to climb in. 'Death to the English pirates,' they shout, ignoring Reid's remonstration. Armed soldiers move in and push the crowd back to clear a space of several yards around the cart.

The crowd quietens markedly. A gun fires to our left. Everyone turns in that direction to see the horses set off. The horses gallop along in front of the crowds and past the cart. They complete one circuit and then another, before hurtling across the finishing line in front of us. A great cheer goes up from the crowd.

'Damn!' shouts one of the soldiers guarding us. 'It's the Regent's horse, the Jamais Arriere.'

Fontane laughs.

'What's so funny in that, Philippe?' asks Cox.

'*Jamais Arriere* means Never Behind; quite appropriate for a winning horse.'

'I suspect it's probably the earl's family motto,' suggests Sawyer.

'Well, it's doubly appropriate, as the Regent's a horse's behind as far as I'm concerned,' says Sinclair.

'Aye, a right horse's arse,' shouts Reid.

We all laugh.

'Well, that's a good deal more spirit and a little less dignity than I had in mind,' I say. 'But so what.'

The soldiers and the crowd look at us wondering what there is for us to laugh at.

The cart jolts forward down onto the sands, with a good section of the crowd surging behind us resuming their chant of, 'Death to the English pirates.'

'It's death to the English and Scottish pirates, you ignorant peasants,' shouts Reid, but to no avail.

'*Non, non*, it's death to the English, Scottish and French pirates,' shouts Fontane, reacting to this continued unintended insult.

We all laugh, but with not quite so much gusto as before.

'I see they've set the stakes way down the beach towards the waterline, and the tide's already turned. If I get the chance to

274

say some final words, I'll try to keep it going until they're wet to their knees,' I say.

'Good for you, cap'n,' say Brocas.

The cart reaches the stakes set in the sand closest to the East Craigs. We are bundled out of the cart and chained to the stakes. I am to the left of the line. Then from left to right: Robert Loutton of Filde, Yorkshire; Adam Sawyer, the surgeon from Penzance, Cornwall; James Johnston of Leith; John Sinclair of Dumfries; Thomas Tailor, alias Benkis, of London, lately of Lowestoft; Philippe Fontane, the Frenchmen, from La Rochelle; Thomas Cox of Worcester; John Norris, the master gunner and blacksmith, from Lambeth; John Crechlaw, alias Brocas, from Pemberton in Lancashire; John Cornish, from Lancashire, latterly from Winterton in Norfolk; Andrew Reid, from the Holyman's Cape, by Aberdeen; and finally Nicholas Long, the cook, from Salisbury Plain in Wiltshire.

A lightweight carriage pulls up nearby. 'It's the Regent,' murmur some of the crowd.

The Regent stands in his carriage and says, 'It's a good day today. I'm ridding the world of some English pirates.'

The crowd cheers and chants, 'Death to the English pirates.'

'And Scottish,' shouts Reid.

'Aye and Scottish,' shout Sinclair and Johnston.

'And French,' adds Fontane, swiftly.

The crowd laughs.

A soldier shouts, 'Silence dogs,' and strikes Reid, Sinclair, Johnston and Fontane in turn.

'And it's been a doubly good day as my horse, Jamais Arriere, won the race,' resumes the Regent.

'Up the horse's arse,' shouts Reid.

Large sections of the crowd laugh loudly, although I suspect they are unaware of the joke.

A soldier moves forward and strikes Reid again. He slumps forward in pain.

The Regent continues, 'You've been lawfully convicted of piracy and condemned to death by drowning here, on Leith Sands. After the sentence has been carried out, your bodies will remain here for three days, as food for fish and fowl, and as a warning to others. After that, what remains of your remains will be interred in an unmarked grave. May God have mercy on your souls.' Then after a short pause, he asks, 'Do you have any last request, or anything you'd like to say, Captain Isted?'

'A last request. Hmm, I don't suppose you'd like to let us go free to die of old age?' I reply.

The crowd laughs loudly. The Regent frowns and a soldier steps forward and strikes me.

'I'll take that as a no. In which case, I've quite a few things I'd like to say.' I raise my head to look towards the Regent and then out to sea beyond him.

'If you've got something to say, get on with it man,' demands the Regent, 'the tide's coming in.'

'Oh, I can't be bothered,' I say, looking the Regent straight in his eyes. 'I suggest you and these good people get the hell out of here, before you get your nice shoes wet. Let us men die in peace.'

'So be it,' says the Regent, looking somewhat taken aback. 'Captain Dalrymple, get your soldiers to disperse the crowd and leave these men alone,' he orders. He then rides off in his carriage.

The captain takes his orders seriously and his soldiers push the shouting crowds back up the beach, leaving us condemned men alone.

'I thought you were going to keep talking until the crowd got wet, cap'n,' says Brocas.

'I was. But a little while ago, I noticed the topsails of a ship moving from behind yonder island.'

'That's Inchkeith,' states Johnston.

'Anyway, the ship was headed towards Leith harbour. I thought little of it, as there's nothing odd in that. It's still a long way off, but, as I was about to speak, I thought I recognised it.'

All the men look out to sea at the ship.

'It's the *Barque of Bulleyn*,' says an astonished Cox, more in hope than expectation.

'Aye, I think it may be. Mr Hills has come to get us. If that's the case, I thought it best to try to get rid of everyone as soon as possible.'

Several of the men laugh and cry at the same time and say quietly but earnestly, 'Please, God, let it be Mr Hills and the *Bulleyn*.'

'You're from Leith, aren't you, Mr Johnston?' I ask, as the water creeps about our ankles. 'How long do you think we've got?'

'With the way the beach falls away, the sea state, the wind direction and the way the waves are breaking, I'd guess we've probably a bit less than an hour,' replies Johnston. 'A bit more for you, cap'n, as you're a bit taller than the rest of us. And a bit less for Nick, whose a bit of a short-arse,' he adds, referring to the inappropriately named Long.

'Thanks, Jim,' remarks Long.

'You're welcome, Nick.'

'That might just be enough time, once Mr Hills has got as close as he dares, gets the longboat in the water and rows here,' I say, 'provided our weakened bodies can sustain us that long in the cold water.'

'But why couldn't they have set off earlier?' complains Loutton.

'It's all a matter of timing, Mr Loutton. Too early and the soldiers will be alerted to what they're doing and put a stop to it. But if they get it just right, the soldiers will be cut off far enough from us by the tide. It's a bold move, typical of Mr Hills. But steel yourselves men, it will be a close run thing.'

'Come on, Mr Hills, come on, Mr Hills. Please, God, that he gets here in time,' says Cox, quietly but earnestly.

'Amen to that,' says Fontane.

'You do realise, that even if he gets here while we're still alive, he's unlikely to have time to release us all,' whispers Loutton, with composure. 'And even if he does, he won't be able to get us all in the rowing boat.'

'I know, Mr Loutton,' I whisper in reply, 'but I'd be obliged if you'd keep that to yourself. We'll deal with that when we have to, and not before.'

The relentless tide creeps ever higher, above our knees, as the *Barque of Bulleyn* makes painfully slow progress across the Firth of Forth.

The *Barque of Bulleyn* turns sharply in our direction and comes abeam us staked out on the beach, further out than we would have liked, as the water laps into my chest. At the same time, it turns to larboard and moves away from the shore.

'No, no, they're turning away and leaving us,' shouts the short Long, with the water lapping into his face.

'No, the ship can't come any closer. They'll have put a boat in the water. See!' I say, as the longboat is revealed, as it is cleared by the ship's stern. 'I think that's Mr Hills in the boat.'

'And it looks like he's got Goliath and Isekeri with him,' reports Johnston.

'Come on, Mr Hills,' shouts Cox.

'Quiet, men,' I order. 'We don't want to alert the soldiers. They'll probably notice soon enough without our help.'

'Come on, Mr Hills; come on, Mr Hills,' say some of the men, quietly, but with increasing excitement and desperation, as the water creeps ever higher.

We can see Isekeri and Goliath row on strongly, with John standing in the stern to get a better view of the beach.

The water steadily rises, and the onshore breeze brings low waves dousing us ever higher up our weakened bodies.

'I think the game's up men,' I say. 'I can hear a commotion behind us on the beach.' I turn around as far as my chains will allow. 'They've been spotted; the soldiers are loading their muskets. But, I think they're to far away to make their shots count.'

'I can't hold on,' cries a breathless Long. He slumps down at the stake, with his eyes wide open and his head turned upwards towards heaven. He slips below the rising water without a further sound.

'Try to hold on men. It won't be much longer,' I shout.

The soldiers fire. We hear the crack of the shot as it flies through the air close by us and splashes short of the approaching longboat.

Three of the soldiers run off up the beach. The other three run along the shoreline to get a better angle, load their muskets and wade into the water up to their waists. 'They'll only get one shot at this and then they're done. Let's hope they miss.'

The soldiers fire. One musket misfires. The powder was probably damp. But the other two go off. One shot hits the boat, while the other hits Isekeri in his right shoulder.

'No!' shouts Brocas, straining on his chains. His knees, weakened by the rack and the cold of the water, give way and he plunges below the surface unable to rise.

The longboat lurches off course. Goliath stretches out his giant hands and clears Isekeri from the oars to allow John to take his place.

The short Loutton, next to me, starts to struggle, thrashing his head about, trying to keep his mouth above the incoming waves of water. But after a little while he too goes the way of Long and Brocas.

'I can't feel my legs,' gasps Cornish.

'Neither can I,' adds Benkis.

'It's the effects of the cold water,' I say. 'They'll be all right as soon as Mr Hills gets us out of here. Just hang on a little longer.'

'I'll try, captain,' cries Benkis, but then he passes out and his life slips away quietly in the rising tide.

'I can't feel the cold no more, cap'n,' says Cornish, with his face turned towards the watery sunlight, with a strange wide-eyed euphoria. He gasps his last and he too slumps forward in his chains.

'Those other soldiers have dragged a boat to the water and are rowing out to us,' shouts Reid, as the waves bring the water lapping ever higher.

'I'd always planned to return home to Leith to die,' gasps Johnston. 'But I didn't expect it to be like this.'

'Come on, Mr Johnston, don't give up,' I exhort. 'You're a man who likes a song. How about raising our spirits with your favourite,' I add, trying to keep the men's minds off the relentless cold, the incoming tide, and the demise of some of our fellows, while John and Goliath regain control of the longboat.

'All right captain, but my favourite is the Battle of Otterburn,' replies Johnston, wearily, 'It's a ballad about the famous Scottish victory over you Sassenachs. He then sings out:

'It fell about the Lammas tide,
When the muir-men win their hay,
The doughty Earl of Douglas rode
Into England, to catch a prey.'

Johnston skips a few verses and then quietly sings out the dying words of the Earl of Douglas:

'My wound is deep, I fain would sleep.'

Then with his dying breath he lets out a mighty shout of, 'SCOTLAND!'

Reid and Sinclair sob at the passing of their brave countryman in such a way.

Fontane who had been affected by a fever, and who had been quiet for sometime, starts to sway, and in a strange voice chants:

'De profundis ad te Domine;
Domine, exaudi vocem meam...'

'What's up with Philippe and what's he saying?' asks Cox.

'It's *De Profundis*, the Latin version of Psalm 130,' says a shivering Sawyer. 'They say it in the Roman Church to commemorate the dead.'

'Oh my God!' exclaims Norris. 'I didn't realize Philippe was a papist.'

'He's not. He's just delirious, which does strange things to the mind.'

'What, turn Protestants into papists?'

'Philippe told me he trained to be a priest, before becoming a Huguenot and then losing his faith altogether,' says Sawyer.

'These events and his delirium have just brought this to the surface.'

'Et ipse redimet ex omnibus iniquitatibus ejus,' chants Fontane. He stops with his head contorted backwards against the side of the stake.

'The soldiers' rowing boat is getting closer cap'n,' shouts Sawyer.

There is a flash of light and a puff of smoke from a gun port on the side of the *Barque of Bulleyn*, closely followed by a loud boom and a splash close enough to the rowing boat to drench the soldiers in spray. As a result, the soldiers turn the boat around and row hard for the shore.

'Well done, Mr Norris. You trained your men well,' I say. 'Now hold fast, men. Nothing can stop Mr Hills now. We're going to be saved,' I shout, joyously.

39

John Hills's Narrative - The Barque Bites Back

Goliath and I heave ourselves over the bulwark of the *Barque of Bulleyn* and collapse in a sodden heap on the deck, as two sailors assist the wounded.

'What happened, Mr Hills?' asks Coggan.

I sit up with my back resting against the bulwark, shivering with cold and rage. 'Fate craftily contrived to deceive us,' I reply, as I hold my head in my hands, screwing my eyes tightly shut in an attempt to blot out what had befallen us. But it is of no use, and there is nothing to do but to carry on. 'I swear I'll exact revenge on the Scots for what they've wrought this day, or my name isn't John Hills,' I shout, defiantly, as I get to my feet.

'What are your orders, Mr Hills?' asks Coggan.

'Take us out of here and set a course for Aberlady Bay, where we saw those ships at anchor yesterday. I've a mood to exact revenge while our blood still boils.'

'Aye, aye, sir.'

'And when you've done that, Mr Coggan, come to my cabin and I'll tell you exactly what happened.'

Coggan knocks on my cabin door and enters as I finish towelling myself down.

'Take a seat, Coggan, and pour us both a brandy,' I say, as I start to put on dry clothes.

'So what happened, Mr Hills?' asks Coggan, in a subdued tone.

'Everything seemed to be going well, once your cannon fire had sent the Scottish soldiers in the rowing boat packing,' I reply, slumping into my chair. I take a sip of my brandy and resume. 'But as we reached our men, and turned the boat beam on, a wave pushed it into Andrew Read – the surviving man on the end of the line. It struck his head, rendered him unconscious and he slumped below the water. Sinclair, further along the line, strained against his chains in a useless attempt to reach his fallen brother-in-law. But he also lost his footing and plummeted below the surface. They both drowned before Goliath and I could regain control of the boat and attempt to do anything to help them.'

'What happened then?' enquires Coggan, earnestly.

'Only the captain, Sawyer, Cox and Norris were left alive. But the waves were beginning to lap into their faces, making it difficult for them to take regular breaths.'

'So what did you do?'

'I asked the captain if they were tied or chained. He said they were chained. I'd feared they would be, which is why I took the blacksmith's hammer and flat chisel with me.'

'And then?'

'I jumped into the water leaving Goliath to secure the boat. The captain ordered me to release Cox and Norris first as they were the shortest and couldn't hold on much longer. I ignored him and told Cox and Norris the captain was my priority. Norris indicated that he understood, but Cox was already too busy struggling to keep his head above water.'

'Norris was a good man – ever the soldier,' says Coggan, sadly. 'And I'm sure Cox would have understood, as well.'

'May be so,' I sigh. 'Anyway, ignoring the captain's protestations, I ducked below the water to inspect his chains. When I surfaced, Cox had already failed in his struggle. I ducked below the surface again and attempted to break the captain's chains with the hammer and chisel,' I add, before pausing to regain some composure.

'And?' enquires Coggan, eager to know the rest.

'I couldn't get enough momentum swinging the hammer through the water to generate sufficient power against the chisel to make so much as a dent in the chains,' I groan, in exasperation. 'And when I resurfaced Norris had also surrendered to the relentless sea.'

'So what did you do then?'

'Goliath leapt from the boat and lifted the captain as high out of the water as he could in his chains, to give us a little more time to think. Then the captain said, "It's no good John, there's not enough time." "I won't give up, while I can still draw breath," I replied. "No, John, not while I can still draw breath," said the captain, with a flicker of a smile. "There really is no more time. I'm spent." I pause, fighting to contain my emotions. 'The captain then reminded me of a premonition he'd had about drowning and said he didn't want to die like that. Then he asked me to put an end to it for him.'

Coggan gasps in shock.

'I told him I couldn't do it. Then Sawyer chimed in to say he was content to pass that way, but that I should do whatever needed to be done for the captain.'

'And what then, Mr Hills?'

'I gave Sawyer a nod of respect. Then the captain told me to tell Hannah, his girl in Hastings, that he loved her; and to give his love to Anne, the lady who you may have seen come aboard while we were alongside at Deptford. He then bent his head backwards with quiet resignation and looked skyward,' I say, pausing with barely controlled emotion. 'Then I propelled myself out of the water, with one hand on Goliath's shoulder, and at the same time struck firmly home with my sword. The captain didn't cry out at all, but momentarily looked straight into my eyes. Then with the water turning red with blood, Goliath stumbled and they both plunged below the surface of the water,' I add, sobbing unashamedly.

Some two hours later, as we reach the mouth of Aberlady Bay, the three Scottish barques are heading north-west towards Gullane Point.

'More sail, Coggan. I want to head them off before they reach the open sea,' I order. 'And open up our gun ports and roll out the cannon. I want them in no doubt as to our intention, if they refuse to comply with my orders.'

'Aye, aye, Mr Hills.'

We pass within hailing distance of each of the Scottish barques in turn, and order them to heave to and prepare to be boarded. They all comply in face of the threat we pose. We come alongside the lead ship. I board it with a strong boarding party and confine everyone in its captain's cabin without resistance.

'Now, Coggan, take your boarding party in our longboat to the hindmost ship,' I order. 'And, Goliath, commandeer the boat from the Scottish barque and take your boarding party to the other one. You both know what to do.'

Coggan and Goliath do as they are commanded, and bring the other Scottish ships alongside one another, outboard of the Scottish barque I am aboard.

They remove from each of the great cabins, the captain and seven of the captive crew, one at a time to make it easier for them to have their way with them without alerting the others to their fate. They knock each man on his head from behind with a cudgel, and quietly gag and bind them hand and foot. I act similarly on the ship I had boarded, but leave its captain alone and bind and gag ten of its crew.

The bound and stunned mariners are carried onto the Scottish barque outboard of the rest.

'Now get the remainder of the captives over here,' I order. 'I want them all to see this.'

The remaining captain and thirteen men are rough handled out of the great cabins to snarls and jeers from the crew of the *Barque of Bulleyn*. Once they're aboard the outboard Scottish barque, they are horrified to find their shipmates in various levels of consciousness lying bound and gagged on the weatherdeck.

'Make sure those men are conscious,' I order, looking down from the quarterdeck. 'I don't want any of them to miss the experience.'

Three men rush forward with buckets of seawater and throw them over the bound mariners, jolting them towards a greater level of consciousness.

'Our captain and some of our men were captured ashore and sentenced to death by drowning, by the Scottish Privy Council, although we had done no harm to them nor to their shipping or their fellow Scots. By doing so, they have declared war on us. So we are declaring war on them and will repay them two for one for the men we've lost,' I shout, loudly, so that all can hear.

The crew of the *Barque of Bulleyn* cheer loudly, as the captive men look on aghast and in fear. The cheers die down. Some of the bound men curl up in foetal positions, trembling. Others cry, some lose control of their bladders and bowels, some are transfixed with fear, some struggle against their bindings, while a few sit there in thoughtful prayer and accept their fate.

'Let's get it over with, Hastings style, and be on our way,' I order.

The crew cheer more loudly.

The first bound man is lifted by two of the crew holding his shoulders and legs. He is swung to and fro a couple of times to gain momentum, and then unceremoniously heaved over the side. Loud hurrahs ring out from the crew hanging in the rigging and other vantage points, as he is thrown, makes a splash and sinks deep into his briny grave.

We play out this scene a further twenty-five times, to ever louder hurrahs from the crew of the *Bulleyn* and ever more muffled panic from the bound and gagged men, and the increasingly horror filled faces of the Scottish sailors we force to observe the fate of their fellows.

As the twenty-sixth man is confined to the deep, I turn to the surviving captain and men from the three Scottish barques, and calmly say, 'You are all free to go in the longboat.' Some of the men are crying, whether in relief of being released, or in sorrow for their shipmates, I neither know not nor care.[63]

'I want you to tell everyone what you've seen this day,' I add, with menace. 'Make sure the message gets to the Regent, and let him know that if there is any further action taken against us it will be requited three to one next time. He has my word on it. I'm John Hills, Master of the *Barque of Bulleyn*,' I shout.

The men cheer loudly in support of my defiance.

The terrified Scottish captain and crew clamber over the ship's side and into the longboat, in silence, then row as quickly as they can towards the shore.

'Get us and our prizes underway, Mr Coggan, and set a course for Berwick-upon-Tweed,' I order.

'You ought to go below and get some rest now, Mr Hills,' says Coggan. 'You must be exhausted with all your efforts of this day. I'll stand watch.'

---

63 Killigrew wrote to Walsingham, on 12 July 1574, to inform him that Hills the Master of Isted's ship had captured three Scottish barques and thrown twenty-six men overboard – Calendar of State Papers, Scotland: Volume 5, 1574-81 refers.

'Thank you, Coggan, but I won't be able to rest,' I reply, trying to still my pounding and sorrow filled heart. 'I think I'll take the tiller for a while.'

I take hold of the tiller from the helmsman and steer a north-easterly course past Gullane Point, with the wind and the Scottish summer evening sun on my back.

Epilogue

There is no record that Robert Isted's accusers, Captain Lucas Zeleson, and Cornelius and Herman Johanson, ever returned to Scotland with proof of their story, or that they were ever paid the proceeds for the sale of their ships and goods. Did they lie? Did Robert Isted have the legal right to take their ships and cargo under a letter of marque issued by the Prince of Orange?

Legend has it that Hannah Clark continued to live at the White Hart (the Stag Inn), well into her old age, from where she protected Hastings from French raids with her witchcraft. She then disappeared, suddenly one dark night, never to be seen again. However, her smoke-cured cats were discovered more than three hundred and fifty years later and are now on display in a glass cabinet in the main bar of the Stag Inn, Hastings. Were they used in a spell to curse Robert Isted?

The Scottish Regent, the 4th Earl of Morton, was later arrested and charged with being complicit in the murder of Lord Darnley, King James VI's father, which he confessed to under 'examination'. He was executed by the 'Maiden', which he had acquired for the execution of others. His body was left for three days, as he had ordered to happen to the bodies of Robert and his men. It was then interred in an unmarked grave in Greyfriars Kirkyard. However, his head was on the spike on the north gable of the Tollbooth, where it remained for eighteen months before it was eventually reunited with his body. The instrument of his death, the 'Maiden', can still be seen in the National Museum of Scotland, Edinburgh.

Queen Elizabeth never resolved the *Great Matter* in the way had hoped. Instead, she kept her cousin, Mary Queen of Scots, under house arrest for many more years. Mary was eventually executed, in 1587, after she was found guilty of conspiracy in another plot to overthrow Elizabeth and replace her as Queen of England.

England maintained its uneasy peace with Spain until the Spanish Armada was sent against it, in 1588. The Armada's utter defeat was perhaps a vindication of Queen Elizabeth's policy of playing for time to delay an inevitable war. Was Robert Isted's apparent abandonment a result of that policy?

The Dutch continued their struggle for independence from Spain, for another seventy-four years, before they finally succeeded in breaking free, in 1648.

Four years after the events portrayed in this book, Henry Knollys joined Sir Humphrey Gilbert in a venture to establish a colony in North America. They gathered eleven ships and six hundred men, many of whom were convicted pirates pardoned on condition of joining the expedition. However, Knollys fell out with Gilbert. As a result, he and Jack Callis, one of the pirates at Lindisfarne when he and Robert Isted were there in 1574, took three of the ships on a privateering expedition off the Spanish coast. They were later joined by some of the other ships deserting Gilbert. Following this, and a failed expedition in support of a claimant to the Portuguese throne, Knollys joined the fight for Dutch Independence from Spain. He died, in the Netherlands, of wounds sustained in battle, in 1582.

Sir John Pelham's financial problems continued. He was committed to the Fleet Prison, on more than one occasion, as a result of his debts.

Thomas Isted moved to Hastings, scaled down his interests in Mayfield, and was the last of the Isted ironmasters. The Wealden iron industry declined from its 16th century peak and no longer exists. However, its history and iron making techniques are the subject of continuing research by the

Wealden Iron Research Group (WIRG) www.wealdeniron.org.uk

Dick Isted married Ann Warnett in c1575. They had five sons and one daughter. Many of the Isteds in the UK, the USA, Canada, South Africa, Australia and New Zealand, along with countless others with Isted ancestry, are descended from them. Dick continued to serve as a freeman and jurat of the Cinque Port of Hastings, until he resigned in 1588. His resignation followed the amendment of Hastings' Charter by Queen Elizabeth, after Hastings had only sent one ship to defend the country against the Spanish Armada. After that, Dick spent more time in Framfield from where his wife came, very close to the old Manor of Isted from which the family takes its name.

Many official records referring to the *Barque of Bulleyn* and its various aliases, during its service in the Tudor Navy, still exist. Some details of them are transcribed in *The Navy of Edward VI and Mary I,* edited by C. S. Knighton and David Loades, published by Ashgate for The Navy Records Society. However, what happened to the *Barque of Bulleyn* and those aboard her, subsequent to the events portrayed in this book, is another story entirely…

THE END